BOY LIKE ME

Simon James Green

Scholastic Press / New York

First published in the United Kingdom in 2023 by Scholastic UK: Westfield Road, Southam, Warwickshire, England CV47 0RA.

Library of Congress Cataloging-in-Publication Data available

ISBN 978-1-339-04587-0

10 9 8 7 6 5 4 3 2 1   24 25 26 27 28

Printed in Italy   183
First US edition, May 2024

Book design by Maithili Joshi and Sarah Baldwin

*For Alice Leggatt
and hero librarians
everywhere.*

A NOTE FROM THE AUTHOR

Some parts of this are completely true, some parts have been changed to protect people's privacy, and some parts have been entirely made up to help the story along. Essentially, though, this is real, and it's about trying to be real at a time when that reality felt terrifying.

A few things before you read on: First, there are scenes of homophobic abuse and violence in this, and that's not my normal style, so I wanted to warn you. But don't worry, it's not all doom and gloom. There's also goodness and wonder and humor and big-time love up ahead. Secondly, my US and Canadian friends, this book is very firmly set in England in the 90s and you're going to come across a few things you're not familiar with—like your beloved "Axe" being called "Lynx" here in the UK. I wanted to keep as much cultural authenticity as possible to highlight one fact: Different place, different time, but we're all still dealing with the same brand of ignorance and bigotry right now. Lastly, I'd like you to cast your eyes over a piece of legislation the Conservative government introduced, which became law in England, Wales, and Scotland on May 24, 1988, and was in force until June 21, 2000, in Scotland and September 18, 2003, in England and Wales. Section 28 of the Local Government Act stated:

A local authority shall not–

(a) Intentionally promote homosexuality or publish material with the intention of promoting homosexuality;

(b) Promote the teaching in any maintained school of the acceptability of homosexuality as a pretended family relationship.

Got it? OK, then turn the page and join me back in 1994 in the UK . . .

Chapter 1

They say ignorance is bliss.

And right at this moment*, *this* ignorant kid was *blissfully* happy and *blissfully* unaware that in just twelve hours' time something would happen, the first domino would fall, leading to his safe little world being blown wide apart.

In narrative structure, that's what we call a *hook*. But let's leave that dangling and focus back in on the present.

Location: my cul-de-sac in the town of Market Wickby, Lincolnshire—*welcome to the middle of nowhere; if you do die of boredom, please try not to cause a scene.*

Our hero: me. I've always hated writing myself into stories in a way that feels autobiographical, mainly because it would lead to awkward conversations with my mother. So, we'll call our guy Jamie Hampton, OK? Sixteen. "An intelligent and sensitive boy." (Not my words—my school report—although I wouldn't disagree.) Average height, slim build, and (according to my mom) handsome.

---

* 8:00 a.m. on a sunny Monday in May 1994. Hi there—yes, we're using footnotes in this one.

I've never liked thinking about my appearance—besides, attractiveness is more than just the physical, as I was soon to discover. (That was a callback to the hook just to tease you, but come on, focus on me for now.) I was a bit too bright to be seen as cool, a bit too popular to be accepted by the nerds—very much in the middle of the social pecking order, and that was an OK place to be—accepted enough that I got invited to most of the parties (even if I wasn't top of anyone's list) but never having to worry about the A-listers never liking me, because I wasn't part of their group anyway. Only one problem: Being in the middle wasn't really what Cambridge was looking for in their applicants, so I had my heart set on making more of a splash. Little did I know quite how much of one I would make by the end of summer semester. Nice bit of foreshadowing for you there. I hope you enjoy all the literary devices in this opening chapter.

What else?

Oh, and dressed in my new rugby shirt—more on that shortly.

Action: I'm walking down the pavement on my way to school. I'm smiling. A bounce in my step. A bit *too* happy for a normal sixteen-year-old. I probably should have been more tortured, more into Camus and Nietzsche, but, I don't know, maybe I've always had unnaturally high serotonin levels.

Soundtrack: "What's Up" by 4 Non Blondes—chiefly because that's what my clock radio was playing when it woke me up, and I couldn't get it out of my head.

Honestly, life was pretty good.

Bryan Adams liked to sing about the summer of '69, but I'd never understood why 1969 was so special (although Mom seemed to think it was, or Bryan Adams was, or I don't know). In any case, it felt like the summer of '94 was going to be *our* moment.* The one *we* would look back on. By "we" I'm only talking about the junior year at Market Wickby High School, but right then, we were all that mattered. I suppose everyone is the center of their own universe, aren't they? I didn't have any idea what it was like being on the cusp of seventeen and living in London, or Manchester, or New York, or Berlin. I only knew this, and this was rural and quiet, with a main street that was dead by five, a local economy that was tanking thanks to the closure of the fat stock market, and a bucketload of old-fashioned attitudes. But that was where we were, and this was us, and somehow it still felt exciting, and it still felt like change. I had a plan, you see. To make a splash, to maybe help get me elected as class president even, and, more than that, to show this town the new generation was going places, we were doing things, and the old ways weren't our ways.

Anticipation fizzed through my veins on the way to school that day. Me half wondering whether I could capture it and write the lyrics to my own Bryan Adams–style song. But how to do it? And how to be better than (or at least equal to) Bryan Adams anyway? And actually, when you account for my complete lack of musical ability, maybe just sticking to writing stories and scripts would be the best bet?

Was something in the air that day, or was I just in a staggeringly good mood? Was it my new rugby shirt? I was feeling pretty pleased

---

* Ahh, the arrogance of youth! 1969 was a hugely significant year—not only was there the moon landing, but also, on June 28, 1969, the Stonewall Inn in New York City was raided, which led to riots and, in many ways, was the catalyst of the modern LGBTQ rights movement. By contrast, 1994 turned out to be a bit of a disappointment.

with it. I'd noticed a few of the guys wearing rugby shirts—even the ones who didn't play rugby—and it gave them a kind of, well . . . *rugged* quality that I quite liked. Up until today, I'd been a shirt with a vest sort of boy. Fashionable, possibly, but also . . . time for a change? Maybe a vest felt a bit shoulder-length hair, leather satchel, scarf and poetry, you know? I'd stared at myself in the mirror that morning and been *pleased*. Not *delighted*, but certainly not *disappointed*. The cut of the rugby shirt made me look slightly bulkier somehow, and combined with sand-colored chinos and sneakers, and my hair mussed up with some Black & White hair pomade, I actually looked like . . . well, I looked pretty much like most of the other guys. Mission accomplished because it's nice to fit in. I'd even turned my back to the mirror, then spun around, to take myself by surprise, as it were, to see what a "first impression" might look like. Not bad. And that had definitely put me in a good mood.

Even so, what I was feeling felt *bigger*. I just couldn't place it.

I was first in to the junior common room, which I liked, and which was why I always left for school by 8:00 a.m. I'd successfully campaigned for the funds to buy a tea kettle for our exclusive little corner of the school, but the finances didn't extend to a fridge (so no milk, just powdered Coffee-Mate) and an attempt to introduce communal tea and coffee supplies was taken advantage of to the point of it being impractical. So now I stored my own jar of Nescafé, sugar, and Coffee-Mate in my locker—but to avoid letting half of my class use my supplies, it was necessary to get in early and make it before anyone else arrived.

(Note to editor: Does that piece of selfishness make me an unlikable protagonist? To be discussed.)

Close-up[*]: a perfect cup of coffee. Rich. Smooth. No one would know it tastes like shit because of the Coffee-Mate.

Enter: Dan—ambling in.

Soundtrack: "Young at Heart" by The Bluebells. It's suddenly playing out of the common room radio. (I didn't even notice the radio was on until then.)

I liked Dan. Or rather, I felt like I *would* like him. I didn't actually know him beyond a nod of vague acknowledgment in the hallways. He'd transferred to the junior class from another school last September, and, I don't know, he just seemed like someone I would get along with. I couldn't explain it. I just got this *sense* that we would click and be best friends . . . so naturally, I'd never spoken to him. Maybe that was because I was so sure we could be great friends that I didn't want to mess up our first introduction, and so I was overthinking it, or maybe I'd just never found what felt like the right moment. He was quite . . . *dinky* as boys go. Small, slim, dark hair—he looked a bit younger than sixteen or seventeen, with a very friendly, open face and a playful sort of grin that told me we'd have hilarious late-night conversations and share witty, sarcastic asides throughout the day. That was all projection. He might have been dumb as shit for all I knew.

But it was weird because I also had this overwhelming urge to

---

[*] Now the cynics among you might think the only reason I'm formatting some of this like a screenplay is my crude attempt to show it'll be ideal for a ten-part Netflix adaptation. But, actually, I've always seen a lot of my life like a movie. Maybe I'm just detached and observing it, rather than living it. Or maybe I'm just a narcissist. Either way, it's definitely not because I hope to be showered in cash. However, I wouldn't complain, and any TV producers reading this can contact my agent via my website.

protect him. Isn't that weird? I wasn't imagining I would take a bullet for him or anything. It was more in a nurturing sort of way. A friendly cuddle if he was feeling stressed about essay deadlines was more what I had in mind. I had no idea why. Maybe it was because he was quite small, but isn't that what friends ultimately do? They're *there* for one another. They help one another. I wanted a friend like that. One that felt extra special somehow. I had Beth, but I would never cuddle Beth, and I didn't suppose Beth would cuddle me. But I also wouldn't want her to. That just didn't feel right. Whereas, weirdly, a cuddle with Dan . . . *did*. I couldn't explain it.

Dan nodded at me.

Despite being the only other person in the room, I felt pleased he'd noticed me.

I nodded back.

He flopped down on one of the soft chairs covered in offensively orange fabric that I suppose someone, somewhere, must have decided was the sort of color "youths" like, pulled out a Sega Game Gear, and started playing.

I noticed his legs were apart.

I subtly uncrossed mine and copied him.

He was engrossed in his game—this jolly, fairground-style music came out of the console.

I bit the bullet. (Something *was* in the air, you see?! Or maybe I was just feeling extra confident in my swanky new shirt.)

"What are you playing?" I asked.

He didn't look up. "Sonic."

I nodded, not that I knew the game, and not that he could see anyway—he was intensely focused on the screen, thumbs flitting over the controls, biting his tongue between his teeth in concentration, which was a little bit sweet and made me smile.

That oddly tender moment rudely interrupted by:

Beth ENTERS, looking like shit, dark brown shoulder-length hair still wet from her shower, baggy, oversized black sweater that comes down to her mid-thigh, black leggings and battered Reeboks, with an air of chaos around her.

"You're looking *way* too happy for a Monday morning," she said, throwing her bag down and collapsing onto the chair next to me, before coughing and blowing her nose.

I tried to subtly edge away from her.

"I was at a party last night; I'm not *ill*." She eyed my coffee. "Ended a bit late." She was still looking at my coffee. "Probably something to do with the four pints of cider I drank." She picked my coffee up and took a sip while I tried not to look offended, upset, or otherwise left out that there had been a party my best friend had gone to, and I hadn't been invited.

"Needs more sugar," she said, putting the cup back down. "And don't do your jilted-friend face, Jamie. It was a Young Farmers Event."

"Sorry, I've obviously missed the moment when you started growing crops and milking cows."

"My cousin's a farmer. You know that. He invited me."

"And your dad was fine with this?"

"Obviously not." Beth cleared her throat. "I may have been vague with the details and suggested it was less of a party and just some of 'the girls' getting together."

We cut away here to the fearsome image of Beth's father—a

tyrant: strict, traditional, full of hatred and venom, and also the local priest. We see him preaching hellfire and damnation, informing his audience they are full of sin and destined for hell.

Cut to: the audience—a group of terrified elementary school children he's giving an assembly for. Some are in tears.

Back to the present.

Because of her dad's job, Beth was pretty much universally known as "the daughter of the local priest" in the same way Adam Henson was "the son of Doctor Henson," Rob West was "the son of Sir Jeremy West MP," and I was . . . just me because no one in my family was anyone remarkable or interesting . . . *yet.** Anyway, that was why, when Beth first started talking to me, I was highly suspicious and assumed she was trying to convert me; it only later materialized that Beth was, in fact, a massive atheist. Unless, that was, she was playing an extraordinarily long con on me, and her plan all along was to trick me and entrap me into the cult. But if that was the case, honestly, hats off to her—I'd probably have gone along with it just as a show of respect for all the effort. Reverend Clayton didn't seem to mind me going round to their house, but we weren't allowed in her bedroom, in case—and these were his actual words—"I couldn't control my manly urges." Honestly, hearing that, I'd never felt so sex repulsed in my life. Maybe that was the point.

Beth ripped open a Spira bar†, dunked it in the coffee, bit into the chocolate, then took another swig of the drink. She shook her head. "Why isn't there more sugar in this?"

---

* You can't get enough of my foreshadowing, can you? You bloody love it.
† Seriously, Cadbury's—just bring them back already. Everyone loved them.

"Because it isn't your coffee."

She stopped chewing and met my eyes. "Oh, shit, sorry, Jamie. My head's a bit all over the place."

I rolled my eyes.

She glanced at the coffee again. "Shall I just keep it now, or what? You know, *germs?*"

"Have it," I said.

A slightly devious smile played on her lips. "Thanks."

"Good night, huh?" Dan was looking up from his Game Gear. "I've never seen anyone do 'The Time Warp,' 'YMCA,' and 'Vogue' quite like you!"

(Definite flashback to Beth doing this, in the TV show version of this story, her eyes focused, face serious, movements erratic and wild, while onlookers clap and cheer her on, reveling in her humiliation.)

Beth shook her head and groaned, and Dan chuckled.

"You went too?" I said. "Are you a farmer as well?"

"Dad is," Dan replied. *"Pigs."*

I nodded. "Well . . . We love bacon over here."

That made him laugh enough for him to throw his Game Gear back in his backpack and come join us. "We've never really met, have we? I'm Dan," he said.

"Jamie," I replied.

And that feels like a good moment to smash cut into the opening credits.

Chapter 2

I was walking out of history at the start of lunch when Debbie King hurried up to me. Debbie was, according to the way I'd heard most of the guys talk about her, the junior class's answer to Cindy Crawford— all glossy hair and luscious lips, tall and slim and legs and breasts. What none of them seemed to comment on, or notice, was the fact she was actually quite funny, pretty intelligent, and really hardworking, and that was why, aside from the fact that for my project to work I needed backup from some top-of-the-food-chain students, I asked her to join the Prom Committee. To my delight, she agreed, as long as her boyfriend, Adam Henson, could join too. Which of course I said yes to; with *both* of them working on the event there was no way it would be a flop. Adam was a rugby and soccer player—all messy blond hair and square jaw, tall and strong with legs and pecs. As such a fine physical specimen, he was universally adored, but what no one seemed to comment on was the fact he also had no sense of humor (every joke went over his head), he was utterly *dense*, and he was lazy to boot. For a while I'd wondered what Debbie saw in him, and then I remembered catching a glimpse of him in the showers after PE in sophomore year and put two and two together and realized, as far as

Debbie was concerned, he most definitely had other very attractive attributes and was almost certainly good at other stuff.

"The posters have arrived!" Debbie beamed. "And they look *fantastic!*"

Yep, more good news! It's almost like I'm being set up for a massive fall, isn't it? Well, don't worry—there isn't too much more incessant, unmitigated joy to get through.

Ten minutes later, Debbie and I proudly pinned a large poster to the middle of the noticeboard in the common room, and the project that we'd been working on for the past couple of months was finally revealed. This, my friends, is what (I hoped) would get me noticed.

Close-up: (because you want to get an eyeful of this, it was brilliant). These posters were properly printed on what had been designed to look like old-fashioned parchment paper, with an illustration in red ink in the center of the fairies from *A Midsummer Night's Dream* by everyone's favorite playwright, William Shakespeare. (Or, as Beth liked to call him, *Willy Shakes*—a "joke" only she found amusing.) Fancy black calligraphy stated:

The Junior Prom Committee 1994
cordially request the pleasure of your company at . . .
A Midsummer Night's Dream
"Awake the pert and nimble spirit of mirth!"
7:00 p.m., July 15, 1994, in the school gymnasium.
Tickets: £20 (single), £35 (couple)

The buzz was immediate—and good, because this was a first. It was traditional for the junior class to hold some kind of end-of-semester party, but in the past it had basically been a shitty get-together in any nearby community center that was prepared to turn a blind eye to underage drinking and all the puke that would end up everywhere, in exchange for making a shit-ton of cash on the bar. But then I heard about the May Balls that happened at Cambridge University from a guy who came to give us a talk last year and thought how good it would be to replicate a bit of that here. Apparently everyone came in tuxes and ball gowns, there were all sorts of food and drink stands, firework displays and even fair rides, as well as sets from well-known comedians and bands. I knew we couldn't do all that, but we could do something a bit similar. Something properly nice, you know? Dare I say, *sophisticated.* I wanted to make a splash—this was it. Something to be remembered by. And if people had a good time, when it came to voting for class president at the very end of the semester, ready for our senior year, maybe they'd remember me? But also . . . I don't know, there was part of me that got a thrill from mixing things up a bit. From breaking the mold. We weren't just a bunch of losers from a nowhere town; we had futures, we were something, and we could party like the best of them. Why not?

"That's a *lot* of money," Jason commented, flicking at the ticket price with his fingers, "for a dance."

Jason: skinny, for one of the guys. But with a vicious streak that made him intimidating. Usually in some form of trouble. Smokes. Likes to fight. Resentful of being in school, even though it was optional after sixteen, so he was there by choice.

His eyes were on me, utterly unimpressed, but Debbie stepped in. "It's not a dance, Jason, it's a *prom*, so the price includes the live band, food, decorations, and other entertainment."

I watched Jason's face soften, his eyes drifting to Debbie's chest, then snapping back to her face again, like he'd just caught himself staring and realized he probably shouldn't be. "What band?" he sniffed.

"All will be revealed soon!" Debbie said, just as Adam blundered in and replied, "Speak No Monkey*, hopefully— Oh, shit, that's still a secret, isn't it?"

I rolled my eyes and wanted to kill him on the spot, but the news caused an immediate furor of excitement that drowned out Debbie admonishing Adam, because yes, we weren't just planning to have some guy with a CD player, or someone's brother's band, this was one of the best Britpop groups out there, this was going to be the real deal—at least, it would be as long as this was the one thing my dad didn't let me down over. When I first mentioned my idea to Dad a few months back, he said he knew Speak No Monkey's manager really well—a friend from school, he said—and he reckoned he could get them to play for us. I'd taken it with a pinch of salt due to previous disappointments (the trip to see *Phantom of the Opera* that never materialized, the forgotten birthdays, and all the times I was meant to see him but he was suddenly busy), but he phoned up the following week and said he'd spoken to his friend, and there might be a gap in their tour schedule that allowed it, and I should write a letter to them explaining about the prom and inviting them to play. So I did. I hadn't heard back yet, but Dad assured me the letter was received, and they were just working out some logistics

---

* Speak No Monkey never existed—it's one of the few things I've made up just because it's easier this way. Speak No Monkey were four cheeky chappies who sang really catchy songs about quite mundane things.

and the whole thing was 80 percent likely . . . which did nothing to stop me focusing on the 20 percent *unlikely*, hence why this was meant to be a secret, for now.

Just like that, Scott (Jason's partner in crime, who *was* a big guy—classic beefcake, all muscle, barely evolved, at the mercy of all his basest urges and impulses—sorry, but some people just *are* stereotypes) ripped open his Velcro wallet, pulled two bills out, bought a couple's ticket from Debbie, then strolled over to Rachel Plimpton (whose standards were so low she would have gone out with a warthog), got down on one knee, and asked her to the prom. That caused cheers, and tears of joy from Rachel, and, despite the individuals involved, it did make me smile, because this was all working out perfectly and it seemed like people were getting on board (no guarantee of that with a bunch of cynical seventeen-year-olds).

Adam nodded in delight too, soaking up the buoyant atmosphere, almost like he couldn't believe it, then announced: "Debbie and I are dressing up as Torvill and Dean!"

"Oberon and Titania!" Debbie corrected.

"Well, whoever, I can't remember all the names."

Debbie smiled at him fondly and gave him a kiss on the lips, which developed into a slightly lingering one, Adam getting far too into it, before Debbie pulled back, probably in the interest of decency.

"Shit, everyone's coupling up!" Jason said. "Who am I gonna take? Jamie?"

"Funny," I said.

"Shit, I wasn't *asking* you, I just wondered who you were taking!"

"I know." (I didn't know.)

"Jamie wants to go to the prom with me, everyone!" Jason shouted.

Assorted cheers, someone retching, and replies of "Gross!"

I swallowed and shook my head, smiling through it.

But Jason came up behind me, arms around my waist, and held me tight. "How about it, huh?" He did a little thrust.

"Funny. Very funny."

"I love you, Jamie."

"OK, I have to put up more posters now, so . . ."

"Nice rugby shirt, by the way," he hissed in my ear. "Looks new. Wonder why?"

I froze, like a rag doll, while he continued to manhandle me for a few moments.

"Ah, *man*, who is *that*?!"

He suddenly released me and headed over to a couple of guys who were holding up page 3 of *The Sun** and admiring the model, and just like that, I was dumped.

Close-up: on me. Relief. And the only time I'd think page 3 was a good thing.

I glanced around. No one was looking at me. No one had thought anything of it.

That's one nice thing about being in the middle. People don't really notice. Even when you've organized a prom for them, they soon find someone—or something—more interesting. I wondered if that

---

* *The Sun* is a British tabloid newspaper that featured topless female models on page 3 until 2015. It was, and remains, in my humble opinion, a repulsive rag.

would change if the prom went well? Part of me craved recognition and minor fame. Part of me hated the idea and wanted a quiet life.*

I took a pile of posters, hurried out, and spent a while pinning them to other bulletin boards around school; it was important to cultivate as much buzz as possible, and keep the prom at the front of people's minds.

"Not there, Jamie." It was Mrs. Prenton. "That's for official notices only."

Mrs. Prenton: the principal at Market Wickby High School. In her early sixties . . . I think, but I was at that time of life where age is meaningless because either you're a kid, a teenager my age, a regular adult, or old. Prenton was hard as nails, took no nonsense, and was terrifying in many ways, even for a woman who was actually quite short and slight. Everything about her oozed respectability and power, from the neat skirt and jacket to the hair that made her look like Margaret Thatcher†—set, back-combed, and sprayed into place. She liked me though. And I wanted her to like me. God, I was such a people pleaser.

I took the pushpins out and removed the poster. "Sorry, miss." I gave her a smile.

"How's the idea going down with everyone?"

"Really well! We're already selling tickets."

She nodded approvingly. "Looks like the gamble might pay off."

---

* This hasn't changed. I've learned that fame is a double-edged sword, and you'll soon find out why. (That's the last of the foreshadowing, I promise.)

† Margaret Thatcher was leader of the Conservative Party and prime minister of the UK from 1979 to 1990. There was no denying she was popular with some, but personally, I couldn't stand her, and her legacy of greed and selfishness lives on today.

I smiled again while my head played the flashback: me in her office, sitting opposite her on the soft chairs while I tried to sell the idea of the prom. No, there wouldn't be any alcohol. Yes, it would be limited to only students from this school. Yes, we had done the math, and yes, we could cover the costs . . . maybe even end up with a surplus we could donate to charity.

She wouldn't commit, and I suspect she'd have turned us down had it not been for Debbie's dad stepping in to underwrite the whole thing. Mrs. Prenton was courting Debbie's father—not in the romantic sense; she was grooming the richer parents for donations toward equipment for a new performing arts wing, and this was probably the opportunity she needed to get in with him.

"I'm impressed with you, Jamie. This is a big undertaking. It hasn't gone unnoticed."

"Thanks, miss."

She smiled at me and walked on while I started pinning up a poster on the next board along, high on what the possible interpretations of "It hasn't gone unnoticed" might be. On the shortlist for class president? Surely!

"And not that one!" she called back without even turning around. "That's PE department only—and they're *very* territorial!"

I chuckled. "Sorry, miss!"

Funny though—despite the reaction from everyone, and despite Mrs. Prenton's kind words, I had a nagging feeling in my stomach. Something like . . . sadness? Something like . . . I'd been so excited about the prom, but now that it was out there the excitement belonged to everyone else and not to me.

I couldn't make sense of it, but after I'd finished putting up my posters, I knew I didn't want to go back to the common room. It felt like I should just let everyone get on with pairing up and finding dates and asking people out. I had some essays to get started on anyway, and with all the hysteria, the library would probably be the best place to focus for half an hour.

I'd hidden myself away at a table behind one of the bookcases, but the librarian, Mrs. Carpenter, found me when she rounded the shelves with a pile of books she was putting back.

"Jamie Hampton! What are you doing lurking here?" She smiled at me. "And do you want a cookie?"

She didn't wait for an answer, just produced a packet she was holding under the books and put two on my table. "I've been hearing the chatter about the prom," she said.

I raised my eyebrows. "Really?"

"Seems to be the thing everyone's talking about!"

"We only put the poster up half an hour ago."

"Well, it's exciting. Biggest thing to happen around here in . . . forever!" She laughed. "But it's nice. A big event to take someone you like to, and all that. Ahh, the romance! Almost makes me want to be a teenager again, except . . . *no*, not quite enough to want that, but it warms my stone-cold heart to think of all of you experiencing that."

I smiled at the "stone-cold heart" business. Mrs. C had the *best* heart. She was funny and kind but also really sarcastic, and I loved that. She also regularly gossiped about school stuff that students weren't supposed to know about, never hiding her feelings about what she thought of certain staff members. And I loved that even more. And stylish? Oh boy. Mrs. C would regularly be seen wearing a leather jacket or faux fur, and I'd even seen her in vinyl pants on a weekend. For me, she was on a par with Kate Moss or Winona Ryder—sure, a little older, but totally rocking the A-lister look.

"So, who are you going to take, Jamie?"

My eyes met hers and I momentarily froze. "Um . . . hadn't thought." I turned to my cookie, twisting the pieces apart and going in for the cream center first.

"Because, if there's anyone you like, you *have* to take them to the prom," she said. "It's a rite of passage."

I concentrated on the cookie. "There's no one I like."

"Aww—"

"Besides," I said, glancing quickly at her, "I'll have my work cut out on the night itself, organizing everything and making sure it's all OK. So."

"Very professional," she said.

I nodded and she turned to the shelf, replacing a few books.

"Is that rugby shirt new?" she said, back still to me.

"Um . . . yeah."

She turned. "I'm used to seeing you in a vest and shirt.*"

"I wanted a change."

"Nothing to do with what happened on Friday, I hope?"

I froze. What did she mean?

"What Jason and Scott were saying?" she continued.

I did not know she overheard that.

***

---

* I promise you, this wasn't a fashion disaster at the time.

INT.* LIBRARY. FRIDAY AFTERNOON. FLASHBACK

Study hall. Jamie Hampton sits alone at his table, finishing an English essay on *Wuthering Heights*. An assortment of other juniors also sit at tables, including Jason and Scott, at a table just behind Jamie. Mrs. Carpenter, behind her desk at the front—surely not within earshot, unless she has super-human hearing?

JASON: You know what's really *gay*? Guys who wear vests.

SCOTT: So fucking gay.

JASON: May as well just carry a sign that says, "Massive Queer."

SCOTT: Massive *hoooooomooooooo!*

JASON: *Hoooooomooooo!*

Close-up on Jamie: *Are they talking about me?*

I shook myself back to the present and swallowed. "I just . . . wanted a change."

"Yes, you said." Mrs. C nodded and replaced another book while I hoped that would be the end of it. Truth was, that *was* why I'd bought the rugby shirt. I'd been mortified. The idea that Jason and Scott would think *that* about me. I suppose I was just clueless about fashion. I'd seen a few people do the casual vest and shirt thing, admittedly more traditionally associated with formal attire, but I liked the look and thought it might suit me. But then again, maybe not.

Not if that was the impression it gave anyway.

---

* INT. is screenwriting shorthand for "interior"—meaning the scene takes place inside. Later you might see EXT., which, you've hopefully guessed, means "exterior." You're welcome.

"Don't let other people dictate who you are," Mrs. C continued.

"I'm not."

"Good. Because you be you. Be who you want."

"I am."

She gave me a smile. "Good!" And she disappeared around the shelf.

Be you.

Who was I anyway?

I mulled that one over for a good few minutes, let me tell you. Nothing like life's big questions to occupy your mind.

I turned to a fresh page in my notebook and wrote *Jamie Hampton* at the top of it. I sat back, tapping my pen, thinking, wondering, then added:

Straight A student.

16.

Friend.

Organizer.

Studying AP English Lit., history, economics.

Kind to animals.

Kind to animals?! I scratched that last one out. Was that the best I could come up with? I admired Mrs. C for her style, her eccentricity, and the fact she was unashamedly unique. How did she get there? Part of me wanted that; part of me was scared of that. And what was this list I'd made anyway? A poem? The edgy sort that didn't rhyme? It wasn't a story. It was . . . just random words. Disjointed. Meaningless.

Boring.

The truth?

No. I was more than that.

Wasn't I?

I drew a box around my list, drew lines from corner to corner, crossing through the text, then added, at the top:

Work in progress.

I mean, aren't we all?*

---

* If you're familiar with teen books and movies, you'll be worried this list will be discovered by someone awful, and I'll be humiliated. Won't happen here, so forget about it. Happy to tell you that, because I want you focusing on the important stuff, and not sweating cheap plot devices. (Oh, I'm such a bitch.)

Chapter 3

Mrs. C stopped me on the way out. The bell had rung several minutes ago. I was already late because I'd just been sitting at the table, staring into space, but, you know, existential crisis and all that.

"Jamie!" She beckoned me over to the desk where she handed me a book called *Wildflowers of Great Britain*. "I think you might enjoy it."

I glanced up from the book and met her eyes. "It's good," she added. "Good read. *Important*."

"I'm not taking biology."

"And that's OK," she said.

I frowned at the book. "But—"

"Jamie, do you trust me, as keeper of the books, or do you *not* trust me?"

I cracked a smile. "Obviously, I trust you."

"Then trust me on this. Keep an open mind. OK?"

I shrugged. "OK."

She smiled, satisfied.

Isn't it interesting (and also terrifying) how one tiny action can completely alter the course of your life? When I think about it now,

I marvel at this, and how, had I not done it, everything could have been totally different, and not necessarily in a good way. *I took out my library card.* How is it possible that such a small thing can ultimately change so much? Well, it's chaos theory, I suppose. The butterfly effect—the idea that one small change can create much larger consequences down the line. Taking out my library card was, however, a perfectly normal thing to have done. Every student had a library account, and the database of who had borrowed what books was kept on the library computer system—a BBC Master Computer with some kind of database software that ran off five-and-a-quarter-inch floppy disks. Each book had a barcode that was scanned, along with the one on your library card, and that way everyone knew if you were the one hundredth awkward and insecure teenage boy to try and steal *Diary of a Teenage Health Freak* because there was a little chart in there that told you how big your willy was meant to be.*

I took my library card out, and I realize now that Mrs. C was shaking her head, telling me not to worry about the card, just to take the book, but right at that moment Mr. Haskins, one of the PE teachers, walked through the doors, about to take a study hall, and clocked us both, so Mrs. C grabbed my card and scanned the book to my account. It was all so quick and easy and normal, I thought nothing else of it, taking the book, my card, and heading off to my English class.

What I didn't know, of course, was that that was the first domino, and now, inevitably, the rest would fall; the wheels were in

---

* Somewhere between five and six inches, in case you're wondering.

motion; it was . . . unstoppable. I'd been thinking about change earlier that morning, and now bigger change than I could have anticipated was happening.

But I didn't understand that.

And nor do you.

And that is called *dramatic tension*.

Let's leave this chapter here. Significant events deserve emphasis, and very short chapters do that, don't you think?

Chapter 4

If someone had told James Frampton he was going to have the prom of his dreams, he would never have believed you. Yet the night was magical. Everything was going just as he planned. The band was electric. The food was delicious. The atmosphere was beautiful and relaxed, and every photograph that he took he knew would be a treasured memory someday. A time when he was young and full of joy and hope about the future and what his life would be.

It helped that she was there, of course.

He liked her.

He really liked her.

James couldn't quite believe his luck when it turned out she liked him back.

And now, here they were, walking hand in hand around the ball together at prom. Enjoying the night. Laughing with friends, but always, however much the laughter, and however fun the friends, ultimately returning to each other, because each other was what really mattered.

They rode the big wheel.

And at the top, they kissed.

Sounds corny. A big cliché.

But why should fairy tales only exist in books?

"Jamie? Your dinner's ready!" (Mom, from downstairs.)

I tore the paper from the pad and stared at it. Why did the words feel so flat? All the romantic elements were there—the location, the lovers destined to be together, and, that staple of any good romance, the big wheel! What more did you need to feel the love? I tried placing different people I knew as the "she" character—seeing if they fitted, like the prince looking for the owner of the slipper. It wasn't Beth. I felt weird and icky even trying to imagine her and me in that scenario. We loved each other, but not like that. And I couldn't imagine being on the big wheel with Debbie either. I felt sure it should be someone, but I couldn't picture who. Maybe that was the problem? I needed to be specific? What did she look like? *Who really was she?*

"Jamie?!"

And why had I called the main character *James Frampton?* Was it me, or not? It all felt so wrong. I ripped the page up and dropped the pieces in the trash. Some work is too bad even to be saved by an edit. I'd revisit it later. Try again.

I hurried downstairs, then took a moment at the closed living room door to steel myself.

I had to make an effort.

I had to make an effort *with Keith.* I'd promised Mom I would.

There are a number of ways I could write about my family situation, but, honestly, what better than this selection from the archive, the ramblings of a thirteen-year-old boy writing poetry that barely scans?

27

Mom kicked Dad out
When she found out about
His secret affair
With the girl with blonde hair.
She was twenty years younger
Mom said it was vulgar
But Dad really dug her
Said she "satisfied a hunger." (I know, it makes me want to
vomit too.)
Now they're divorced
And Dad lives in Stoke.
I don't really see him
And we are flat broke.

Not my finest work, but it does the job. All was doom, gloom, and
bills with scary red writing until last year, when Mom started
seeing a "certain someone" who eventually turned out to be Keith
Davidson—a man who sold vacuum cleaners, which were the only
things that sucked more than he did. Keith officially moved in three
weeks ago. I'd stood next to Mom in the open doorway and had
watched as Keith sprang out of the driver's side of his Ford Mondeo,
trying to keep the fake smile plastered on my face, despite the
sight of a middle-aged man with blond highlights, a mullet, tight
Wrangler jeans, and slip-on shoes offending me to the point of
nausea.

Keith had looked at my mother like she was an angel (and not a
desperate fortysomething with a questionable perm), and then at
the house, like it was nirvana (and not a tiny new build on a bland

acre of land). He drank it all in, smiled like the cat that got the cream, and said, "It's a beautiful day, you're a beautiful woman, and this is the start of a beautiful thing!" Which didn't in any way sound corny and rehearsed, but, huh, if he did write that himself, then I supposed I owed a tiny bit of kudos to a fellow creative.

It's true, I hadn't gelled with Keith. He was very much an alpha male, very much the "big I am," but beyond that, I couldn't really say what my objections were, and I was aware it might come across all a bit *Freudian* and "the son not being happy about his mother finding a new man," and all that, so I was *trying*. I was trying.

Dinner was steak, which was something we ate a lot now. Either Keith really liked red meat, or he had a sketchy cut-price butcher contact. Either way, I could feel myself becoming more vegetarian by the minute. Something about the way Keith closed his eyes in ecstasy whenever he started chewing a piece of sirloin, combined with Mom's little moans of pleasure at the taste, really irked me. It was like some hideous meat-based foreplay and I didn't want to see it.

I took a breath and went for it. I "took an interest," just like Mom had asked. "So, is business good, then, Keith?"

"Never better," he replied.

"He works hard for it though," Mom quickly added, as though my question was a trap and his answer needed justification.

"I do, I work hard for it. S'why I have to spend periods away from home—saturated the local market and I have to expand my territory."

I tried not to wrinkle my nose at "territory." That was something dogs marked by pissing everywhere. For some reason, I could imagine Keith splashing urine over various streets around the UK while declaring, "I sell hoovers here now!"

(Note to TV producers: We don't need to see that in a fantasy sequence. *Or should we?* Might really highlight my revulsion in a very visual way—to be discussed.)

I carried on. "Mom says they're expensive? The hoovers? How much are they?"

Keith put his cutlery down and fixed me with a stare. "They're not 'hoovers.' Hoover is a brand name for a vastly inferior domestic suction device. I know most people use the word generically, but it's not right." He sniffed. "They're eight hundred."

"*Wow.*"

"Last you a lifetime though. Unparalleled cleaning quality."

I nodded, feigning interest. "Still, eight hundred!"

"But that's where I come in. They're not just buying a SuctionMax 2000, they're buying Keith Davidson: charmer. Raconteur. Purveyor of hopes and dreams. Plus, your average bored housewife can't resist a certain handsome man." He winked at my mom. "Just lucky that god gave me the right tools, you know?" He cast his eyes toward the ceiling. "Thank you, Jesus!"

"Thank you, Jesus, for Keith," Mom added.

I wasn't sure whether we were all about to break into some evangelical-style prayer situation. We'd never been a religious family—never went to church or anything—but Mom clearly thought Keith was some sort of divine gift. Whereas I saw him more as a cult leader—and if he could charge eight hundred bucks for a hoover, then he was clearly adept at persuading people to drink the Kool-Aid.

"How's the prom going?" Mom asked.

"Fine."

"Never had that sort of thing in my day," Mom continued. "We'd be lucky to have a sweaty dance."

"Who are you going to ask?" Keith said. "Who's the lucky lady?"

"What about Beth? She's a lovely girl!" Mom added.

"Mom, really? She's my best friend. It would be like incest."

"Me and Keith were friends at first," Mom replied.

"Friends, Jamie, make the best lovers," Keith said. Seriously, he was full of advice like that.

"I'm in charge, so I'll be pretty busy on the night," I said.

End of conversation. Cut to: dessert and good night, please?

No such luck.

"Seems a shame," Mom said.

I shrugged. "Someone's got to do it."

"Word of advice," Keith said, swallowing down a mouthful of steak and fries, and jabbing his fork in my direction. "These are the best years of your life: You've got freedom, you can play the field, mess around, have some fun. Trust me, that's what you should be doing."

"Well, maybe I don't want to. Maybe I've got other priorities."

Keith shrugged. "All right. *Fine.* But you've got to at some point, else people will start to think you're a bit weird."

So, there we had it. We spent the rest of the meal in virtual silence, while I contemplated if this was true: Was I just weird? Other people were enthusiastic about taking a date to the prom. Even Mrs. C had wanted to know who I'd be asking.

Why couldn't I get myself together in that regard?

I couldn't even picture the girl I would take in my wildest dreams.

Was there something wrong with me?

After some ice cream, Keith disappeared for a few minutes, returning to announce he had a "surprise" for me.

Montage sequence: Keith covering my eyes with his hands. Keith guiding me up the stairs with Mom following behind. A ridiculous amount of anticipation—even from me, always a sucker for a "surprise." I did have high hopes. I really wanted my own CD player. Tapes and LPs were fine, but this wasn't the 80s, and CDs looked futuristic, and they were so much more convenient—easy to carry around, and you could skip ahead to songs easily. Not to mention the sound quality! I mean, the Channel Tunnel had just opened, for god's sake—you could go from England to France *through a tunnel*—and here I was, still listening to songs on what basically amounted to a gramophone.

"No peeping! No peeping!" my equally excited mother said.

Finally in my bedroom, Keith removed his hands from my eyes. "TA-DAH!"

And there, in front of me, stuck up on my wall, was a giant, poster-sized, glossy picture of Electra from ITV's primetime Saturday night show *Wave Warriors.**

Wave Warriors featured members of the public competing in

---

* OK, kids, you're going to need to suspend your disbelief here. Yes, there was a very famous "sports entertainment game show" on ITV in the 90s, but using it here would be problematic (and could get me sued), so just go with me on this, OK?

water-based challenges in a huge pool against a team of athletic "Wave Warriors" who were named after mythical figures and sea creatures—including the fearsome Poseidon, scary twins "the Sirens," Nessie (whose swimsuit was tartan), and glamorous Electra—goddess of storm clouds, and favorite of pubescent boys everywhere, to the extent she even had a heavily laminated calendar dedicated to her.

(Note to legal: Can I get away with this?)

"*Electra*," Keith said.

I stared at the vision.

"Great, big, massive *Electra*."

It's true, she was huge.

"What do you say, Jamie?" Mom said.

"You've been in my room?" I managed to spit out.

"Wanted it to be a surprise," Keith said. "Don't worry, I didn't find your stash of *Playboys*."

By reflex, I glanced at the bottom drawer of the set under my desk.

"Thank Keith, Jamie," Mom said. "He went to a lot of effort to get that poster. Had to save up tokens from a lot of crispy pancake boxes."

"Fifteen boxes," Keith added. "Plus, postage and packaging."

I took a breath. "Thanks, Keith, it's . . ." I tried to find the right word. One that Keith would like, that sounded like I was pleased and grateful. For some reason, I opted for: "Fabulous!"

Wrong choice. They both stared at me.

I nodded, because sometimes it's best just to double down on this stuff.

33

"I have some homework to finish," I managed to say. "Thanks again. I love the poster. I'm . . . really happy."

They left me to it.

I sat on my bed and stared up at Electra.

She was posed thrusting her chest forward in a red sports bra type thing with sheer-cut red—I didn't know what you would call them—bikini bottom things? Undies? Except this wasn't underwear; it was a sporty swimwear outfit, only it wasn't like anything most people wore when swimming. This seemed . . . I dunno, designed to titillate?

Well, it wasn't titillating me.

And I knew it should be.

Was I weird?

I stared at her really hard. I wondered if I should try imagining her naked, but it didn't seem right. It felt . . . disrespectful. I think I would have preferred just a magazine interview with Electra. It would have been interesting to know how she'd got into this line of work, about her hobbies, or her favorite food, stuff like that. Maybe one of those photographic tours of her house would be good? I would've loved to have known what kind of place she'd be living in after finding fame on primetime Saturday night television. With the extra cash, I bet she'd got a private gym set up, maybe even an indoor pool so she could get extra practice in.

Back to Electra. I knew I needed to find her sexy, like every other guy did.

What was wrong with me?

I zoned in on her.

So focused.

Image blurring.

Like one of those 3D Magic Eye pictures they printed in the *Daily Mail* weekend supplement. When you stared hard enough, for long enough, suddenly they just became 3D—real—jumping out at you because of some kind of optical wizardry. Maybe if Electra was more real, maybe things would click for me and I'd fancy her, want to . . . whatever boys like doing with . . . people who weren't boys.

I sighed. It wasn't working.

Nothing was changing.

And then, honest to god, her eyes moved.

Electra's eyes moved.

I rubbed mine.

Staring too hard?

But I was still looking, and I saw it again. Her eyes—flicking downward, as if . . . looking at something, as if . . . she was showing me something . . . drawing my attention to something . . .

I followed her gaze down to my schoolbag, and the book that was poking out the top of it.

Wildflowers of Great Britain.

I looked back up at her, and, I'm not lying, she seemed to nod.

She . . . wanted me to look at the book?

I shrugged. OK, *Electra*, whatever, I'll look at the damn book.

And at 8:00 p.m. on a Monday night in May 1994, pretty much exactly twelve hours since this story began, when I'd walked down the street on my way to school feeling like change was in the air, I picked up the book, opened it, and settled down to read.

And change well and truly grabbed me by the throat and did not let me go ever again.

Go on, at least one more chapter; you know you need to know why.

Chapter 5

The front cover said *Wildflowers of Great Britain*.

There was no title or imprint page inside, and, even more weirdly, the text just started . . . and it was *all* text, no pictures or diagrams of . . . well, wildflowers.

Intrigued, I read on.

This was not a nonfiction book about botany.

This was a story about two boys.

About friendship.

Strange. How did the insides end up not matching the cover?

Then, within the first forty pages, something really resonated with me. The main character, Hal, tells this story about how he watched a children's TV program when he was younger, about two boys who find a can of magic beans, and it enables them to time-travel, having all sorts of adventures and solving all sorts of problems along the way. And he recounts how, at the end of the first episode, the two boys swear allegiance to each other, cutting their hands and becoming blood brothers, and how he realized how much he wanted that sort of total, complete, no-holds-barred friendship with another boy.

And I thought: me too. Me too, Hal! That's what I'm looking for. A boy to share a can of magic beans with. To be my confidant, my always-there, my loyal sidekick, and me his. But where to find him?

I'd gasped, and then I'd smiled, because for the first time, I was reading words that described almost exactly what I was feeling.

Remember I told you about Dan earlier? How I felt this need to protect him? Well, that's what this was, only now more eloquently put, and now with the added hope that maybe what I was feeling wasn't so weird, but had been felt by others before me, by Hal, and so . . .

I read on.

And soon I realized.

This wasn't just a story about friendship between two teenage boys.

This . . . was a love story.

Between two teenage boys.

And, honestly, maybe those last two sentences should be individual chapters on their own, one each, because they deserve that emphasis, because this was huge.

Never had I ever read anything like this before.

I didn't even know this existed.

It felt . . . *illegal.*

And yet I couldn't stop reading.

Then . . . *shame.* And panic. Because I read a section, an . . . *intimate* section, and I think I was enjoying it a bit *too* much because it had an effect on me that should have happened when I was looking at Electra.

I closed the book. And in the TV show of this story, this would be an abstract, kaleidoscopic moment, with thoughts and visions appearing and intruding at random, like . . . why did Mrs. C give me this book? It was a mistake, right? Because she thought it was about wildflowers? She didn't think I'd be interested in what this really was, did she? Because if she did know . . . Is this what she thinks I am? How did she reach that conclusion? And how do I prove her wrong? People can't think that of me!

Cut to: Jason in the library, laughing at me for dressing gay.

Cut to: newspaper headline I saw when I was younger: *"I'd shoot my son if he had AIDS," says priest.*

Cut to: "Who are you taking to the prom?"

Cut to: that photo of Freddie Mercury, gaunt and emaciated, before he died from AIDS—a surprise that shocked everyone.

Cut to: "Be you!" (Mrs. C).

Cut to: Who the hell am I anyway?

And I didn't know, didn't know any of the answers, except that I *did* want to find a boy to share a can of magic beans with, and if it was just to share magic beans, was that the same thing, because that wasn't anything sexual, it was just magic beans, and was that so wrong?

I glanced up at Electra. I was clearly in some sort of *state*, because her eyes moved again, guiding me again, to the book.

I picked it back up and read on.

It was just a book.

It wasn't real.

Just because it was about a certain *thing*, it didn't mean that I was also that thing. Reading a book about an astronaut didn't make me an astronaut, merely an observer of someone else's life.

That made me feel better.

Keep an open mind, Mrs. C had told me. Good advice.

And what was I thinking anyway, imagining boys with cans of magic beans? *What was I? Five?!* Grow up, Jamie. And, of course, fairy tales are for books; no, they aren't real life, how can they be? I'd lose that line from my rewritten story. This rose-tinted, sentimental mindset wasn't helping me.

I'd almost convinced myself, reading on, the story getting somewhat darker—don't worry, I won't spoil it—until about three-quarters of the way through when I came across some hand-written words scrawled in blue ink in the margin.

Really?!

Because I couldn't believe this:

I feel like this too.

Then, just under that, in black ink:

Anyone else?

And then, finally:

Just me then.

And just like that, the story wasn't fiction anymore. It was real. Because someone else had been here, reading these same words, and they felt maybe something like what I was feeling. I realized, in horror, that nagging in my stomach . . . it had been loneliness. Because now I felt better. Realizing someone out there was a bit like me.

More shame. More guilt.

I didn't know *who*, of course, and I didn't know when. For all I knew, these words could have been written years ago. Whoever it was could have been long gone by now. Except . . . the ink looked bright. *Fresh.*

I stared at the words.

An invitation.

I couldn't quite place *why*, but it felt like a can of worms I shouldn't (couldn't?) open.

But the words . . .

Anyone else?

Just me then.

They sounded so lonely. The sense of hope and then the crushing sadness. No longer a question, a statement of fact.

Was it a fact? Was it just them?

Either way, I felt bad for the writer. And like I'd felt with Dan, I had this weird urge to protect whoever it was—or, if not protect exactly, then to help them.

Except . . .

I feel like this too.

Like what? Like the characters in the book, presumably.

As in . . . they're a boy who loves other boys?

Was that really something I could (should?) help with?

"What are you waiting for?"

My head snapped up and I froze. That had been a woman's voice. It had come from . . . My eyes flicked to the poster. *Electra.* Obviously, it couldn't have been. And yet, those words had been clear as day inside my head. Was I losing it? Was I so deep in creating my little story worlds in my notebook that the lines between fantasy and reality had become blurred? Virginia Woolf, Ernest Hemingway, Leo Tolstoy . . . they'd all suffered from mental illness . . .

I stared at Electra, the light from the setting sun glinting off her high-gloss lamination, basking her in a warm glow.

"What if he's your boy with the can of magic beans?" she asked.

A little squeak escaped from my mouth. It wouldn't have been a good idea to scream. A scream would have meant Mom and Keith coming up. And then what? *Mom, I'm hearing voices!* I wasn't sure where that admission would end, but I felt like it wouldn't be in a good place.

I released an unsteady breath. Then took another deep, slow one.

Come on, Jamie. When you write stories, you hear character voices in your head all the time. This was just that.

Wasn't it?

"Jamie?" she said.

I would go with it. Why not? See where it leads. "Uh-huh?"

"You want to find a boy to share a can of magic beans with. What if that's him? And what if you're about to miss your chance? Wouldn't that be sad?"

"If I write a message back, it would be like I was admitting something," I whispered.

"If a tree falls in a forest, and no one is there, does it make a noise?" she replied.

"I have no idea what that means."

"If you write in the book, but no one knows it was you, did you really write it?"

"Ohhh. Makes sense. It would be anonymous. There'd be no proof it was me. No one's going to do a handwriting test. And, hey, I could deliberately fake my handwriting anyway, and, huh, maybe I'd only be doing this because it's intriguing. I'm intrigued. Messages in a book *are* intriguing, they're—"

"Seriously, kid, dress it up however you want, I'm just saying, now's your chance."

I grabbed a pen from the jar on my desk and told myself, what the hell, it didn't matter, even if I did put this out into the universe, it would be so easy to backtrack. I never even had to look at this book again if I didn't want to. In the scheme of things, this was utterly insignificant. But what words to put in reply? I was a writer. Words were my thing. I'd written so many—played around with form and structure, metaphor, juxtaposition, iambic pentameter—I needed something beautiful and moving and perfect for this.

I thought and thought and thought.

And in the end opted for what must be my most disappointing piece of work ever, because nothing felt right and everything was either too much, not enough, or all-out pretentious:

Hello!

Yes, even an exclamation mark.

God, Jamie, maybe writing *isn't* your thing.

Chapter 6

Of course, I couldn't stop thinking about the identity of the mystery note writer.

Detective work: There were three date stamps in the front of the book. The first was September 23, 1988, when I would have been in sixth grade. That was a lifetime ago, and it was highly likely that student would have left by now. But the second stamp was dated just three months ago. Of course, I couldn't be sure if the person who wrote in the book was the same person who was second to take the book out, but it was the best I had to go on.

And, of course, by the following morning I'd devised numerous scenarios about how this would play out, and so . . .

Dream sequence.

Me and mystery note writer communicate over the course of a few weeks. We get to know each other. It's clear we share the same sense of humor. He turns out to be a misunderstood guy in my year, secretly lonely, adrift in the confusing sea of finding yourself and working things out—it can be *a lot*, don't you think?— and he just needed someone to be there for him. Difficult, when boys are expected to be so macho and hard all the time. He needed someone to be vulnerable with, someone he could just talk about his feelings with, with no judgment and no one making fun of him. That person is me. I put my arm around his shoulders and hold him close. He likes that. It's just as friends, nothing more, but we both know if anyone saw they'd probably get the wrong idea. So we only meet in secret. It's nice. He feels better being with me. I help him. Maybe he is Dan.

Tuesday. Exterior shot of me walking toward school that matches yesterday's shot, only maybe a bit *less* of a bounce in my step. That's due to the book and the notes. I'm deep, deep in thought. I have a rugby shirt on again, but it was three for two in Burton*, so this one is different colors: green and burgundy, if you're interested.

My plan was to return the book first thing, before homeroom, but even just carrying it into school felt like I had a bomb with me. The actual text was one part of it: If anyone found me with a book about two boys having a relationship, I knew I'd pay for it. Nobody reads that sort of thing except for perverts. But then there were the notes. And *they* felt much more dangerous.

Cut to: me walking into school. Eyes on me. Or so it feels. Whispering behind my back? Or am I imagining it? How could they know? They couldn't.

Cut to: slipping the book into the returns box, acting like an MI5 spy, glancing over my shoulder, checking the coast is clear. Nobody sees. At least, I don't think they do.

---

* A popular menswear store in 90s UK. Most of my clothes came from there.

Cut to: me walking along the hallway, passing different students. *Is it him? Could it be him?*

Cut to: "Jesus, Jamie, you need to see this."

Debbie King dragged me into the common room and over to the bulletin board. There, in the center, was the prom poster. And scrawled across it, in black marker, the words *RIP OFF!*

My stomach tightened. It had taken less than twenty-four hours for the cynics to show themselves. My biggest fear with the prom was that people would dismiss it as over the top. I hadn't accounted for them thinking it was too expensive.

"People are asking where all the money's going," Debbie told me. "Saying we must be pocketing some of it."

"Do they know your dad's sponsoring it? And that if he wasn't, even with the ticket revenue, it wouldn't be happening?"

"That's just making it worse. They're saying if we're already getting it sponsored, why is the ticket price still so high?"

"It's a prom!" I howled.

Debbie shrugged. I blew out a breath. People had no idea. Damn it, you try to do something different for people, something nice, an event where everyone can have a pretty special time, that it's optional to come to anyway, and some people still have to shit on it.

"Who's 'they' anyway?"

"The usual troublemakers." She met my eyes. "Jason."

"Of course."

"I'm thinking we nip it in the bud. Me, you, and Adam, in assembly this morning—and we set the record straight."

Well, that sounded horrible, but what choice did we have?

Half an hour later I was standing at the front of the hall, looking into the cold, soulless eyes of two hundred juniors. Plus Electra.

What?! I did a double take. It wasn't Electra. My mind was still playing tricks on me. Bloody hell.

"Hello, everyone," I began. "Um . . . It's come to our attention that some of you are questioning the cost of the prom tickets, so we just wanted to say that it's a big event, there's lots going on, and it's going to cost a lot of money."

"We're very happy to publish the budget!" Adam piped up, grinning at everyone. I glanced at him, tight-lipped, because we hadn't agreed we'd do that, and while we didn't have anything to hide, that felt like a lot of work and extra scrutiny that we didn't really need.

"What we're also saying," Debbie added, "is that if there is any profit whatsoever, we'll donate it to charity. Just like Bob Geldof and Band Aid."

"Prom Aid!" Adam announced, sounding really pleased that he'd come up with that.

I sighed. "Just to reiterate, this is much more than the usual junior class party, and we've got some really brilliant stuff planned."

"Like a set from Speak No Monkey!" Adam shouted. "Seriously, you'd pay more for a ticket to see them, and we've got so much else too!"

I briefly closed my eyes. He shouldn't have mentioned Speak No Monkey again. I really needed to phone Dad and see if he'd heard anything from his friend. The point was, it was a long way from a done deal, and dangling that as the big carrot made me nervous because if for any reason it didn't work out, and that was why people had bought tickets, we were screwed. That was why we'd agreed to keep it secret—and just to tease an "exciting band" because that was open to interpretation, and it allowed rumors to spread that we couldn't be held accountable for. Only that plan was wrecked now.

I gave everyone a smile anyway. "Tickets are selling fast," I lied, "so don't leave it too long. And we've got more announcements to come!" Also, a bit of a lie, but hopefully we'd figure something out. "It's going to be a really good night."

I had no idea why nobody looked like they believed me. Not one person was looking back at me enthusiastically.

When we were all dismissed, Beth made a big show of bounding up to me. "I'd love a ticket, please!" She presented me with a check made out for the full amount. "A couple's ticket!"

I raised my eyebrows. "Have you found a date?"

"Not exactly."

"So, maybe?"

"I remain *hopeful*."

"So, is there someone?"

"Jamie, I'm just trying to be optimistic!" she hissed. "Bloody hell, take the check. If I can't find anyone, I'll just come alone, and I won't even ask for a refund."

I smiled, plucked the check from her hands, and tore a ticket from my pack.

"Are Speak No Monkey really playing?" she asked.

"I mean, that's the plan. Dad's trying to work it out for us."

"Your *dad*?"

Close-up: Her face says it all. She can't hide her horror. She knows how many times he's let me down in the past, so she understands that this was a high-risk strategy with one inevitable outcome.

Close-up: me, keeping a poker face. Absolutely not ready to admit this because everything is totally fine and Dad won't disappoint me this time.

I was thinking about it all through morning lessons—oh, not the likely humiliation with Speak No Monkey, but Beth buying a couple's ticket. Our friendship had been forged in the fires of a shared sense of humor, atheism (I would never forget her refusing a free Bible when the Gideons came to try to indoctrinate us with the line, "No, thank you, my shelves are already full of fiction!"), and the fact we had both always been *single*. Everyone else was coupling up, going out on dates, and often doing more, and I would doubtless be feeling left behind were it not for the fact that Beth wasn't doing any of that either. If we were going to be weird (as Keith would have it), we could be weird together, and that didn't feel quite so bad. We had discussed the topic of romantic possibilities many times, but there were no suitable candidates. Why was everyone in the school so awful? We would lampoon weddings we'd each been invited to over the years, how laughably patriarchal they were and how pathetic and depressing the notion that somehow you aren't complete until you have a partner. "My other half," as though you couldn't possibly be *whole* without someone else. And did people really want to partner up, or did they just feel like they *had* to, like it was *expected*, the *respectable* thing to do—you had to have someone, settle down, do the right thing—because didn't that explain why Mom was with Keith? And probably why she married Dad originally, even though they weren't right for each other either? So, the idea that Beth was now "optimistic" about finding a date for the prom irked me.

It spoke of things changing, moving on, and I did not like that one bit.

Yes, change was exciting. I'd felt that excitement only yesterday.

But change was also scary. I was feeling it right then, realizing that certainties were in fact far from certain.

And, oh boy, I had *no idea* how many certainties would become uncertain in the coming weeks.

You can almost hear the ominous background music, can't you? (Well, you will in the TV adaptation.)

My mind wandered back to the notes in the book. What would it be like if I went to the prom with whoever had written them? Not as a strict couple, like Debbie and Adam, say, just as . . . two close friends. Two boys with a shared can of magic beans who liked each other so much they wanted to go to the prom together and enjoy the night. And it's cheaper with a couple's ticket. What then? And I thought: *Why are you doing this to yourself, Jamie?!* Because I knew that couldn't happen, wouldn't happen, and however innocent and lovely *I* might think it would be, and how much he would too, other people would get the wrong idea, and say things, and the whole situation would be horrible.

EXT. THE PROM. NIGHT. FANTASY SEQUENCE

Jason stands pointing at Jamie and his Mystery Pen Pal, who are in matching tuxes and bow ties and just happened to have come to the prom together to save money, no other reason, really.

JASON: GAAAAAY!
SCOTT: HOOOOMOOOOO!

Fade to black, their slurs still ringing in the background.

All hypothetical anyway. I'd be too busy at the prom—logistics and all that. I'd probably have a walkie-talkie and a clipboard, and be running around, checking the refreshments were OK, the band was ready . . . Oh god, the band. Don't think about the band.

The library was quiet at the start of lunch—everyone was busy getting food, and normally I would have been too, but, ever the optimist, I thought there might be a chance he'd responded and the whole situation, his potential identity, was utterly captivating. This boy (I'd decided it was a boy, although technically it could have been a girl) walked among us. He might have been in my classes. I could have spoken to him in the hallway.

"Jamie!" Mrs. C came right over to me as I walked in. She was wearing a leopard-print blouse. Amazing. She lowered her voice conspiratorially. "What did you think of the book?"

"It wasn't about wildflowers."

"*I know,*" she said.

I immediately panicked. She knew. *Great.* What else did she know? Or think she knew?

She glanced over her shoulder, then back at me. "It's actually called *Dance on My Grave,* and it's by Aiden Chambers."

"Right. Well. It was good." I nodded. "Sweet story."

"I knew you'd enjoy it."

"Yeah." I kept it neutral. Nonchalant. Take the book or leave the book, but, damn it, she *knew* I'd enjoy it?!

Action replay (in my head):

"Jamie!" Mrs. C came right over to me as I walked in. She lowered her voice conspiratorially. "What did you think of the book?"

"Mrs. C! God, it was fantastic! I didn't know there *were* books like that! I loved it!"

"I knew you'd enjoy it!"

"Enjoy it?! Seriously, best thing I've ever read—I've never had a book give me a hard-on before! Sorry, too much information, but honestly, just *wow*!"

But the reality was that I was a bit frustrated that Mrs. C thought she knew me that well, that she thought she knew something about me that wasn't even true, and if I gave her too much, well, she'd just think she was right. She wasn't right. It was far more complicated than that, and not something I could really explain. All that "Be you!" business yesterday—was that meant to be some subtle way of telling me I should just embrace being a homo?

No thanks.

I casually made my way over to nonfiction, which was helpfully shielded from view of the rest of the library at the far wall, behind several rows of tall bookcases. It didn't take me long to find *Wildflowers of Great Britain*. Good thing Mrs. C was an efficient reshelver. I flicked to the page with the notes on it, but there was no reply. I shouldn't have been surprised, the book had barely been back on the shelves for a few hours, but I still felt a twinge of disappointment.

I placed the book back on the shelf. The problem was, if the original notes had been left a while ago, the writer might have lost hope by now. They might not even bother checking the book for replies anymore. I couldn't do anything obvious to draw attention to the book*, but I pulled it out a little bit so the spine wasn't flush with the others, in case he might see, realize someone must have touched it, and might be intrigued to look. Honestly, this felt like a longer shot than getting Speak No Monkey to play at this point.

I was hungry, and I should really have gone to get some food, but I didn't want to leave the book. I wanted to wait. I wanted to know who it was.

So I sat down at a nearby desk and got some homework out. Far enough away to not put someone off if they wanted to be unobserved; close enough that I could see anyone walking around to the nonfiction section.

An hour later, I left none the wiser and a whole lot hungrier.

---

* Not sure what that would have amounted to anyway—fairy lights?

Chapter 7

Wednesday. Long shot of me, Jamie Hampton, still our hero, but doesn't look it as he plods toward us, head bowed, a lot clearly on his mind, e.g.:

- Are Speak No Monkey going to play at the prom? Dad did not pick up when I phoned him last night. I really needed some reassurance.
- Are we going to sell enough tickets to even have a prom? The phone rang last night during dinner. Mom never picks it up after five because she knows it'll be for me.

    "I've only sold five, how about you?" It was Debbie, her voice tense.

    "One," I replied. "Oh, shit," she said.

    "It's early days," I told her. "It'll be fine."

- Does being an optimist actually damage my chances of success? That is, does my assumption that things will be OK mean I don't take action to ensure they in fact will be?
- Is Beth going to find love and leave me behind?
- Why can't I be happy that Beth might find love? Why can't

I encourage her? Help her, even? Am I possessive and controlling? Why? Is that weird? Am I the unlikable protagonist of my own story?

- Who is my Mystery Pen Pal? And is he even a pen pal if he never replies? And has he not replied because my reply was just "Hello!" and it was so pathetic and uninspiring that he's lost the will to live?

Day three, so it was my third rugby shirt. Two-tone blue: baby blue and navy, if you're interested. That was another thing. What the hell was I going to wear tomorrow?

Popped into the library before homeroom—the book was still sticking out slightly and nothing more was written inside.

Popped in during break—still nothing.

Each time, Mrs. C's eyes followed me in through the door, and found me again after I emerged from around the bookshelf hiding nonfiction. She said nothing, but she didn't need to. She seemed to know what I was up to and was happy to leave me to it.

But I didn't like to think about that.

It was English Lit before lunch, and at least that was something to look forward to. Aside from liking the subject itself, we had quite a nice class, and a very small one too, which always gave lessons a more informal, chatty sort of feel.

AP English Lit.

The cast:

Me, Jamie Hampton (Obviously excited, wants to be a writer one day)

Beth (Sits next to me)

Debbie (Aspires to work in journalism, so English is an obvious choice)

Adam (Openly admits he took it because "he thought it would be easy" and because "Debbie's doing it")

Zara (Intelligent and brilliant to the point of being intimidating. Once wore a beret, and has never lived it down. Often has extra books on feminism in her bag. Bloody *loved it* when we did *The Handmaid's Tale* by Margaret Atwood)

Rob (Complete mystery—usually absent anyway)

Ms. Wilkins (Fresh out of her student teaching, really passionate about the subject and wants to change lives.* Adored by Zara. Intimidated by Rob, although we all get the sense she fancies him a bit)

For once, the cast was all present, but Ms. Wilkins decided to "mix things up" and put us in pairs we don't normally work in to devise a family tree and plot summary of *Wuthering Heights*. Beth was put with Debbie, Adam with Zara (you should have seen her face— completely appalled—and his, *terrified*), and me with Rob.

Just great.

If there was ever going to be a group project, you could guarantee everyone else in my group would let me down, and I'd end up doing all the work. So, on that note, meet Rob West: He'd only joined at the start of junior year last September, having been "transferred"

---

* She left teaching after three years and retrained as an aromatherapy practitioner.

from a private school down in Surrey, which was widely interpreted to mean "kicked out." The rumors were unsubstantiated, but too juicy not to spread like wildfire: fighting, drinking and drugs, basically. And something about a possible prostitute. He'd kept his head down since getting here, but he still had a reputation. He was generally considered to be trouble—frequently absent from class, always in detention, and a nasty temper to boot—but because his dad was the local politician (Sir Jeremy West), it had never got to the point of him being suspended or actually expelled. He was the Teflon kid—the bad stuff just didn't stick.

He looked me up and down as I approached his table. Judging me.

He made me nervous because I couldn't work him out. On the one hand, Rob had this bad-boy reputation. On the other, he had this preppy, clean-cut look (Ralph Lauren polo shirt and chinos, dark brown hair: short back and sides), he lived in a massive house on the edge of town, and his father was *knighted* for goodness' sake. It would have been so much easier if he'd just conformed to some sort of *Breakfast Club* stereotype—leather jacket, long hair, ripped jeans, broken home—at least you know where you are with that.

He kept his eyes on me as I sat down. Yes, he had the intimidating thing down to a T.

Time for an icebreaker, I thought: "Got your prom ticket, Rob?"

He took a slow breath in and out. "You might like to know there are rumors about people sneaking in."

"What? How?"

"By climbing over the fence at the far end of the field and then blending in with the crowd."

"We're having wristbands," I said quickly. "We have that covered."

He shrugged. "Who's monitoring it though? Who's checking? And if half of the juniors from Louth High turn up, what you gonna do?"

My eyes widened. "Louth High? Is that what people are saying? Other schools are gonna sneak in too?"

Rob nodded.

I closed my eyes. *Shit.* Another problem to talk to Debbie and Adam about. I'd given Mrs. Prenton my word that everything would be OK—specifically, no trouble—and I felt like all this was ultimately on my head.

"Now you know, you can do something about it," Rob said flatly, not looking or sounding like he cared either way.

"Yeah." I released a breath. "Anyway! Got your ticket?"

He rolled his eyes. "No offense, but it's really not my thing."

"It'll be a fun night!"

"No, it won't."

"But—"

"I'm not coming, Jamie."

I left it there.

But I would work on him.

I would work on everyone.

I had to. I didn't want the prom to be a massive humiliation I'd be remembered for forever.

There was too much on my mind. I set myself up in the library again at lunch, but no one went anywhere near the book. A quick check at the end of the day, and still nothing.

I was starting to lose hope. And I couldn't work out, when I got home that evening, why I was so angry. I'd allowed this situation to build and build in my head; I was thinking about it far too much, and why? I'd only written a friendly note back to someone who sounded like they could use a pal. If they didn't want to reply, then so what? Why did it matter so much to me that they did? Why was I acting and feeling like some lovelorn twelve-year-old who wanted to pass love notes in class?

Pathetic!

Grow up, Jamie!

What are you even thinking?!

It was Electra. *She's* the one who put the idea in my head in the first place. Whatever was going on with me, seeing her and hearing voices, it needed to stop. I needed to get back to some kind of normality.

I slammed through the front door, threw my backpack down against the wall, charged up the stairs, into my room, and raised my hands to rip down and destroy Electra—

"Have you considered," she calmly said, "that he might be as scared as you?"

"Huh?"

"Have you considered that he's seen your message, and he's wondering not just *how* to respond but if he even should?"

"Why would he be wondering that?"

"It's one thing writing something, but it's an entirely different ball game if someone actually responds. If he replies, everything changes, *he knows that.*"

"Nothing changes," I said.

Electra smiled a smile that said *Oh, you naive child.*

"Nothing changes, Electra!" I insisted. "He replies, maybe I reply, what's actually gonna change? It's not like we would ever meet and . . ."

She arched an eyebrow.

"I'm not talking to you anyway," I muttered. "You don't even exist."

I ignored her chuckling like I'd amused her in some way.

"I only wanted to help him," I told myself. "That was all."

For some reason my throat and chest tightened, and I could feel the tears pricking my eyes. I had to get a grip. What the hell was wrong with me? Was this stress? Had I taken on too much with the prom and all my schoolwork? Was I having some sort of breakdown? Zara's mom had a breakdown a few years ago. They found her walking in the middle of the high street talking to imaginary geese. It seemed like I was dangerously close to something similar.

"Whoa, fuck!" I jumped. *Electra.* She was sitting opposite me now on a chair! As real as day! In the flesh. *Electra.* No longer a voice from a poster, but . . . an actual person!

I stared, unblinking, terrified, but also unable to look away—rubbernecking my own car crash of a mental state.

"You know who you remind me of, kiddo?" she said. *"Holden Caulfield."*

We did *Catcher in the Rye* last year. I remembered one of the essay titles: "Is Holden Caulfield a narcissist?" Electra clearly didn't think much of me.

"He talks about standing in the rye, catching small children so they don't fall over the edge of the cliff," she continued. "That's a bit like you, isn't it?"

"Because I want to help him?"

"Bit similar, isn't it?"

"It's nice to help people. That doesn't make me like Holden!*"

She leaned toward me slightly and lowered her voice, making me lean in too. "What's interesting though, is *why*? Why does he want to catch them? Because one argument, that you yourself explored in an essay, Jamie, is that Holden is suffering from trauma and he wants to save others from similar trauma. He wants to protect them."

"I haven't suffered trauma," I said quickly. "Holden did, I agree, but not me."

"Sure about that?"

"Yes! Yes, I'm sure. What—my parents got divorced? I wouldn't count that as trauma."

Electra nodded. "Maybe have a think. And maybe consider the notion that fear is a terrible thing but facing it with someone else might help. And that's why it's worth being patient."

What? Just as I was about to tell her to leave, she vanished anyway, back to staring down at me from the poster on my wall.

I went downstairs. I needed some real human company, a bit of reality, even if it was Keith and Mom. He was busy watching an old *Wave Warriors* episode, repeatedly hitting rewind on the VCR

---

* I like Holden and won't hear a word said against him. His detractors are the same people who hate protagonists who are anything less than perfect—i.e., phonies, which is ironic.

so he could assess all the strategies and moves . . . or maybe just to ogle the female athletes emerging from the pool in their swimsuits some more.

I grabbed a packet of chips and a slice of cake from the kitchen, flopped down on the sofa, and picked up the newspaper sitting next to me, idly flicking through a few pages while munching on some cheese and onion, before finding a headline: *Are We Being Run by a Gay Mafia?* The comment piece was all about gay politicians and people in positions of power, and suggested these men had a secret agenda to indoctrinate the public into thinking being homosexual was a good thing.

I stopped crunching on the chips. I felt sick.

I'd seen so many pieces like that over the years. The headlines flashed in front of my eyes, a montage sequence . . .

Gay Sex Lessons for Schools!

Britain Threatened by Gay Virus Plague

Articles about how hardly anyone thinks gay people should be allowed to marry. *Repulsive.*

Immoral.

A symptom of a sick society.

Slimeball MPs keen to lower the gay age of consent.

Margaret Thatcher, at the Tory party conference, October 1987—I'm ten years old, but I see her on the news: "Children who need to be taught to respect traditional moral values are being taught that they have an inalienable right to be gay."

Perversion. Corruption. Dangerous. Pedophiles. Sick. Threat.

So many headlines.

So many speeches.

Years upon years upon years of them.

My attention was drawn by Electra being interviewed on the TV show after winning her contest. She leaned into the microphone and looked directly at me through the screen.

"You sure you've never experienced any trauma, Jamie?"

Chapter 8

Actually, Electra, thanks and everything, but I think I'm pretty trauma-free.

Yeah. Back then I was really good at burying stuff I didn't want to think about.

But right then I was thinking, *Why do I need to complicate all this with psychoanalysis?* I was just helping a fellow student who perhaps felt lonely. No big deal. Nothing to get all angsty about.

To prove it wasn't an issue, albeit only to myself, I resolved not to check the book the next day. Because I could take it or leave it.

Close-up on me. Not a care in the world. Totally stress-free. Mind clear. Back to normal.

Thursday, I convened a prom meeting at lunchtime to discuss what Rob had told me yesterday. Debbie had a minor drama on the student newspaper to attend to, so I was left with Adam, who listened to my story thoughtfully while eating his chicken salad sandwiches. It was like having lunch with a gentle giant—Adam was so much taller and broader than I was, but the more I was getting to know him, I was realizing he was essentially harmless, even if he was (unintentionally) annoying and the type of person who just blundered into things and wrecked them.

"We need bouncers," he said. "Security guys. Patrolling the perimeter with flashlights. *And batons.*" He balled his fist and made a hitting motion.

"I agree. But we don't have the budget."

Adam nodded, thinking. "I could ask some of the guys at rugby practice. They're all pretty big and scary. We'd have to pay them something, but not as much as a professional security company."

This was the first useful thing Adam had offered up in several months of prom committee meetings, and thank god. "Really? That would be great."

Adam looked pretty pleased too. "OK! I'll ask them! What do you think? Thirty bucks each?"

I nodded.

"And we could give them each one of those fluorescent vests so people know they're official. And we'll need walkie-talkies. I'm pretty sure the Boy Scouts have a set they use for expeditions. I know the guy who runs it, I can ask him too?" He met my eyes. "Why are you looking at me like that?"

"It's just . . . this is all really *helpful.*"

He frowned. "And I'm not usually?"

"It's not that, it's just—"

"No," he said, putting his hand up to stop me. "I know I'm pretty useless. Debbie tells me that too."

"I didn't say useless."

"But I am. I know I am." He shrugged. "It's just anything I *do* say, Debbie makes a mental note of, and yells at me about later."

Wow. "Really?"

"Yeah, but I never seem to get anything right. So, she's got a point—it's better for me not to speak, because then no one can tell how dumb I am."

I wasn't sure how to respond to that. The idea that someone like Adam would feel bad about themselves was strange enough, but the idea that the school's golden couple might not be as perfect as they seem together was even stranger.

And then, sitting opposite me, lunch box on his knees, sipping a juice through a straw, wasn't the popular, strong, handsome, toned guy I'd always known, but someone weaker, a bit more vulnerable, and dear god if I didn't have that familiar urge to protect him too. To stand in the rye and bloody catch him. I really had to stop Holden Caulfield–ing it up. Who did I think I was, trying to save everyone? Frigging *Jesus?*[*]

Adam scratched the back of his head and looked sheepish. "On that note, can I ask your advice? Debbie wants us to go to the prom as Overon—"

"Oberon."

". . . and Titania. And she keeps going on about whether I've figured out my costume yet, but I've no idea. What should I wear? What does Orbison—"

"Oberon."

". . . wear?" He looked at me expectantly, as if of course I'd know the answer.

---

[*] What I didn't notice, at the time, was that everyone I was trying to "save" was a boy, of course.

66

I blew out a breath. "Well, he's king of the fairies, so—"

"You see, that already sounds a bit—"

"It's a play. It's fiction."

"Can't he be more of a *sprite* or something?"

"If you want. But the point is, he's . . . ethereal."

Adam's face was blank. He just stared at me.

"Otherworldly," I explained. "So your costume needs to speak to that. How about a long coat, but adorned with foliage?"

"Fo-li-age?"

"Leaves and twigs and bracken. Maybe some flowers? And makeup," I said, my mind straying to David Bowie in *Labyrinth*. "You'll need makeup."

"No. No makeup. I don't want to poof it up."

His words stabbed me for a second. The way he said that, so casually, not even a hint of malice in his tone, just factual. I swallowed. "Think of it more like war paint, then. Oberon and Titania are basically at war anyway, through a lot of the play."

His eyes lit up. "Like that stuff the army uses for camouflage on their faces?"

"Exactly."

"I like that!"

I smiled.

"Thanks, Jamie."

"That's OK. Thanks for offering to figure out the security problem."

He gave me a salute and stood. "Roger that, boss. I have to go. Soccer practice."

"OK. Oh, hey, Adam?"

He turned back to me, eyebrows raised.

"For the record . . . I don't think you're dumb."

His face softened, his eyes dropping down to the floor for a moment. "Thanks, Jamie." He gave me a small smile, checked his watch, then perched back down on the seat. "Everyone has that idea about me, and I'm not saying I'm Einstein or anything, because I'm most definitely not, but . . . I read. I bet you didn't know that? I read books."

The hairs on the back of my neck tingled.

He continued conversationally, "I go to the library sometimes, but usually when no one's going to see me, because if the guys knew they'd give me so much shit. I really like nonfiction. Airplanes fascinate me. Really wish I could be a pilot, but I'm taking all the wrong classes.*"

I nodded and he smiled while I tried to weigh up this new information . . . a handsome boy . . . who liked hanging around nonfiction . . . who might also be familiar with a book about wildflowers . . .

"But you can't tell anyone," he said. "I would . . . never live it down. It's why I told everyone I was doing English because it was easy and because Debs was doing it. I actually really like it. But it's just easier this way."

"Why's it easier?"

He gave me a look as if it was the most obvious thing in the world. "'Cause everyone would say I'm a massive queer otherwise."

---

* About five years later, I was on an EasyJet flight to Corfu and who should be one of the flight attendants? Adam Henson! I'm happy he sort of got his dream job—although I believe he only stuck at it for a few years.

I watched him go.

Adam Henson.

Could it be him?

Cut to: fantasy sequence. A wall in my bedroom. Mystery Pen Pal represented by a silhouette in the center of the wall. A piece of red string linking that to a photo of Adam Henson and a question mark.

Fun, isn't it? Was that a clue, or a massive red herring?

Time will tell.

Either way, all of that, and the talk of books, was like hurling copies of *Playboy* at a sex addict—and I needed my fix. I hadn't even lasted twenty-four hours, for god's sake.

I headed to the library, begging myself not to every step of the way, beating myself up for my weakness, because what would this solve? It would just be more disappointment. More frustration.

The double doors to the library nearly smacked me in the face they were thrown open with such force.

I froze.

And when he saw me, he froze too.

I knew it was weird him being in there at lunchtime, and, by the startled look on his face, I imagine he knew that too.

"What are you staring at?" Jason snarled.

I didn't reply because in these situations I'd learned it was best not to.

He stared at me for a good five seconds longer, shook his head, muttered, "Gay wanker," and pushed past me.

I let him go, let his words go, then walked inside and headed straight for the book.

It wasn't pulled out to the edge; it was just aligned with the books next to it. Someone had moved it, at least to nudge it back into the row.

The fantasy: I open the book, a choir of angels sing, light streams out of it, bathing the room in a beautiful, warm glow, and the world is suddenly a better place.

The reality: I open the book. It's just the book, the same book it always is.

Only now there are some words written in the margin which weren't there before:

Are you real?

No choir of angels, no light, and no warm glow, but it didn't matter: The world *was* suddenly a better place! I stood staring at the words—written, so lightly, in pencil, like they were tentative, and could just be erased if necessary.

He'd replied.

The words were real.

He was real.

Forgetting all pretense of playing it cool and not caring, a smile spread across my face, and I had to stifle a laugh.

He was real! He was out there! In this school!

I didn't know why, but this meant so much. This was everything.

Breathless, I reached into my backpack and clumsily retrieved a pencil—that seemed to be the medium we were using now. I tapped it on the book. What to write? I considered the question again.

Are you real?

I didn't know. Was I? What was real? And even if I was, I felt my reply should be more than just "Yes." I'd already given him the stunning effort of "Hello!"—what sort of writer was I if I could only manage monosyllabic responses? Poetry, Jamie! You need something poetic!

Of course, he probably didn't mean literally real, more likely he was asking if I was *for real*, as in, I meant this, I hadn't replied as part of a joke, or a trap.

But then . . . I still couldn't be sure his original message wasn't a joke either. What if I was the one being trapped here?

I remembered Jason and a prickle of something nasty danced up my spine.

A coincidence that he'd just been in the library, and now there was a reply in the book?

I doubted very much he also had a slightly adorable obsession with flying machines like Adam.

I glanced over my shoulder. Was it even safe to write a response?

And was I just falling for a long con?

I had to proceed with caution. My hands wouldn't stop shaking, but I managed to scrawl a reply I felt worked:

As real as you.

I was quite pleased with that. It sounded a bit mysterious, and it worked both ways: I was real if he was real. But if he wasn't being real, then I was saying I wasn't either.

God, I was good.

I wanted to ask more, of course. I wanted to write: *What year are you? What's your name? Do I know you?!* But I knew I had to take it slowly.

I stared at my reply, then closed the book and placed it back on the shelf.

And the waiting game began again.

Chapter 9

"We've got something to show you!"

Mom had pounced on me the moment I'd walked in through the front door, using a hushed and excited tone that could only mean a baby, or maybe a puppy, awaited me on the other side of the living room door. She was wearing jogging pants and a matching top in offensively bright green with *en vogue* emblazoned across the front, as though saying it in French made it true.

She put her finger to her lips to ensure my silence and led me in.

Keith was sitting on the sofa, his hair blonder than usual, which meant he must have had his highlights done. He was staring, dewy-eyed, at a black rectangular block on the coffee table.

"Is that a mobile phone?" I asked.

He nodded. "Motorola. Isn't she a beauty? Set me back fifty bucks, but this, *this*, Jamie, is the future. I can theoretically be any-where in the country with this—on the road, in a field, any town, any city—and you could call the number and you'd be able to speak to me."

I glanced at it. "Can we phone it now?"

"Unfortunately not. Cellnet doesn't have any reception here, but parts of Lincoln have some, and there's a patch on the road between here and Grimsby."

"Oh. Right."

"Tell him how many phone numbers you can store in it, Keith!" Mom piped up.

"Fifty phone numbers!"

I nodded.

"Good battery too—standby time is ten hours, or a full hour if you're actually talking on it."

I supposed it was pretty impressive. The idea of being able to have a conversation with someone else, and not be tethered to the phone line in the living room so everyone could hear what you were saying, was certainly appealing. How many times had Mom moaned about me chatting on the phone to Beth "about nothing"? It wasn't nothing; it was usually English homework, or some drama at school, but how much better it would be if I didn't have to monitor what I was saying all the time? Privacy! My god. Even so, I wasn't quite as in awe as Keith and Mom were, but I managed "It's beautiful!" which Keith seemed to appreciate. However, as he started demonstrating how the antenna pulled out of the top of it and talking about a function that was being developed (but wasn't available yet) where you could send a short, typed message to another mobile phone, I zoned out. Not that I didn't want to live in the future or anything, it was just the *now* was feeling pretty exciting as it was.

Close-up: me, Jamie Hampton, eyes glazed over, a fixed expression on my face.

The image blurs. Shapes, colors, but no definition.

The sound becomes incoherent, just vague tones and noises. Keith droning on. Mom's occasional giggles.

And POP! We're inside my head.

The notes between me and Mystery Pen Pal have been going on for a while. Soon, we progress to late-night telephone calls . . . using mobile phones, which we both have. I can talk with him under the duvet, and it's like he's there with me, except he's not, so it isn't weird or anything. In time, we progress to meeting up in person. We lie on my bed and we talk—not about school, but about big stuff. The future. Hopes and dreams. Sometimes I put my arm around him as we lie there; it's not weird, it doesn't mean anything like that, it's just caring, and it's OK, we'd just never do it in front of anyone at school because people would get the wrong idea. One day, we go out on a lake . . . a rowboat . . . It's a warm afternoon with a gentle, sweet breeze . . . The water is calm, just the splash and ripples from the oars as he rows us to the middle of the lake. And then stillness, silence, peace. As he pulls the oars in, we lie back in the boat, and we just . . . drift . . . timeless . . . infinite . . . staring up into all that beautiful possibility . . .

"Jamie?"

I was back in the room.

"Did you even hear what I was saying?" Mom asked.

I released a breath. "Sorry. I was miles away."

"Your dad's had to cancel seeing you this weekend. He's got to be in Manchester, apparently."

My breath caught. This was meant to be my chance to nail him down about Speak No Monkey. I still hadn't been able to get hold of him on the phone, since he never seemed to be at home (something else a mobile phone would solve!) and I needed answers.

"OK," I said, weighing up how I was going to deal with this.

"Very magnanimous of you, Jamie," Keith said with a sniff. "Personally, I think a good measure of a man is his ability to keep his word."

"Yes, all right, Keith," Mom said.

"You can come fishing with me, if you like?"

"Thanks, but I'll be OK."

"Go on, Jamie," Mom said. "It might be nice to go fishing."

"I . . . can't fish."

"I can teach you!" Keith smiled. "Be good to have some time together, just the men. Chew the fat. Your mom tells me you've been lacking a male role model."

I glanced at my treacherous mother and saw that fixed smile on her face, as always. Seriously, I could have told her Russia had launched the nukes at us, and I swear her expression wouldn't falter. "I'll think about it. I might have something, I don't know, but thanks."

I retreated to the safety of my bedroom while Keith went to stand in the garden, his mobile phone in one hand and a wire coat hanger in the other, to see if he could entice any reception our way.

I pulled the notebook out from under my desk drawers and wrote down the story so far, before adding:

I had a nice girlfriend. I really enjoyed spending time with her. In fact, he had a girlfriend too. In that sense, we were regular guys. But we also had each other. And with each other we could talk about anything, and just be there for each other, in a way no one else could. Real, true friendship. That could never be broken. I'd often joked with Beth about weddings, disparaging married couples who say they've found their "other half." How sad, I'd thought, that you are not enough as you are. Yet, being with him, I realize something. I was missing something myself. I was incomplete. Part of me was empty, and now, with him, it's there. And it feels so good.

I put my pen down and reread my words. I was pretty pleased with them. It was a nice story. *Comforting.*

I glanced up at Electra, half expecting her to say, "Play it cool!" or "Don't come across as too needy and scare him away," but she was silent.

I read my words again, the shame starting to seep in with every sentence, and every cloyingly pathetic moment. It didn't matter how many times I'd emphasized we were just friends, it felt like I was protesting too much, and the more I read, the more disgusted I felt with myself. This wasn't normal. Normal boys don't lie next to each other, talking and cuddling. The boys who do that are the boys they talk about in the newspapers, and they are despised, and dirty, and usually end up dead.

Why couldn't I just be friends with a boy, and it be normal?

I grabbed my pen and scratched it all out. Violently. Hard. The paper tearing as I forced the nib down, destroying every single word.

No one must ever read this.

And I had to stop thinking it.

Pervert, I told myself.

Chapter 10

The badge said *Student Librarian.* .

It was being worn by Beth, who was sitting behind the main desk, the BBC Master Computer at her side, presiding over the library in a red plaid miniskirt, black tights, black patent-leather Doc Martens, Nirvana tee, and black biker jacket, none of which I'd seen before. Beth and I didn't do fashion. Now, apparently, she did. And good for her, but I also hated it. *Change*, you know?

(Note to editor: Everyone hates a petty protagonist—but I can't help being bitter and afraid of change that risks leaving me behind. Best to lie? Could write scene where I embrace Beth in style of camp gay guy and wax lyrical about her look? "O-M-G, you look fabulous!" etc. To be discussed.)

"What are you doing?" I asked.

"Extracurricular," she replied. "It occurred to me I really should have something I can put on my college applications. This seemed like the least effort." She glanced over at some sophomores. "Silence in the library!" she barked, then looked back at me. "So easy."

"Why didn't you just join the prom committee?"

She laughed.

That was her entire response.

"OK, well, I'm just going to get some stuff done."

"Plus, I get to see you more," she said. "You seem to spend all your time here, even when there's the junior class study area."

I moistened my lips. "Yeah, I just like being near the books. I find it helps."

She met my eyes and nodded. "Whatever floats your boat."

I glanced at her outfit. "Is this all . . . new?"

She nodded. "Trying a new look out. Thoughts?"

"Nice."

"God, Jamie! Do you have to be so over the top?! Please! I'm thrilled you like it, but just tone it down a bit, can't you? It's embarrassing how enthusiastic you are!" She gave me a sarcastic smile.

"Yeah, OK, I do love it actually."

She held my gaze for a moment. "What's going on with you?"

"Nothing!" I cleared my throat. "Nothing."

"Is it the prom? Speak No Monkey hasn't confirmed, have they?"

I nodded. "Right. Exactly. There's a lot on my mind."

"Hence why you're hiding away in here?"

"Can't keep anything from you, can I?"

She tapped her head. "Female intuition."

It wasn't ideal, Beth being a student librarian. It was bad enough being watched by Mrs. C, but at least—if she did suspect anything—she was keeping it to herself. If Beth started suspecting things, she would start asking me things. I didn't want to be asked things. Especially when I didn't know any of the answers.

I headed off to do a quick flyby of the book and check for messages. I rounded the bookshelf and bumped into a figure lurking near nonfiction.

"Dan!"

"Oh, hi, Jamie."

I don't know, his sweet face, so open and trusting, his little nose (he had a little nose), or that red-checked flannel shirt he had on, over a white T-shirt, my heart just swelled at the sight of him. "What are you doing here?"

"Books?" he suggested.

I met his eyes. Fine, it *was* a library, but he looked . . . guilty? Or was that projection? He was shifty, certainly, his cheeks taking on a pink tint. Like I'd just walked unannounced into his bedroom and caught him doing *you know what.*

I probably didn't need to think about that.

I let my eyes drift to the shelf where *Wildflowers* was sitting, then back to him.

He put his hands in the pockets of his cargo pants. *Way* too casual. It looked fake.

"Actually, I was hoping to find you," Dan said. "I wanted to buy a prom ticket." He pulled a crumpled check out of his pocket, smoothed it down, and handed it to me.

"Great!" I glanced at the amount written on the check. "A couple's ticket?"

"Please."

I pulled my book of tickets from my backpack and tore one off.

"Not that I have a date yet," he added. "But who knows!"

Beth's voice sailed across the library. "I can hear *talking!*"

80

I handed him the ticket, then he glanced back at me. "Are you going with anyone?"

My heart rate doubled. "Um . . . hadn't really thought about it."

"You have to go with someone!"

"Not really. I'll be busy with . . . everything. Although . . . I'm not saying I wouldn't. Just that I . . . haven't thought about it."

He smiled at me. He had, without question, a lovely smile. Gentle. Sweet. "What about Beth?"

"Oh, we're just friends. I mean, we *could* go together, as friends, but that would be all."

"I wasn't sure."

"OK. Well, yeah. That's us."

"*Someone* is *still* talking!" Beth shouted again.

Dan cracked a smile, then whispered, "I don't even know why I bought a couple's ticket. I'm crap at asking people out. In fact, I've never done it."

I smiled too. "But you went with a couple's ticket anyway?"

"Maybe I'm trying to force myself to try it, under pain of losing money?"

I laughed.

"Silence for the books!" Beth bellowed.

"She's getting angry," Dan whispered. "I don't suppose you want to get some lunch in the cafeteria? I hate eating by myself."

Close-up: me, trying to hide my facial expression, which basically reads: *You bet I bloody do, hooray, hoorah!*

If you wanted a definition of cognitive dissonance, have me. I'd stumbled across the phrase in a psychology textbook I'd been idly flicking through while skulking in the library, and kind of wished I hadn't. Once a condition has a name, it's more real, isn't it?* But there I was, ticking all the boxes for it. Absolutely one hundred percent straight. Yet made so giddy and happy—heart fluttering, stomach fizzing—by being in the presence of a sweet boy and him wanting to have lunch with me. But that didn't make me gay! Oh no, no. That's what friendship is, you see? Really close male friendship. It's easy to see why some people could get confused. But not me. I was not confused.

It's normal to feel pride when walking alongside another boy in the hallway.

It's normal to guide him around a chicken and mushroom pasty that someone had dropped on the floor, and that he hadn't seen, so he didn't step in it, getting an endorphin shot just from touching him briefly.

It's normal to order the same thing for lunch, even though you would have preferred the casserole, because there's a part of you that admires him so much you want to be like him, and while you're thinking about it, where did he get that shirt because it's nice and you might like one too?

Normal.

Sausage, fries, and baked beans.

A boy with a can of beans? Or a boy with a *plate* of beans?

Either way, another suspect for the murder wall, right? I was dying to know whether I'd interrupted Dan just as he'd finished

---

* To be fair, any medical condition I've ever read about, I immediately feel I have. I regularly diagnose myself with all manner of horrible diseases, although, to date, inaccurately every time. One day, I'll be right though, won't I? (You see? That's how I think.)

writing in the book! I hoped my impatience didn't show as we chatted over lunch, but I couldn't think of much else.

Beth watched me as I ran in at the end of lunch. "Think I dropped something!" I explained.

"We're closed!"

"I'll be so quick!"

I scurried around the shelves to nonfiction and pulled the book out.

There was no reply.

My heart plunged.

But maybe I'd interrupted him as he was *about* to write in the book. Was my obsession with finding out who this was going to scare him off and ruin things for me? And was that my enthusiasm or did I actually *want* to scare him off?

But why would I self-sabotage?

"Because part of you can't deal with what might happen if this goes any further," Electra said plainly, standing opposite me in the library.

I froze. Being in my bedroom was one thing. Appearing, at random, in the world at large was another. One minute you're hearing occasional voices, the next, tanned, swimwear-clad athletes from TV shows are standing opposite you, and they're still there no matter how much you blink and rub your eyes?

"There's nothing to 'deal' with," I hissed at her. "Because nothing is happening. We're not even friends. I'm just trying to help. Furthermore, you have no business—"

My eyes flicked to Beth, suddenly in front of me, Electra now gone, and I froze. What had just happened?

"Please," she said. "Don't stop on my account. You seemed to be having a lovely conversation . . . with yourself."

"Like I said, I have a lot on my mind."

"Are you OK?"

"Couldn't be better."

Our eyes met. She didn't believe me, I didn't believe me, and she knew I knew she knew that.

That's the thing with good friends, isn't it? *They know.*

She also knew she wasn't going to get anything else out of me, so she turned on the heel of her flashy new Doc Martens and went to admonish some freshmen who were still hanging about despite the late bell having already rung forever ago.

Time-lapse montage sequence: me, Jamie Hampton, sitting in economics.

The teacher, Mrs. Prince, talking about supply and demand.

Me, on edge, leg bouncing up and down, pen tapping.

The clock, ticking, every second painfully slow.

Flashback to Electra: "You can't deal with it!"

Flashback to Dan: "Do you fancy getting some lunch?"

Me: beads of sweat on my forehead.

Flashback to Adam giving me sexy eyes: "I want to do things with you."

WHAT?!

I shook my head. That categorically did not happen.

It was a long, painful lesson, made worse because I knew I *should* be focusing, I needed to, I had to, I wanted an A, I had to concentrate, but I couldn't. I was out of there like a shot when the bell rang.

To the library, for one last check.

Bingo!

My heart leapt when I saw the words. He'd replied:

As real as me? Well, I don't know who I am, so not sure that tells us much.

That made me smile, the slightly sardonic and self-deprecating tone. I liked that. I could relate to that. This was the first little hint of his personality, and it made me feel a little bit closer to him. Underneath that, more words:

No identifying details. No names. No year groups. Deal?

I held my breath. *Oh.* I mean, absolutely, I had no problem with anonymity, it was just . . . this was an acknowledgment. That we shouldn't be doing this. That it was wrong. If anyone found out, our lives would be made hell. The risks were sky-high—we could talk, but we could never really *know*, because anyone could find this book and then anyone could work it out . . .

But work *what* out?

What was this?

Two people who had found each other in the pages of a book. That was all. And I don't know why I felt shame as I did it, but I pulled out a pencil and wrote:

Deal.

And then, since we were talking now, I added:

So, what did you think of the book?

That felt safe. That didn't feel like we were doing anything wrong. No identifying details.

I carefully put the book back in its place and wished the books could talk, could tell me who he was. It was funny to think that he would have been standing there, exactly where I was, writing in the book like I had just done, here, in this space, just—

I froze when it hit me.

I'd returned the book at the end of lunch. And the message had appeared by the end of the school day—exactly one hour and fifteen minutes later.

The only students who were allowed in the library during lesson time were juniors and seniors.

And since the seniors had all gone on exam leave . . .

He was a junior too.

More than that, I knew last period was a study hall for some people because Beth had one then.

Which meant there was also a list somewhere of exactly who was in that class, and therefore who was in the library at the time the note was written.

But did I really want to know?

Because you know what they say?

Ignorance is bliss.

Chapter 11

Just five days ago I'd been in total ignorance—of the book, the notes, and Mystery Boy. Now Pandora's box was well and truly open, and all sorts of shit had flown out. Confusion, questions, shame, guilt, fear, panic, risk, danger . . . and real-life Electra talking to me and offering advice, apparently. Life had felt a hell of a lot easier before.

Despite that, I resented the weekend getting in the way of me being able to get back to the book and check for further correspondence. More of that cognitive dissonance! Hated what was happening, felt it was bad for me, but wanted more, telling myself that whoever it was really needed me, and I would help them, and that was all that was happening here, that it was anonymous because admitting you needed help could be difficult, it could be seen as weakness by some, and so on, and on, and whatever other bullshit I was telling myself to justify all this.

Keith took me fishing on Saturday. He wore stonewashed jeans, a fluorescent windbreaker, and seemed genuinely excited, prattling on about bait as he drove us over. The old brick pits were located on the way out of town, behind the woods. When they took the clay away years ago to make bricks, they left huge pits that were now filled with water and were good for fishing, supposedly. It was probably about an acre in all, with reed beds and lily pads, surrounded by banks with wild grasses and beyond that, trees. The serenity of the place turned out to be just what I needed, and once Keith had set me up with a pole on a stand and attached a gruesome-looking worm to the hook, I was able to sit back, stare out into the water, and think . . .

Scenario: Following detective work, it turns out to be Dan.

"I've always wished from afar to be your best friend," he says. "I just didn't know how."

Cut to: friendship montage. He stays over, we talk late into the night; when he's tired, he drifts off to sleep next to me. He feels like he's different from other boys too, so we understand each other.

Scenario: It turns out to be Adam.

"I know I'm with Debbie, but that's because everyone expects boys like me to be in a relationship. I'm being crushed under the weight of societal expectations, Jamie!"

No, scrap that, more like:

"I don't know what I'm supposed to want, or who I'm supposed to be. Soccer player. Hero. Role model. *Great big fake?*"

"I understand, Adam," I say.

And we don't need any more words, because we get it.

Scenario: It's freaking Jason and the whole thing is a trap. Close-up: his sneering face, dripping with hatred.

"Queer little gay homo," he snarls, brandishing the book. "Now everyone's going to know!"

Close-up: me. Why was I so naive? How could I be so stupid?

I shuddered. Of course, those were only three options. There were about a hundred boys in the junior class, and it could have been any of them. Although, I'm sure you're hoping I'm not such a bad story-teller that it ends up being someone we haven't even met yet. That would be cheating, wouldn't it?

Stories have rules.

Life, on the other hand, *doesn't*. It's a free-for-all.

Chaos, basically.

I wonder if that's why I've always found real life to be so scary?

After an hour or so of silence, with no fish biting, Keith cracked open a Thermos and poured us both some tea, this also being a pre-text to open a conversation with me, which is exactly what I'd been dreading. The idea of anything described as "man to man" turned my stomach. My own father had always steered well clear of any discussion about sex or puberty, and for that I was enormously grateful. I wasn't sure Mom was as convinced I didn't need some sort of "talk" though, and my fear was that *that* was what all this fishing business was really about.

I was going to get a "talk."

And I did get one, a bloody awful one. Here are the highlights:

EXT. THE BRICK PITS. AN OTHERWISE LOVELY DAY

Keith, a middle-aged man with an upsetting penchant for a

slip-on shoe, is pontificating. Jamie, our hero (even if he doesn't feel like it), stares out across the water, afraid to make eye contact because it's all too gruesome, but occasionally shrugs by way of some sort of response. He wishes someone would "kill him now." But they don't, so he has to sit there and endure it all.

KEITH: Your mom and I were wondering why you haven't asked anyone to the prom, Jamie?

KEITH: Is it because you're nervous around girls?

KEITH: That's normal, Jamie! Girls are mysterious. They can be intimidating. But . . . they can also be the most wonderful thing to happen to a man.

KEITH: Now I don't mean to boast, but my whole life, I've had a lot of success with women.

KEITH: Don't tell your mom, but I lost my virginity at thirteen.

KEITH: That's how successful I am.

KEITH: She was called Pam.

KEITH: Great legs.

KEITH: Are you a "legs man," Jamie?

KEITH: Well, you've got time to work out your preferences anyway.

KEITH: Point is, I could give you the benefit of my experience. Give you some advice. Would you like that, Jamie?

KEITH: I'll take that as a yes.

KEITH: Never come across as desperate; women love a confident man. And never act like *you* have anything to prove to *them*. A good line is to approach the lady in question, say at a bar, or, in your case, the classroom, or wherever, and say: "You're not usually my type; I don't go for blondes, but for some reason you caught my eye." And, if you see what I'm doing there, I'm suggesting that she's lucky she's got my attention, but in a flattering way, like she's special. She'll love that.

Electra flopped down on the grass by my side. "She'll *hate* that, but I think you know that already, Jamie. For the record though, this is horrific advice."

"I know."

Keith turned to me. "You do? Well, great! I'm glad you know. There's hope for you yet. And that makes me happy, Jamie! Know why? Because I want *you* to be happy. I want you to find a nice girl, settle down, have a couple of kids, and . . . I dunno, be happy. Because that's what happiness is." I felt him studying me for a few moments. "Assuming you want a girlfriend, of course," he said quietly.

"Uh-oh," Electra muttered. "Up to you, but I don't feel this is the best moment to come out of the proverbial closet."

"Why would I come out?" I hissed.

"What?" Keith said.

Shit!

"Why wouldn't I want a girlfriend?" I asked him, but then immediately realized I'd only made things worse, furthering this conversation in exactly the wrong direction.

He shrugged and looked away. "I dunno. Some people are queers or whatever they call themselves." He stared out at the expanse of water.

91

"I don't think they call themselves queers*." I swallowed. "And anyway, I'm—"

"Oh! We've got a bite! We've got a bite!" Keith sprang into action, grabbing his fishing rod and starting to reel the line in. "It's a big 'un! I can feel it!"

I sat back in my chair and sighed, watching the fiasco. "I'm not—"

"Jamie," Electra said, touching my leg to stop me, "just leave it, OK? You don't have to explain yourself to anyone. You don't owe anyone anything. Unless you *want* to say something?"

I shook my head.

"Come on!" Keith was saying, still reeling. (We both were, in a way.) "Oh, she's gonna be a beauty!"

I turned to Electra. "But, just to say, I don't think I'm—"

She raised her eyebrows.

"No, OK then," I said, sitting back again.

"Carp!" Keith said, dangling the flapping fish aloft. "Nice one too!" He sniffed, unhooked the poor gasping creature, and chucked it back into the water.

I was glad the fish got to live, but at the same time I didn't understand what the point of this whole expedition was, because I'd naively thought we were going to catch a fish and eat it for dinner but apparently not.

"Good chat," Keith said as we were packing up, half an hour later. "Good to talk. Man to man."

---

* It's changed now, but back then, nobody I knew would call themselves "queer"—it was very much a slur.

And I realized, maybe that's what real men did. They talked, but only if they had an activity to do that gave them an excuse to talk. And real men asked girls out, and they liked girls, and they found them sexy, and they might be "legs men" or other-body-parts men, I supposed, and they went to bars and they pulled "chicks" and they went fishing and handed down man wisdom, generation after generation, because apparently the whole point, the whole reason we are here, is to find a mate and reproduce, and I know I don't owe anyone anything, and I don't have to explain myself, but . . .

What if you don't want to do that?

Chapter 12

The book was good. One of them dies. Sounds about right.

The response had settled my mind a bit. Over the weekend I'd got myself steadily more worked up. I didn't want to be different from everyone else. I wanted to be normal. I sometimes wonder what I would have done if I'd walked into the library on Monday lunchtime and found anything other, anything more suggestive, than a chat about literature, because I think I might have lost my nerve there and then, for who knows how many more years?

I'd made the decision not to do any digging about who was in study hall on Friday. I couldn't think of a way of doing it that wouldn't arouse suspicion anyway. Beth was the obvious choice, since she was in that class, but it would have been an odd request. She would have known I was up to something. But I didn't want anyone to know anything about me, because the first person who really should have known . . . was me.

I reread his words, tracing my finger over them, feeling good because it made me feel close to him somehow, and then was immediately overcome with shame because *what are you doing, Jamie*?!

Sometimes I hated myself.

Why did I have to be so sentimental and emotional and feel things I knew I shouldn't feel?

I read the words again.

I wasn't sure about the "dying" thing; it made me uneasy—was it a veiled threat? Self-hatred? A morbid joke? So I scribbled back:

What do you mean?

That was enough for now. I was still being noncommittal. I could still back away from this and leave no trace of myself. Short of spy cameras, I knew it was unlikely anyone could work out who I was.

I snapped the book shut, placed it back on the shelf, rounded the corner of the shelves, and bumped straight into Dan.

"We must stop meeting like this," he said, a smile playing on his lips. "Don't suppose you want some lunch?"

I glanced over at Beth, who was busy with two freshmen at the desk: "The fine is calculated weekly, or *part thereof.* I don't make the rules!" she was saying.

I felt disloyal, leaving her in there, but then she was a student librarian now, and I wasn't, so what could I do? It wasn't like Dan was replacing her or anything. It wasn't like I was cheating, even if it felt like I was.

Over our chicken pies and fries, I gathered up the courage to ask him: "Found anyone to go with you on your couple's ticket yet?"

He looked down at his plate, sighed, and shook his head. "This'll sound stupid, because I know I'm supposed to know this, but . . . how are you supposed to actually do it? Ask someone to a prom?"

I laughed.

"I'm serious!"

"No, I know you are. I'm not laughing at you; I'm recognizing the problem."

"Every scenario I can picture is ridiculous. I went to see a movie with my parents last week—it was called *Four Weddings and a Funeral*. It just came out. Have you heard of it?"

I nodded.

"So, it had all these people who have crushes on each other, and I thought it might be useful, you know? It might be a template for . . . dealing with romance. But it was so over the top! Weddings being stopped, people in love with the wrong person, heart attacks . . . sorry. I shouldn't spoil it."

"I mean, the title gives a certain amount away."

Dan laughed. "Oh yeah. Anyway, none of that is me. All that drama! I just want things simple."

"Me too," I said. Simple sounded good right then. Who wanted their life to be dramatic and tense enough to make a work of fiction out of it?*

Dan chewed thoughtfully on some of his pie. "There were two gay characters in it too."

I suddenly became aware I was staring at him, and quickly looked down at my food, forking a cube of chicken. "Oh yeah?" (So casual.)

"One of them dies."

I froze.

---

* Well, we wouldn't be here otherwise, so in some ways, dramatic is good.

"Sorry, I'm spoiling it again," he added.

I looked up, met his eyes, and he smiled, gently, at me. "It was actually quite a sweet storyline, although I don't think my dad was too impressed. But why not, huh?"

"Exactly. Why not?"

Dan nodded.

We ate in silence for a bit, while thoughts crashed about my head, like:

What do I say now?!

One of them dies?! That cannot be a coincidence!

Why bring that storyline up anyway?!

"So?" Dan said softly.

For some reason, I turned ice-cold. "What?"

"Any tips on asking someone out?"

"Like I said, I'm no expert."

"Still." He cocked his head and smiled.

I scrambled around for an idea. Having listened to Keith's advice on Saturday, I felt like I had one thing to offer: Just do the opposite. Keith's approach was all game playing and bluffing and tactics and tricks to try to engineer some sort of result. It sounded exhausting. It also sounded wrong. "My tip," I said, swallowing, "would be to just be real. Just be yourself." And what I didn't say: *"Because you are perfect as you are, Dan."*

"You're assuming I know who I am."

"I mean . . . yeah."

"OK. So who am I?" His eyes were sparkling, as if he was enjoying this.

"You're . . . Dan . . ."

"Good start."

"You're sixteen?"

"Until July."

"Baby of the year, like me."

"Who *am* I though?"

I blew out a breath. "I dunno, you're . . . nice?"

He guffawed while I went red.

"You are though," I muttered, looking down at my food.

"Jamie Hampton, you'd better not be flirting with me!"

"'Course not." I shrugged, but my brain was about to explode with thoughts and feelings I didn't know what to do with. "I'm just saying you're a nice guy, be real, that's enough."

I met his eyes again and he smiled at me, again. "Thanks," he said. He pushed a few fries around his plate. "You have to be a bit brave, don't you? To put yourself out there? As the real you?"

I wanted to hug him. How was he feeling all the things I was feeling? I didn't hug him. There was a table between us anyway. "Yeah. I think you do."

"Because then you're actually saying this is me, this is every-thing, and if they reject you, then that's personal. I don't know, some of the guys, they swagger around, talking about 'this chick' and 'that chick' and how they asked her out, and maybe she said no, but they still laugh about it, as if it's nothing, doesn't matter, the loss is all hers, and I could never be like that. I'd be devastated."

"I don't think anyone would reject you."

He nearly choked on the fry he was eating. "You're really good for my ego."

"Happy to help," I said.

"Be brave?" he said.

"Be brave."

What would I do?

What would I do if Dan was Mystery Boy?

Dan had been hanging about the library. Very near to the book. I'd bumped into him twice now. He was kind, and he was sensitive—exactly the sort of person who would enjoy a book like *Dance on My Grave*.

He'd mentioned the gay characters in a film.

Why?

Testing the water?

Was my heart beating faster because I liked the idea of that or because I was terrified of it?

What did I want? I wanted someone like me. Someone to talk with. Someone who got me. It wasn't anything more!

What if Dan asked me out?

Would he?

But he wasn't like that. He only mentioned it.

But what if he was brave?

And yet . . . that would just be weird.

Wouldn't it?

I could still be friends with someone though, even if they were gay, couldn't I?

I mean, you get the picture, right? I was a mess. I didn't know who Dan was, or who I was. I didn't know what I wanted. Or what I even hoped for. I think when you're that scared of it, when you're that deep in denial, when you've refused to answer anything you've asked yourself honestly, then, of course, you don't see it. Even if *you* can see it. Which I'm sure you probably can.

I was hooked on wanting to know more though. I might not have known *me*, but I wanted to know if it was Dan.

So, I tested the water in the exchanges in the book that followed:

I don't believe in happy endings

That was him. I didn't like that reply. There was a darkness about it. It didn't *sound* like the Dan I knew, but actually aren't people full of surprises? I thought Adam Henson was one thing, and he was something else. At least in part. Everyone's got layers. Bits they keep hidden.

I scribbled back:

That's a shame. I do. I think I do. But I don't think they just happen. Even in fairy tales. The prince had to go out and find Cinderella, right? I think you have to take action. Be brave.

There. I'd mentioned being brave. I felt sure Mystery Boy's response to this would provide me with the big clue I needed.

His reply:

Brave? Love the idea of that. Asking someone of the opposite sex out? That might be brave. Asking another guy when you're a guy? In this school, that's not brave. That's suicidal. I could ask you . . . but I

don't even know who you are. And you don't know me. Might not even
like each other. Although I kind of love the idea of finding out . . .

There we had it. The first time "liking" each other had been mentioned. An admission that this wasn't just friends chatting about
books. This was (could be? might be?) something more. He liked
guys. And he assumed I did too.

He didn't know me; that much was right.

And yet it still felt like he knew too much.

Or he thought he did.

And he might be up for taking the next step. What else could
those ellipses mean?! It was what was left unsaid that was the scari-
est here.

I slammed the book shut and got out of the library as fast
as I could.

I was terrified.

Chapter 13

"So, it's you?"

He'd rounded the corner without me realizing and caught me red-handed, pencil poised in the copy of Wildflowers.

"I hoped it'd be you." Dan smiled at me.

"And . . . it's you?" I replied.

He nodded. "Never in a million years did I dare to hope the boy I loved having lunch with, but who I was too scared to ask out, would be the same boy I was getting on so well with in the pages of that book." He held his hand out.

And I took it. "Hello, Jamie."

"Hello, Dan."

Look, I was a writer. I was just playing around with ideas, situations and possibilities. It was artistic expression. It didn't mean anything. Authors don't have to be like the characters in their books. They don't have to agree with them.

I slammed my notebook shut in frustration and hid it back away. What felt easy and beautiful in fiction was scary and ugly in real life. I could have written it down, dismissed it as a creative work, but carrying on in the pages of the book, with a boy who might potentially like me, felt like really admitting something.

Who was I to tell anyone else to be real?

I wasn't real. I didn't know what I was, but I had this nagging feeling I might be a phony.

Holden would hate me.

Days went by without me looking at the book, and I was grateful for more prom-related dramas to keep my mind off it.

INT. THE LIVING ROOM. AFTERNOON

Jamie Hampton is on the phone, waiting anxiously for his father to pick up. So far it has rung fifty times. Maybe he's in the shower? On ring fifty-three, and just as Jamie is about to hang up, there's a click . . .

DAD: Yeah?

JAMIE: Dad? It's me. Jamie!

DAD: (Groaning) Jay. I was asleep.

JAMIE: It's four p.m.!

DAD: I'm working nights.

JAMIE: Oh. Sorry. Um . . . just quickly, have you heard anything from Speak No Monkey?

DAD: What?

JAMIE: For the prom? You spoke to their manager.

DAD: . . .

JAMIE: About them playing?

DAD: . . .

JAMIE: At the prom? The prom I'm organizing at school?

DAD: Oh. Yeah. Haven't they been in touch yet?

JAMIE: No, and I really need—

DAD: You wrote the letter?

JAMIE: Yeah, I wrote the letter, but—

DAD: All right. I'll try to give him another call. OK? You OK?

JAMIE: Yeah, but—

DAD: We'll catch up later, OK?

JAMIE: OK.

Shit.

And then . . .

INT. JUNIOR CLASS COMMON ROOM. DAY

Adam looks mournful and preoccupied, sitting by himself in his rugby gear.

"What's the matter with *you?*" I asked.

He glanced up to check the coast was clear and indicated for me to sit down next to him. "Debbie says I shouldn't have asked the rugby team about providing security. She says everyone's complaining they won't be able to smuggle alcohol in, and that's more of a problem than some threat of people sneaking in."

"I don't want to know. I promised Mrs. Prenton there wouldn't be any alcohol."

Adam shrugged. "There won't be. Officially. You can't be held responsible for what other people do."

I put my head in my hands. "Oh god."

He nudged my shoulder with his. "Cheer up. We're in this together. Debbie says there's a fine line between safety and overpolicing, which would be intimidating, so she's sorting it all out now." He sighed. "Adam messes up again."

"You didn't mess up. It was a good idea."

He smiled sadly, like he didn't believe me. Then Debbie came in along with a few of the other rugby players, and he perked up and was his usual jolly self again.

Maybe I wasn't the only one not being real. Or not being able to. Other people's expectations crush us all a little bit, don't they?

Zara made a beeline for Debbie, Adam, and me as soon as she walked in. "I'd like to buy a prom ticket!" she chirped.

The fact she "chirped" was significant. Zara didn't chirp. She was never normally this happy, so I knew something was afoot.

"A *couple's* ticket," she added loudly.

So, OK, we went through the transaction, I got my book of tickets out, I tore one off, she handed me a check for the correct amount, and just as I reached to take it, she snatched it back a bit.

"Oh, just one thing," she said. "It's fine if the person I bring is another girl, isn't it? Same-sex couples are allowed?"

I froze.

And the whole common room froze with me.

Some eyes on me. (How would I react?)

Some eyes on her. ("So, she really is a lesbian?!")

She was eyeballing me, challenging me. *My expectation* was that people would bring a date of the opposite sex on a couple's ticket, because . . . that's what always happened. Nobody had ever turned up anywhere with a same-sex boyfriend or girlfriend. It just wasn't a thing. And even though, in the wilds of my imagination, I'd been picturing something similar, that was where that idea was going to stay. Of course it was. How could it be any different?

Debbie took control. "The prom isn't really the time to get political."

"Political?!" Zara replied. "I'm asking about taking someone to the prom. How's that political?"

"It's making a statement," Debbie said.

"What? That I like someone? Isn't everyone making that statement if they take a date?"

"Most people disagree with same-sex couples, Zara. It'll make everyone uncomfortable."

Zara laughed scornfully. "You must be joking?"

"What do you think, Jamie?" Debbie said.

Then it was *all* eyes on me. The prom president.

The

final

word.

But what was I to say? What could I say? I was scared of Zara; she was bold and brave, and she told it like it was, no shame, no fear, she was *real*. I agreed with what she was saying.

But I also knew how people would feel about it, but then . . . how would it even affect them anyway? Like if I went with a boy . . . except, I wouldn't . . . and if I supported Zara, then people would make assumptions. They would say I agreed to it because . . .

So, coward that I was, I took the easy way out. "I think we need to discuss this with Mrs. Prenton."

***

Cut to: Mrs. Prenton's office. Debbie, Adam, and me sitting in front of her desk. I feel tiny with Mrs. Prenton looming over us, like one of those film shots taken from a low angle to make her seem larger and more intimidating.

I haltingly explained the situation.

Mrs. Prenton's face gave nothing away. She waited for me to finish. She gave it a moment to make sure I had. Then, without hesitation:

"No."

"That's what we thought," I babbled. "We just wanted to check."

"I'm surprised you even had to ask me, Jamie," Mrs. Prenton said. "I thought I'd made it clear to you that the prom could only go ahead if you gave me your assurance there wouldn't be any scandal?"

"You did. I'm sorry."

"What next? Pupils asking to bring their pet horse to the prom?"

I took a sharp intake of breath at that. I couldn't help it. It was like a gut punch. "I know. Sorry, miss."

She indicated for us to go.

"Why did you say *we* wanted to check?" Debbie said as we walked along the hallway. "I thought I'd made *my* position clear?"

"I just thought we needed to be sure."

"What's there to be sure about?!" she howled.

"Aw, come on, Debs," Adam said. "It's not that bad, is it? Zara bringing some other girl?"

Debbie stopped in her tracks. "Are you serious? My dad is sponsoring this. He's not going to want his money associated with some sort of lesbian festival. He's got his reputation to think about. You're so naive."

She stormed off, Adam in pursuit, offering apologies and clarifications.

Me? I just stood there. People swirling around me in the hallway while I stared into the middle distance.

Disgust.

That's what I felt. I had done the wrong thing, when, in my heart, I had known what was right, even if "right" was something everyone else thought was wrong.

Zara was only being real.

In the pages of the book, Mystery Boy was only being real.

I'd let them both down because I was afraid of real.

But right then, that was all I wanted.

I wanted real.

I turned and headed to the library, pushing through the doors and heading straight over to the book, not even caring who might be looking or watching. I grabbed it off the shelf, flicked it open, and saw his extra note after I hadn't replied for days:

Sorry. I scared you off, didn't I? Sometimes I feel so lonely, I imagine what it'd be like, just being with someone, another boy, like me. Even if I know, in my heart, it would never happen.

Please don't disappear.

Fuck it. Time to be real. I grabbed my pencil and scribbled back:

Meet me.

Chapter 14

Over the next few days, the volume and frequency of our messages increased. It felt like I was getting closer to him, although it also felt like he kept pulling away. His first reply:

You've got to be joking?

And my next one:

No. Let's do it. You said you wanted to.

Him:

I said I love the IDEA of it. Not the reality. Absolutely not. I can't. You don't understand.

I wasn't sure why he thought I wouldn't understand. Surely we were going through similar things and had similar fears?

Try me.

His response to me was a body blow:

I'm taking a swing and assuming you're a junior like me. Were you in the common room the other day? When Zara asked Jamie about taking another girl to the prom? See the reaction? Not one person thought it would be OK. And that would be just the start of the problems.

I'd already worked out he was a junior, but the confirmation was good. And he clearly didn't know who I was. But my head spun, mind ablaze with trying to remember who was in the common room that day, blasting with excitement that *he* was among them—I was close to him, I just didn't know how close—mixed with complete devastation that he'd watched me as I failed to stick up for Zara. And that was what hurt the most. My own uselessness. My own cowardice.

Did I even want him to know who I was now? Would he even want to know me?

I needed to think.

And I needed to talk it through with Electra that evening. (Yes, we're now at the point where we're acting like that's fine and normal. What is reality anyway? Do you know? Does anyone? I don't.)

"Mmmm, okaaaay," Electra said, looking at me over steepled fingers. "You're ashamed you weren't being real. You worry he'll think less of you. And yet, getting it wrong, our imperfections, are what make us human. In that sense, you are completely real." She smiled at me. "If you were some shining example of perfect

judgment, pure of heart and mind, who never put a foot wrong—
well, then I would say you weren't real."

"I feel like this is just twisting words to make me feel better."

"Then answer me this: Do you want him to like you for who
you really are, warts and all, or do you always want to have to pretend
around him?" She raised her eyebrows. "We know the answer, so
let's move on, kiddo. You haven't even worked out who it is yet; god
knows how many clues you need; why haven't you even checked to
see who's in that study hall on Fridays?"

"I'm respecting his privacy."

"No, you're scared. Scared of making it too real. Which loops
us back around to the first point, but also connects with my third:
Fear is a rational, human response. But do you know what, kiddo?
You need to feel that fear, and you need to do it anyway."

"And if I don't?"

"Well, you'll just be miserable, won't you? You'll live a life of
lies, and you'll sink in them. You deserve a shot at happiness, Jamie.
You're a good guy. I've grown to like you."

"Really?"

She nodded. "Uh-huh. I hate the way most other boys your
age are only interested in one thing. You actually engage with me,
we talk, it's very refreshing." She met my eyes. "So? What are you
going to do?"

"Feel the fear. And do it anyway."

She smiled. "Anything you're ready to tell me yet?"

"I can't."

"That's OK. You don't have to."

"I want to."

"Sometimes saying it out loud can help. There's no one here. Just me and you. No one can hear. No one will know. You can just try it out, see how it feels. Think of it . . . like trying on a new shirt. Maybe you'll like it, maybe you won't. Maybe it'll feel right, maybe it won't. But you can't be sure . . . until you've tried it."

I nodded.

And I swallowed.

"Electra . . ." I stopped and sighed. "Do you have a surname?"

"No, I'm just Electra."

"It just feels like I should use your full name—for a big moment?"

"You're building it up too much, kid."

I took a breath. "Electra, from primetime Saturday night ITV show *Wave Warriors*?"

"What is it, Jamie Hampton?"

I stared at her.

And she smiled back at me.

"I'm gay."

Chapter 15

Well, that particular "shirt" wasn't such a bad fit. I didn't hate it. I wouldn't say I was entirely comfortable in it; it felt a bit weird, it wasn't *quite* right, but perhaps I would get used to it?

After I'd said the words that electric Friday night, Electra and I had partied. We put my Pet Shop Boys cassette on my hi-fi and Electra had shouted, "Wave Warriors, splashdown!" and I'd replied, "Contenders, splashdown!" and now I supposed it was time to do this thing.

First stop on Monday morning: the library. I went straight for the book and, before I had time to talk myself out of it, wrote a reply underneath his about what happened with Zara in the common room:

I know. I felt sick. And I wish I'd been brave enough to say something. Honest truth: I'd like to go to the prom with a boy and have it be no big deal, have it be like it is for any other couple. More honest truth: Even though I don't know who you are, I sometimes think about going with you.

I was breathless. Exhilaration mixed with . . . relief? Meanwhile, I was determined to find him. I still didn't want to ask Beth who was in that study hall on Friday—the fewer people who suspected anything the better. I'd have to wait and see for myself in four days. But that didn't stop me trying to catch him between now and then. I went back to the library at break to watch the bookshelves from afar, and at lunch, but I came up blank. By the following morning, he'd replied, making me wonder again who exactly he was and how he was always managing to evade me.

Are you wondering that too?

How does that work, huh?

Intriguing clue, isn't it?

The answer's there, but you hopefully haven't joined the dots yet.

I am *so* going to write a full-on murder mystery sometime soon.

Back to his reply though for now . . .

You are a hopeless romantic, my friend! This is no fantasy novel.

Did he know how close he was to working out who I was? Had he already guessed? I pressed on, because this was happening now, and I was going to see it through:

I admit it, yes, I am. I know it could never really happen . . . except in a way, it could? What if there was a way we could both be there, together, and we would know, but no one else would?

He'd replied by the start of lunch:

How?

I smiled and wrote back:

Both turn up wearing the same color handkerchief in the lapel pocket of our suits. Red, let's say! Then we'll know who each other is. No one else will know the significance. Deal?

He didn't reply to that. Silence again.

But no, no, no. He wasn't getting away that easily.

On Friday afternoon, at exactly 2:45 p.m. (I had to promise myself I'd do it at a set time, otherwise I'd just let it slide and slide, and it would be too late), I told Mr. Higson, my history teacher, that I was feeling unwell and asked to be excused for a few moments. I made my way to the library where the final Friday study hall was taking place, and acted like I was looking for a reference book.

The room was silent.

Mrs. West was the teacher in charge, and she was known for being strict.

Beth had her head down working on an essay. But it was the boys I was interested in.

The camera. From my point of view, panning across the room. Around twenty students in all, most of them minor characters, but three stand out, not because I've had interactions with them (that was irrelevant since they didn't know it was me they were writing to), but because I'd seen them all in the library, sometimes on multiple occasions, and that surely had to be significant:

Adam

Dan

and Jason.

Feel the fear. Do it anyway.

I had to know. I had to either end this, or start this, or otherwise complicate this, one way or the other. The notes had been good. But I was ready for more.

I was ready for change.

I went around to where the book was and scribbled my final note. This was it. He could take it or he could leave it, the ball would be finally in his court. I was ready. It was just a question of whether he was too:

I want to meet you. Monday. 1:05 p.m. Bench in the corner of the yard by the yew tree. I'll be there. I only want to talk. I'm scared. Maybe you are too? Let's be scared together.

Chapter 16

It was the weekend. Don't worry, I won't torment you with two days' worth of filler before we get to the good bit (or what we hope is the good bit, right?). *I* had to endure thinking of nothing else and winding myself up imagining terrible outcomes, but there's no reason you should too.

Things were not helped by writing an English essay on Saturday about the main themes of *Wuthering Heights*. Side note to add: The essay was late; it had been due on Friday. I'd completely forgotten about it, which wasn't like me at all, but the reason was obvious, and, ironically, also the main theme of the book: It was love, wasn't it? Burning, pining love. And the torment of being denied it. I'm not saying that what I had in the margins of *Dance on My Grave* was love, but how was it possible to feel *so much* for someone when I didn't even know their identity? I suppose it was just the power of shared experience. Of finally finding what I didn't know I'd even been looking for—a boy like me. (Note to editor: Possible title? Would hit harder at the end of a chapter. Oh well.)

The other thing to mention (I'll keep this brief, I promise) was on Sunday. Mom and Keith had gone out to a conference about home-based business opportunities, since we were quite the entrepreneurial family now, and, like they were YUPPIES (Young Urban Professionals—although *middle-aged* would be more appropriate in their case), the house now had a fax machine and Mom had a pager (two mobile phones would be too expensive), which was constantly hooked to the waist of her jeans. Worried how I would cope left on my own, I called Beth's house, and luckily she was home, so she came over. I had promised her we'd watch one of the Police Academy films, but my foggy brain hadn't registered that it was Sunday, so all the stores were closed, including Blockbuster.* So that left us with the one movie I'd recorded on to VHS when it was on last Christmas. A film I *adored* (and I think Beth liked too), and that we knew pretty much all the words to.

Labyrinth.

As I watched Bowie's spandex-wrapped perfection gyrating on our 14-inch TV, with his gender-bending glam-rock vibe, it occurred to me that the writing may have been on the wall for some time—I just didn't spot it. Had Beth spotted it? Did Beth already know about my sexuality but was just letting me say something in my own time? *Should I tell Beth?* Admitting it to myself had been hard enough. Admitting it anonymously in the pages of a book was also hard. But face-to-face? That felt impossible. But then . . . it was Beth, my best friend for *years*, and surely it would be OK? Surely it wouldn't change anything? *But could it?*

---

* It wasn't until August 26, 1994, that the Sunday Trading Act finally allowed all stores to legally open on a Sunday. Imagine that!

I'd assumed Debbie was a progressive sort. Didn't have her down for being against gay people, but it seemed she was.

The fear came rushing back in. I had a big can of gasoline, I'd taken off the cap, and I was about to light a match. There was every chance I was going to blow my world apart.

I didn't have to, I knew that, but hiding is so lonely. And it's hard work.

So, I opted for something tentative. And that's how, during the glittery fever dream of the ball in "As the World Falls Down," I ended up muttering, "Bowie has such magnetism, doesn't he?" and Beth didn't take her eyes off the sumptuous ball on the screen, with all the costumes and masks. She just replied, "Is it his magnetism that you like, or his jaw-droppingly tight pants?*" She glanced at me, held my eyes, smiled, then turned back to the screen as her hand found mine and she squeezed.

And that was it.

She knew.

And she was OK with it.

Nothing more needed to be said.

She held my hand through to the end credits, me, fizzing and breathless, unable to focus on the rest of the film, even if everything was OK. Just as I'd bent down to press Rewind on the VCR, she hit me with it.

"Actually, Jay, there was something I wanted to tell you. What's that look for?!" she exclaimed, seeing my stricken face. "It's nothing bad! I'm not . . . dying or anything!"

---

* This is objectively true whatever your sexuality.

119

When people wanted to "tell" you things, when they had "news," it normally heralded change, and change was something I was having a bit too much of. Anyway . . .

"There's someone I really like," she said.

"Yeah? Who?"

She smiled coyly, as if remembering just how much she liked him. "Dan."

Close-up: me. Conflict and turmoil. But you wouldn't know it, 'cause I have the biggest fake smile plastered all over my stupid face.

That'll be the end of an episode in the TV adaptation, but let's drive this on to the messy conclusion we're all now expecting.

By the time I was looking at myself in the mirror on Monday morning, I was a mess. Not a physical mess—my god, I was washed and preened and hair waxed to within an inch of my life—but mentally I was wrecked. I didn't know if he was going to show; I didn't know if he'd read the message; I didn't know what I was going to say to him or even what I really wanted out of this. More to the point, I was worried he would be disappointed. That it was me. And maybe, in his head, he'd built his Mystery Boy up to be someone popular and buff and much more handsome than I was.

What then?

"Let's just be friends."

Oh god. How humiliating.

And then, what if it was Dan? What would that mean for me and Beth? *Thanks for stabbing me in the back and shattering my heart into a billion pieces, Jamie! How very loyal of you.*

Oh god.

Every class that morning was a painful exercise in clock-watching and time going unnaturally slowly, punctuated with a conflicting wish that time would just stop so I could think everything through a bit more.

But those dominoes were falling, inexorably, toward whatever lay at the end.

Economics passed in a blur.

History was just words in no meaningful order.

In English, Ms. Wilkins told me she was "disappointed" when she'd discovered I hadn't handed in my essay on Friday (I hope you know how much those words were a blow to someone like me), before moving on to confronting Rob about having blatantly copied his essay straight out of York Notes. Apparently, he'd come up with a very specific angle on how *Wuthering Heights* was actually about loss, not love—too coincidentally the same as the argument made in the study guide. But not even them having a row and Rob telling her to "fuck off" (which landed him straight in detention with Mrs. Prenton) was enough to stop me thinking about what lay ahead in just under twenty minutes.

Debbie stopped me as I bolted for the door when the bell rang. "Jamie, they're saying they can't do cotton candy *and* the doughnuts; can you help me and try speaking to them on the phone?"

"OK."

"Great, thanks." She started leading me off.

"Whoa. Not now. I can't."

Debbie scowled at me. "This is important. It has to be confirmed *today*."

"I could do it . . . later? I have something."

She sighed in frustration. "Forget it. Adam?"

"I have something too!" he pleaded.

That's when I think my heart stopped.

He met my eyes, looked back at her, saw she was serious, then sighed. "Yeah, OK then, I'll talk to them," he said.

As she marched him down the hall, he glanced back at me, face mournful. I gave him a small smile.

It couldn't be.

Could it?

It was cold that lunchtime. I remember because I felt it to my bones, sitting on that bench, waiting.

And waiting.

I knew he would come. I knew he'd show up. I felt it.

OK, perhaps he wasn't great at being on time.

Or perhaps he was building himself up to it.

But I knew he would show.

I waited.

And I waited.

I waited all lunchtime.

No one came.

Chapter 17

So, that made me feel bad about myself. All that wasted worry. All that hope.

And then stood up! That was the first time I told myself that boys were the worst.[*]

But there was something I didn't know.

Remember when I talked about an earlier action being the first domino that fell (page 24, if you need to refresh your memory)? And then this course was unleashed that would continue and continue, and I couldn't stop it? If you've ever seen a domino run, you'll know that sometimes a line can fork, and two lines can run in parallel, falling simultaneously, until they join back up again with double the force. What I didn't know then is that a short while ago the line had forked. Something else was going on, right at that moment, in parallel, that was about to crash back into my life with considerable force.

There you go, a bit of dramatic irony to keep you going. *It's*

---

[*] And definitely not the last.

important to keep going, I told myself that afternoon. I'd given things a chance, they hadn't worked; it was time to get back to what I did best: keeping myself busy, being an A+ student, polite, mature, an Oxbridge candidate.

The common room was deserted when I got there at the end of the day. Fine by me. All I wanted was to quietly go home and lick my wounds. I twisted my key in my locker, pulled the door open, and the note fell out.

His handwriting.

Hi Jamie,

So it's you? It's funny to finally know that. I'm sorry I didn't show, but I couldn't. You looked me right in the eyes today, but I guess you still don't know which eyes were mine.

I don't mean to be cruel. I'm not trying to tease you. I was all set to come.

But actually, thinking about it, it's a bad idea. Really bad. Everyone thinks I'm someone I'm not. And for reasons you will never understand, it's impossible for me to change that. I won't ever be able to be honest about stuff. So, this isn't me being cruel, it's me saying you'd be better off forgetting about me, because I won't ever be able to be who I want to be, and who you want me to be, who you deserve me to be, and me and you could never be anything anyway because that's not the way the world works and it's definitely not the way my world works.

I'm writing this to say goodbye. It's been a lot of fun and I'm glad we talked. I'll remember it forever. But it's time to move on, and we should both pretend none of this happened. Trust me—that's the only way.

But Jamie? Just for the record, because you don't strike me as someone who sees it, you're really cute. You're smart, and you're kind, and I know you're a sweet guy. I do really like you. When I saw it was you waiting on the bench, it made me smile. It felt good because I don't do much smiling these days.

x

Chapter 18

Obviously, I was going to ignore his wishes. Who gets a letter like that and just says, "Oh, OK then, it sounds like you might be really nice and you clearly think I am, which is frankly amazing by itself, but I'll just leave it"?

I had a free period first thing on Tuesday, so I went straight to the library. The plan: I'd write a new message in *Wildflowers*, show him that he might be saying goodbye, but I certainly wasn't. And if he really meant any of the stuff he'd said in that letter, then surely he wouldn't be able to resist one more look in the book itself? I couldn't guarantee it, of course, but I reckoned it was a good bet.

But *Wildflowers of Great Britain* wasn't there.

Gone.

My chest tightened. It was always, *always* there. I checked the books on either side, and either side of that—maybe one of us had shoved it back in the wrong place in a hurry—but no. Checked the shelves on either side, above, below . . . round the corner . . . nothing.

He'd taken it.

If the book didn't exist, neither did we.

He was erasing us.

I wanted to kick something. *What the hell do I do now?*

Nothing. There was nothing I could do.

"Jamie, you're giving up too easily," Electra said, appearing from behind one of the shelves. "Perhaps you need a different strategy? *Wave Warriors* is all about strategy*—you could learn a lot from me."

I stared at her. *Don't keep me dangling, then!*

"You know someone else took the book out before you because it was stamped," she continued. "If it was stamped, there must be a record on the computer. It wouldn't be definitive evidence of anything, of course, but it would be a very strong lead—especially if the name matches up with one of your chief suspects." Then, just like that, she vanished.

"Holy fuck, Electra," I muttered. "Of course!"

Cut to: me, Jamie Hampton, standing in front of Mrs. C's desk, doing his very best nonchalant acting, as though none of this was an issue and he wasn't remotely bubbling over with excitement.

JAMIE: Mrs. C? Hi. Would it be possible to have a look at the checkout log in order to find out who took the book you recommended out before I did? It might be someone I can fall in love with, you see?

MRS. C: Of course, Jamie! No problem.

---

* Not really true—it was mainly about hitting one another with giant inflatable . . . um, oars?

[She merrily taps away at the computer keyboard and squints at the screen.]

MRS. C: Ah, yes! Here's a name you might recognize, it's—

Cut to: actual reality.

"Let me stop you there, Jamie," Mrs. C said. "I can't."

My eyes widened.

"A fundamental principle of librarianship is a reader's right to privacy," she continued.

"OK, but—"

"Some people might not want other people to know they're into wildflowers. Some people might be unsure and might just have wanted to read about them to test the water. Do you understand what I'm saying?"

"OK, but what if they left notes saying they *were* interested in wildflowers and wanted to know if anyone else was?"

A smile spread across Mrs. C's face. "Oh god, did they?!"

And a smile spread across mine. We both knew what we were talking about, and she was fine with it. More than fine—she seemed excited.

"Well, Jamie, I think that's wonderful news. I think it's brilliant."

Those words meant more than she would ever know.

"But still, the answer's no."

My smile dropped. I glanced at the computer again.

So close, and yet so far.

"The person you're looking for might not be in the system

anyway. Some people scan it out like every other book because that feels safest to them, especially if it's in a stack of other books, but I deliberately turn a blind eye to students who take the book but don't, for obvious reasons, want to officially check it out."

Electra was immediately by my side. "Hang on. *You* checked it out."

"Some students just quietly take it, you see."

"But not you," Electra said. "In fact, Mrs. C checked the book out for you."

"There's no magnetic strip in *Wildflowers*, so it doesn't set off the alarm," she continued.

"Ask her!" Electra insisted.

"But I checked the book out!" I bleated.

Mrs. C opened her mouth, but then froze.

"I know you did, Jamie Hampton," said a voice behind me. "That's exactly why I've come to find you."

I spun around.

Mrs. Prenton was staring at me.

"How fortuitous I should find you so quickly," she said, giving me a smile laced with poison. "My office. *Now*."

I met Mrs. C's eyes. They were wide. *Worried*.

"Oh, kiddo," Electra said. "Oh dear. This is bad, bad, bad."

I turned back to Mrs. Prenton who was gesturing for me to walk.

Cut to: me, Jamie Hampton, not a hero, but a shackled convict in an orange jumpsuit, handcuffed, being led to his fate down an austere, clinical, institutional hallway. He passes cell doors, the sounds of banging from within and shouts of "QUEER!" and "HOMO!" Head bowed, he walks on, his jailer saying nothing.

Fantasy or reality? It was hard to say. Electra scurried up behind me, juggling court papers, law books, and a briefcase. "Something about *you do not have to say anything, but anything you do say can definitely screw you over, so probably best to shut up?*"

Shutting up was one option. Denying everything was another.

Minutes later, I was standing in front of Mrs. Prenton's desk while she glanced me up and down. "Tell me about *Wildflowers of Great Britain*, Jamie," she said.

She fixed me with an emotionless stare while I froze.

Questions: How did she know? How *much* did she know? *Why* did she know? Why did it matter? Who told her? She wouldn't just *know* about it; someone must have said something.

Answers: *shit shit shit.*

I swallowed.

Her stare didn't waver.

She was enjoying this.

And every second of hesitation was another step away from being able to plausibly deny everything and plead innocence.

"I . . . don't really know. I . . . took it out but never had time to read it."

That was, I kid you not, the first time I'd ever lied to a teacher.

Mrs. Prenton nodded thoughtfully. "Quite a niche subject area, isn't it? Wildflowers?"

"I . . . suppose?"

"And you're doing English, history, and economics, so it's not relevant to any of your classes . . ."

I met her eyes, then quickly looked away.

If I hadn't read it, I hadn't read it. She couldn't prove I had.

"No matter," she said. "I checked the lending records first thing this morning, and it seems you weren't the only young man to check the book out recently . . ."

Why did you check the lending records?

"Hopefully we'll get to the bottom of this inexplicable interest in wildflowers among a certain cohort of junior boys," she continued. "We'll see if your coconspirator can shed any light on all this."

I stared at her. Then I looked around. Well . . . where was he, then? Who was he? Was this . . . *him*? Was I about to meet *him*?

The phone on her desk rang. "Yes?" she said down the handset.

I watched her, straining to hear the voice on the other end.

"Excellent. You can send him in."

She replaced the handset and gave me another poisoned smile. "Here he is now, Jamie."

So, this is it, folks. The big reveal. Did you manage to guess? Did you spot the clues, ignore the red herrings, and work it out? You know a good way of hiding who someone is from a reader is to make sure you don't give them much screen time, right? It's a bit of a cheat that, I always think. Oh well.

The prickle of fear in my stomach was replaced by the fizz of anticipation.

The wait felt like a million years.

Eventually, I heard the squeak of the doorknob being turned.

This was it.
The moment.
This was Mystery Boy.
The door swung open.
And in he walked.

Chapter 19

There must have been a mistake because none of it made sense. I couldn't have been communicating with *Rob West*.

Rob West couldn't possibly think I was "cute" or any of those other (really sensitive) things the letter said. Rob West wasn't even *into* books—he attended English in the most reluctant and sporadic of ways, doubtless only taking AP thinking it would be a breeze compared to math or chemistry or something—had he ever even been in the library?

Everyone is wrong about me . . .

Yeah, but not *that* wrong, surely?

I don't do much smiling these days . . .

Well, OK, no, you don't, but then—

I'm sorry I didn't show, but I couldn't.

Because you were given detention and sent to see Mrs. Prenton . . . Ha! So then you were *here* during lunch, which means you couldn't have seen me sitting on the bench, so—

I glanced through the office window and froze. Mrs. Prenton had a fantastic view of the whole yard—doubtless designed so she could keep eyes on everyone. Standing where I was now, you had a direct line to the bench I had been sitting on. He *could* have seen.

No, wait, it couldn't have been, because I'd established one of the notes had to have been written during Friday afternoon study hall, and I'd been in there myself. I'd seen who was in that class, and Rob hadn't been . . .

Except he was known for cutting classes. He wasn't in the class because he hadn't turned up and I hadn't accounted for that possibility.

I glanced at Rob.

Just . . . *no*. Not possible. He wasn't gay.

He didn't seem at all gay.

Expectations.

What was gay anyway?

I knew nothing.

Nothing.

About anything.

Rob wasn't looking back; he was staring straight at Mrs. Prenton, stony faced, frozen, almost like a soldier.

Maybe it was all a mistake. Maybe Rob wasn't Mystery Boy. Maybe Rob loved gardening, and he did take the book out legitimately thinking it was about flowers.

"Eyes on me, Jamie," Mrs. Prenton said.

I felt my cheeks heat up in a flash.

"So who's going to tell me what *Wildflowers of Great Britain* is really about?" she continued.

Neither of us spoke.

"I have plenty of time," she said. "Robert? Let's start with you."

"I've no idea about the book. I don't even remember taking it out," he said flatly and without hesitation.

Mrs. Prenton nodded. "And yet you *did* take it out because there's a record of it on the library system."

"I lost my card for a while. Maybe someone else used it," he replied.

I mean, if that wasn't true, then shit, he was a good liar.

"A remarkable coincidence," Mrs. Prenton said. "Meanwhile, you, Jamie, claim you *did* take it out, but never read it?"

I nodded.

"So then, why would you be frantically talking with Mrs. Carpenter about taking the book out and trying to find out who else had taken it out?"

Out of the corner of my eye, I saw Rob flinch.

Meanwhile, I was clearly fucked.

"Sorry," Rob said. "I honestly can't understand what the problem is here. It's a book. It's just a book."

Mrs. Prenton gave a smug little laugh. "By all accounts, and despite the misleading title, it's a book riddled with homosexuality and a deeply inappropriate relationship between two teenage boys."

"And?" Rob said.

"*And*, Robert, an easily led young person reading that sort of trash might be persuaded into thinking such a thing was a good idea. They might be seduced into a sordid lifestyle leading to god knows what. As a school, we have a duty of care to protect all of you from dangerous ideas like that."

Rob shrugged. "I thought school was about exploring ideas."

"Ideas, Robert, not perversions. And this isn't a debate. It's the law. I'm sure you've heard of Section 28—your father himself voted for it."

"What's Section 28?" I muttered.

"Legislation banning books featuring gay characters from schools," Rob replied matter-of-factly. I stared at him, trying to compute what he'd said. There was a law banning gay books? Really? "And yes, my father was a big supporter," he continued.

I can't ever be who I am . . .

"You *do* know, Robert. Of course you do. So you understand the problem here?"

"Not really, because like we said, neither of us has read it," Rob said, his voice calm. How was he managing it? "But . . . *you* have?"

My mouth fell open a bit. Did he have a death wish? Rob wasn't showing the slightest bit of fear. He was staring Mrs. Prenton down.

Her mouth twisted. "The book found its way into the hands of a freshman, who, I'm told, showed it to his friend. His friend was understandably upset, and shocked, and told his mother about what he'd read. The mother contacted the school this morning."

"So no one's read the book?" Rob said.

"The mother assures me it's pornographic and certainly illegal."

Rob frowned. "Oh, I see. The mother *assures* you."

"Yes, Robert," Mrs. Prenton said, giving him a cruel smile. "But I don't need her assurances because I have it here!" She produced the book from the drawer of her desk, waving it in front of us, like the finale of a magic trick. "I'm a busy woman, gentlemen. I have a governors' meeting this afternoon and a Rotary Club dinner tonight. I don't have the time or inclination to read this sort of filth. But I don't need to, do I? When you could just tell me."

"We've never read the book!" Rob said, incredulous.

"Oh, Robert, I'm sorry if I wasn't clear—I don't believe a word you say. I'm not surprised by you—we all know your history—but just because your father is an MP doesn't make you immune to consequences." She turned to me. "You, Jamie, I *am* surprised by. I thought better of you. I thought your future was bright. Perhaps I was wrong." She sniffed dismissively and placed the book back in her desk drawer. "Why don't you think about what's best to do? If you just admit it, and perhaps give me some idea if anyone recommended this book to you—especially if that person is a staff member, as that could really be putting our students in danger—we could come to an arrangement that doesn't involve me having to telephone your parents and telling them you've been reading homosexual pornography. I have my suspicions about who is ultimately behind this, of course, but I need proof. No reason why you two should take all the blame, is there? After all, maybe you're both victims in all this too. Take twenty-four hours to examine your conscience. Now get out, both of you."

Chapter 20

I was out of there in a flash. On autopilot, I don't know, I didn't wait, I just charged along, barreled through the door of the boys' toilets and slammed open the first cubicle door I got to. "Oh! Sorry! Oh—it's you."

Electra was sitting on the toilet. "It's OK, I'm not peeing; you can come in."

I grimaced and shut the door behind me.

"So. Plenty to dissect there," she said.

I groaned.

"Mrs. Prenton wants you to rat out Mrs. C, she obviously has her suspicions about her, and if you don't comply, your mom will be summoned, she'll probably bring Keith because she'll need the moral support, he'll hear everything, you'll be outed as a massive homosexual, your mom will tell your gran, who will be *appalled*—literally, she worshipped the ground Maggie Thatcher walked on—everyone at school will find out, my god, *the bullying*, it'll be horrific, and there's absolutely no way they'll make you class president next year now. Leaving all that aside, how do you feel about Rob West being Mystery Boy?!"

I blew out a breath. I wasn't going to think about *that* at a time like *this*.

"No, but he's *hot*, Jamie. He's a *fine*-looking young man."

Exactly. *Too* fine. A guy that looks as good as Rob would not be interested in a guy like me. That's really not how things work.

"Well, I think you've landed on your feet! And to think how much worse it could have been—it could have been Jason in some sort of internalized homophobia scenario." She winced. "Ghastly. Plus, Jason has such bad hair. *Scraggly.* Absolutely gruesome."

I heard the main door push open and determined footsteps come in, pace around, and stop outside the cubicle door. "Jamie? I know you're in there."

"It's Rob!" Electra gasped. "Answer him!"

I didn't want to.

"Talk to him!" she hissed.

And say *what*?

"We need to talk," Rob said. He tapped on the door, and I heard him sigh. "Please," he muttered.

I glanced at Electra. She cocked her head. "He said 'please.'" She did a little pout like that was the sweetest thing in the world. "Adorable."

I chewed my lip, then slid the bolt. I glanced back at Electra, but she'd gone. I sighed, opened the door, walked out, and came face-to-face with Rob.

For a while, we just looked at each other.

It really was him. This felt like a dream, and bearing in mind my mental state, and Electra, and so on, it really felt like it could have been.

Rob West.

How did I miss the clues?

Did I miss the clues? Or was this all a big mistake?

Eventually, he muttered, "We meet at last."

"Hi."

"It's not how I would have planned it."

"In the sense that you didn't want it to happen at all?"

He met my eyes. Connection. *Electricity.* Something jumped, deep inside me.

I took an unsteady breath. "Is this even real?" I asked. "Because I don't know what is and isn't anymore. Was it you, writing the messages?"

He nodded.

"You've read the book?"

"Of course I've read the fucking book."

"Prove it," I said. "Prove you're for real."

He sighed. "Fine, ask me about it."

"OK." I thought for a moment. "What is Hal wearing when his boat capsizes?"

"Red jockey briefs with 'a fetching white trim.' I love that that's the thing you asked me."

"I love that you answered without hesitation."

He smiled. Just quickly, but he smiled, and for a second, the world seemed a tiny bit lighter. But, just as quickly, the darkness was back. "Jamie, my father . . ." He sighed, searching for words, giving me a chance to reflect on how formal the word "father" sounded, and how respectful—especially coming from him, a boy so quick to anger, who didn't seem to care about anyone or anything. "He's a horrible bastard. I mean, not in public, then he's caring and kind and bizarrely quite humorous, opening new libraries with a funny anecdote, kissing babies and whatnot, but at home . . ." He whistled and shook his head. "And, I think, this time, he might actually kill me."

I frowned. *"This time?"*

"It's why he took me out of Abbott's—my last school."

"Because you were fighting . . . and the prostitute."

He stopped and stared at me like I'd just slapped him. "Prostitute? Wha—"

The main door opened, and we sprang apart, Rob doing a swift one-eighty and heading straight to the urinals as I flipped around and bolted back into the cubicle, sliding the lock. I rested with my back against the door, listening as someone walked in. I took a breath, then glanced across at Electra, who was back opposite me, perched on the toilet.

"Halftime assessment," she said. "It's definitely him; he's read the book, so it's nice you have Hal's underpants in common; slightly worried you might have offended him with that bit about the sex worker; did you need to bring that up now?"

I winced. Probably shouldn't have done that.

"No one's talking about the elephant in the room!" Electra grinned to herself.

I crossed my arms and stared at her.

"I mean," she continued, "he literally wrote you a letter and said you were cute. That boy is standing there, talking to you, and he wants to jump your bones."

It didn't necessarily mean that. It's one thing writing

something like that in a letter that he thought he'd never act upon, it's another actually going through with it. Maybe he was just being kind, letting me down gently?

"Jamie, you *are* cute," Electra told me. "I'm sure he meant it."

"Stop!" I hissed. "We're in shit."

She put her hands up in contrition. "You're right. I'll leave you boys to sort it out. But later, kiddo, we party. Because this is progress." She leaned forward. "I'm proud of you. You've come a long way."

And right now, I wish I could go back.

She vanished.

I heard the tap running, some paper towels being pulled, then footsteps, the door creak open and closed again.

Seconds later, Rob was tapping at the cubicle door.

I opened it, pulled him inside, and slammed the lock again.

"What do you mean *prostitute?*" he said.

We were almost nose-to-nose. I'd underestimated the amount of space inside a toilet cubicle. I tried backing up a bit, but hit the rim of the toilet seat.

"That's just what people said," I whispered. "About why you were kicked out."

"What do you think I am?"

"I don't know who you are, Rob! I don't know who I am, let alone anyone else. I'm confused. All this . . . is messed up."

Rob took a couple of heavy breaths. He was wearing cologne. I could smell it on his neck now he was this close. "I wasn't kicked out. My father *took* me out because the chaplain found me . . . with someone."

"With . . . another boy? Doing . . . oh, right."

"*Right.*"

My stomach twisted. What the hell was that feeling? Jealousy?

"Couldn't have that, what would the *Daily Mail* say?" Rob continued. "My father has ambitions for a *cabinet position*; he's out there talking about family values; he can't have his son be a disgusting homosexual. So, we pretend it's just a phase, keep it hush-hush, he removes me from the school, invents some story about me being kicked out—clearly exaggerated by the rumor mill—and it's all water under the bridge." He leaned back against the door, his face pained. "Fucking hell."

"I'm sorry."

He released a breath, then opened his eyes. "And all that's before Mrs. Prenton reads the book and finds a lot of notes between two boys, suspiciously in our handwriting."

My chest tightened. Prenton would assume it was us no matter how the writing looked.

He shook his head. "So that's my situation. What's yours?"

"No idea! Never even discussed it with my dad, I mean, why would I? He finds Julian Clary* funny—maybe that's good? My mom . . . I don't know, I think she wouldn't be happy about it, but I don't think she'd hit the roof. It would be a kind of low-level disappointment, steeped in worry. Her new boyfriend though . . ."

"Would?"

---

* I hope you know him, but if you don't: Clary is an openly gay comedian who refers to himself as a "renowned homosexual." He hosted a very camp game show on Channel 4 in the early 90s called *Sticky Moments*. If you want a laugh, Google his infamous appearance at the British Comedy Awards on December 12, 1993.

I nodded.

"Heterosexual men are the worst." He met my eyes and we both cracked a smile. It was funny, hearing him say stuff like that. A boy who I'd just assumed was straight, was borderline dangerous, would hate someone like me, and no . . . he was actually . . . just like me. I kind of . . . loved that? I wasn't sure exactly what the feeling was, but it bubbled up inside me, like when you've downed a Coke too fast, a rush, a bit of a hit, and it made me slightly lightheaded.

"All right," he said. "So, we need a plan, and—"

The main door creaked open again, and we both held our breath. Being found in a toilet cubicle together was not the finale either of us needed right then. I was standing absurdly close to him. Desperate to mitigate the awkwardness, I looked down at the floor. He was wearing brown boots of some kind—not Doc Martens, something less flashy. Dark blue jeans—but not baggy, like most people wore, and not wrecked with rips or holes or acid-washing, just fairly smart and more of a regular fit. His navy-blue polo shirt (practically a trademark garment—and Ralph Lauren, like always) was rucked up slightly over his brown leather belt. Then . . . his neck again . . . maybe it was the cologne that drew me there, but the curve of it into his shoulder . . . it seemed tender, somehow . . . his cheek . . . the merest hint of stubble just below his sideburns, but otherwise baby-faced and fresh, his dark hair— neat, preppy, short back and sides—blended into his neck. Back to his neck again.

I adjusted my gaze to his face, accidentally made eye contact, and quickly looked away again.

In my peripheral vision, I saw his eyes drift down my lips, then back up.

Whatever was going on outside, I couldn't hear it. Just the gentle in and out of his breathing.

Our eyes met again.

And then the heavy thud of footsteps, the door creaking open again, and, finally, shutting.

We both released a breath.

"We need to get rid of the book," Rob said. "Before she has a chance to read it. No book, no evidence." He thought for a moment. "Prenton clearly wants us to implicate Mrs. Carpenter."

"She's only implicated if we say she gave it to us—you're saying we rat out Mrs. C?"

He smiled. "No, of course not. But that freshman might. Mrs. C needs our help. We should at least warn—"

There were footsteps and we heard the main door open again. Wrong way round. That meant . . . The last person who came in was actually *two* people, and one of them had just heard everything we said!

Rob screwed his eyes closed. *"Fuck!"*

We could only hope. Hope they didn't hear. Or hope they didn't care, that they wouldn't make sense of any of it.

But one thing was clear: Whatever it was that we'd started, we were already being nowhere near careful enough.

Chapter 21

Mrs. Carpenter's face was a picture when she clocked us walking into the library together—trying to keep the surprise in check while she worked out if we both knew who the other was. In a split second, she must have known we did and that something was up, because she said, "I've just opened a new pack of cookies in the office—you're in luck, boys!" and escorted us past the main desk and into the small room at the back, where she closed the door.

"Sit!" She indicated a couple of chairs.

"Mrs. Prenton knows about the book," I said. "She knows Rob and I took it out, and she knows some freshman had it." I explained the rest of the story: the friend who told his mom, the complaint, and the fact we were all about to be outed unless we told Prenton who had recommended the book to us.

Mrs. C took a deep breath. "This was bound to happen eventually."

"Why did you risk it?" I asked. "There's a thing called Section 28, you know!"

"Jamie . . ." She chuckled. "It's a great book; it deserves to be in the school library, whatever certain people say. Why shouldn't you be able to read a book that features gay characters? Gay people exist, after all." She smiled at us both and I looked down at the floor.

"Our backs are against the wall," Rob said. "My dad voted in favor of Section 28, and he will—"

"I know," Mrs. C said. "I know he did, Rob. I know who he is, what he stands for." She smiled again. "Shall we all have a cookie?"

She got up and retrieved the packet.

I glanced at Rob and held my hands out—*why isn't she worried?*

He shrugged, as baffled as I was.

She offered us each a cookie, and I was delighted that Rob, seemingly on autopilot, immediately twisted the two halves apart and began by licking the cream section first.

"I wish I'd never checked the book out," I muttered. "Mrs. Prenton would never have known, then."

"I was going to suggest you just take it," Mrs. C replied, "but then Mr. Haskins walked in, and you already had your library card out. It might have looked suspicious. And I wasn't anticipating Mrs. Prenton accessing the checkout log like some secret agent."

"There's a way out if we can get rid of the book before she reads it," Rob said. "Destroy it, burn it, I dunno."

Mrs. C nodded. "OK, first, we don't burn books, you utter heathen, so let's get that straight. Second, the book mysteriously and coincidentally goes missing from her office? Right after you two have been identified as being persons of interest? How do you think that's going to look?"

"Suspicious," I conceded. "But still, if there's no evidence . . ."

Mrs. C put her hand up. "Let me stop you there. You're assuming bigots care about things like evidence. *They do not.* They only care about their agenda."

"Did you just call Mrs. Prenton a bigot?" Rob asked, amused.

"I don't know, did I?" Mrs. C replied, deadpan. "The point is, this is a school, not a court of law. A parent has complained, so she already knows what she needs to know about what's in it. So even if the book disappears, trust me, you'll be the fall guys, as will I, of course." She smiled and leaned forward conspiratorially. "This isn't the first time I've flouted Section 28—because, frankly, fuck the Conservatives."

I just stared at her. It felt like Mrs. C had gone fully rogue— and I thought that was utterly *amazing.*

"Sorry, Rob," she added. "I know your father is a Conservative MP."

He shrugged. "Well, he's an asshole. But what are we going to do, then?"

Mrs. Carpenter stared out of the partition window into the library beyond for a while. Eventually, she turned back to us. "I'll take the bullet," she said plainly, like it was nothing. "Tell her it was me, I'll confess, I'll say I brought it into the library, I gave it to you, I shouldn't have done it, and I'll offer my resignation. She will get what she wants: someone to blame. The parent will get what they want: petty revenge for daring to show their child the world is a diverse place and that not everyone thinks alike. And I'll get what I want: protecting two students who haven't done anything wrong."

***

148

"It's over, we're screwed," I said as Rob and I left the library. Luckily, it was a sunny day—everyone was out soaking up the rays on the field, and the hallway was empty.

Rob grabbed me by my sleeve, pulling me back as I was about to charge through the double doors. "We can't let her take the blame."

"What can we do? I really like Mrs. C, but we've broken a *law*. Aren't you worried about what'll happen? What people will say? What the repercussions will be?"

He shook his head. "Technically, we haven't broken the law, the school has."

"You're splitting hairs. Like Mrs. C said, facts don't matter here."

"Look, Jamie, I don't want to be in trouble, of course not—" He frowned. "What's that look for?"

"You're in detention every other day."

For a moment, he glared at me. "I have a really low tolerance for bullshit. That's why. The point is, in this instance, I'm not ashamed. I got over that a while ago. That's just what they want you to feel. The law is wrong, not us, and Mrs. C shouldn't be fired over it."

"But—"

"Power and control," he said.

"What are you talking about?"

He glanced up and down the hallway to check we were alone, then he met my eyes, and I felt it again—that weird connection. That spark. "The world is full of people who want power and control. But they have to use fear and ignorance to get it, because nobody in their right mind would support them otherwise. Keep people afraid by giving them a common enemy, and keep them uneducated so they never know any better, and you'll always control them!"

I leaned against the opposite wall to where he was. I'd never seen Rob like this. I'd always known he was good-looking, but I'd never really been into him like this. Now though . . . saying this stuff? OK, I'm a writer, words will always be sexy to me, but this was something else. "Okaaay . . . ?"

He smiled, and he walked toward me slowly. Meaningfully. Never taking his eyes off me. "Well, take gay people. The right-wing press and the politicians tell everyone we're a threat. Being gay will corrupt innocent kids. It spreads disease. It contributes to some kind of moral decline. Society will burn, basically. People are scared. They don't want that. Enter our heroic politicians and religious leaders—they will protect us! They know what's right! And as long as we, the general public, support them, they won't allow those nasty, evil gay people to have their wicked way. All will be well!" He flipped himself around so he was next to me and put his arm across my shoulders in one swift movement, while fending off imaginary attackers. "Keep back, evil gays! Jamie isn't interested in your sordid lifestyle choices!" He laughed, then took his arm away, sliding his hands into his pockets. "Oldest trick in the book—history is riddled with people like that—that's what the Nazis did, they blamed all of Germany's problems on minorities. Jewish people, the disabled, gays—anyone they considered unclean. Impure."

I couldn't take my eyes off him. It was part surprise—that he was this eloquent—and part sheer admiration. What he was saying clicked for me. It made sense. It felt dangerous, but it also felt like . . . *truth*. And that was exciting.

Plus, whenever he touched me, I got an endorphin hit. So much so, I was fuzzy-headed and could hardly keep track as he kept talking.

"Now that breaks down if the people know too much. If they get too much understanding, if they, god forbid, learned some empathy and saw that, actually, being gay wasn't evil, it wasn't bad, and it didn't lead to bad things, what then? See, people like us? We're a threat to the power hoarders, Jamie. We're different, so we've dared to think for ourselves! We've read a book that might give the impression it's OK . . . to be gay! If others saw that, if they saw we were also *happy*, what message would that send? That being gay wasn't bad after all? That there was nothing to fear about gay people? That gay people were not going to hell? Oh no! Did the people in power, the people telling us what's right and what's wrong, lie?! It doesn't take much to destroy a system that's based on a tissue of lies. Give too many freethinkers a voice, and the whole pack of cards comes crashing down. And too many powerful people have skin in the game to let that happen."

I blew out a breath, trying to compute it all. Everything he was saying made sense. And it was making me angry. But there was another feeling too, and it felt like a hug, full of reassurance and strength, from being with someone who was talking like this. Someone who was happy to admit "we're different" and use the word "gay" just normally, in a sentence, and it not be a cruel punchline or an insult.

I realized he was looking at me. He gave me a soft smile, then reached out and adjusted the collar of my rugby shirt. "It looks better popped," he said. He studied my face, and I'm not sure what my expression was as so much was racing through my head, but he frowned and said, "You OK?"

"They won't ever accept us," I muttered. "They can't."

"Mm, they will, occasionally, if it suits them." He slid back round beside me with his back against the wall. "But they'll stop accepting us again if it doesn't."

"The system sucks . . ."

"Now we're getting somewhere . . ."

I stared straight ahead, my thoughts suddenly laser-sharp. "Fuck the system!"

He laughed.

And then I managed a laugh too. Somehow, a little bit of weight had lifted. I understood that I'd been fed a lie. Worse, drip-fed poison over years and years and everything I'd thought . . . simply wasn't true.

"The book needs to vanish," Rob said.

"But Mrs. C was right, it'll look obvious if—"

"OK, but what if it doesn't go missing? What if it's just the interior pages that go missing? Replaced by something that no one could object to?"

I turned the idea over in my head.

"The book will still exist," he continued. "*Wildflowers of Great Britain* will still exist. It's just the contents that make it illegal . . . won't. She made it sound like the complaining parent only heard about what's in it, and Prenton's busy for the rest of the afternoon and evening. If she leaves the book in her desk—and no, we can't be sure that she will, but it's worth the risk—then finds something else under that cover, what can she do then? What's she

going to call our parents in for if all she's got is a rumor and a book that's really about wildflowers?"

I shook my head. "Nice idea, but impossible. It's in her office. We can't get to it."

"Well, not now we can't. But she gave us twenty-four hours."

"I don't understand what you're suggesting," I said, although I did have a creeping dread.

He glanced up and down the hall again. We were still alone, but he lowered his voice anyway. "We break in. Tonight. We swap the book. We get out. No book, no problem." He met my eyes. "You game?"

My mouth fell open.

How could I do this? Break in to school? If it went wrong, if we were found, that would be the end of everything. I'd worked so hard for so long. I'd always kept my head down. I had, according to everyone, a "bright future." Now I was in danger of throwing all that away.

But if I didn't risk it . . .

I could lose it all anyway.

"Fuck the system, right, Jamie?" he said.

I met his eyes again. He was smiling at me. Willing me to do it.

"Why should we play by their rules, when the rules are so unfair?" Rob added.

"I know, I know, it's just—"

"Trust me. I won't let anything bad happen to us," he said. He reached out and he gave my arm a gentle squeeze.

For the first time, it wasn't me sorting something out, running a project, or going the extra mile; someone was helping *me*.

I glanced at his hand, then back at him.

He took his hand away, almost apologetically, and swallowed.

I wished he'd kept it there. It was . . . comforting.

"How? How do we break in?" I asked.

For a moment, he looked sheepish. "I have detention after school," he said.

I rolled my eyes and he smiled. "Set fire to a globe in geography with a lighter," he explained. "I call that a metaphor, a lot of people would probably call it *art*, but Mrs. Swain calls it vandalism. Anyway, it'll last an hour. That takes me to four forty-five. If I pack up slowly, I can still be here at five. I can find somewhere to hide out—if they've cleaned the toilets by then, I can hide there, and if not, a classroom. I'll make up an excuse about losing something and going to find it if anyone stops me on the way. As long as I'm on the inside when they lock the main doors, then I can let you in via the fire exit by the drama classroom later."

"It's not alarmed?"

"No, it's not."

"Wait," I said. "After-school detention? You have them a lot, right?"

He shrugged. "Teachers don't like to be challenged, what can I say?"

"That's how you managed to write all the notes in the book without me spotting you! You were still in school after I'd left."

He gave me a quizzical look. "Were you spying? Trying to find me out?"

"Um . . ."

"Unbelievable."

"I was just intrigued."

He gave me a wry smile.

I thought it best to gloss over all that and press on with the plan. "When should I be at the fire exit?"

"Around eight? Everyone will be long gone by then. If I haven't let you in by ten past eight, assume there's been a problem and get out of there."

He was offering to sacrifice himself to save me if need be. That was . . . incredible.

"Won't Prenton's office be locked?"

"That won't be a problem."

I stared at him. *Who was he?*

"You want to know too many things," he said, raising his eyebrow slightly at me. "Trust me, Jamie, OK? Just bring some stuff so we can swap the books over—glue, scissors, I don't know."

I nodded.

"And don't look so worried. We're outlaws now, like it or not. Don't let me down."

He winked at me, then turned and disappeared through the double doors, leaving me alone and wondering what the hell had just happened and what I'd become.

Change, huh?

Chapter 22

The fire exit door opened at eight on the dot. I slipped through the crack, and Rob gave it a firm push to shut it behind me. The noise rattled and echoed around the stairwell at a million decibels.

"Oops!" Rob shrugged.

"Has everyone gone?"

"Hope so."

I didn't like that one bit. Way too vague for me, and I didn't need any more uncertainties right then. I felt completely unmoored, totally at sea, too much new information (Rob was Mystery Boy!), too many new ideas (they vilify us because they need an enemy!), and too out of my comfort zone—what the hell was I doing, breaking into school? That's not the sort of thing a class president candidate does!

"Come on," he said.

The hallway was in darkness, and we walked along in silence. So weird, the school being totally deserted. Exhilarating, but maybe that was more the fear of what would happen if anyone found us. A pair of breaking-and-entering suspected homosexuals—it wouldn't look good and would only strengthen Mrs. Prenton's belief that we'd both descended into immorality.

The whole of this was dangerous, but the first part seemed like it would be the worst: getting the book out of Prenton's office. We walked along the edges of the hallways, keeping in the shadows, pushing silently through the doors into the staff area. We stood in silence and stillness for a moment. All was quiet. Rob headed straight for Prenton's door, which had a doorknob with an integrated lock. He tried to twist it but, of course, it wouldn't open.

I released an unsteady breath.

"Relax," Rob told me, without looking over his shoulder.

He reached into the pocket of his jeans, took out his wallet, and removed a bank card, which he slid into the vertical crack between the door and the frame, drawing it down until it hit the latch. Then he tilted the card, pressing it toward the doorknob, so it was almost touching it and threatening to snap in half. Jiggling it about, he was able to insert it farther into the gap. He leaned against the door, wiggling the card until . . .

Click!

The mechanism released and the door popped open.*

Rob turned to me and waggled his eyebrows, dead pleased with himself.

Close-up: me, Jamie Hampton, absolutely in love with this utter hero.

"The name's West, Rob West," he said.

"Where did you learn to do that?"

"Boarding school. Come on."

We padded into the office, and Rob slid the desk drawer

---

* Security was genuinely shit in the 90s, kids!

open and pulled out the book. "Part one complete."

Making sure not to let the office door close behind us, we headed out and retraced our steps, until we took a right, our shoes echoing on harder floor that marked the start of the new wing where the library was housed. Rob led the way, pushing open some double doors and then up the stairs. He paused at the top, checking that the coast was clear in the next hallway, before we stalked across and straight into the library.

Breathing a sigh of relief wasn't really appropriate, since the danger was far from over, yet we both did. He smiled at me. "You OK?"

"I've been better!" I hissed.

He smirked. Then he gave my shoulders a quick massage. "I'm quite enjoying myself."

I shook my head. "We need a book roughly the same size," I whispered. "Ideally about wildflowers, but any sort of flowers or botany-type subject will do."

The task was far from easy. We couldn't put the lights on, and even though an orange glow from the floodlights outside came through the windows, it wasn't enough to really help. If anything, it made the shadows worse, making it hard to see the titles of books and work out what they were without holding them up at various angles and squinting. Additionally, most of the books actually about botany were larger than the paperback edition of *Dance on My Grave*.

"We need a plan B," Rob sighed. "Did you bring any food?"

"Um . . . *no*. I have some fruit Polos* in my bag?"

---

* These are basically a hard candy in assorted fruit flavors. I munched on them regularly as a teenager.

Rob nodded. I fished them out, handed him the roll, and he crunched into one hungrily. *Should I have brought food?* I hadn't seen this as a social occasion, but now I thought about it, he'd stayed in school for *hours* while I'd gone home, had dinner, and come back. Oh god, I was a terrible person.

"I'm sorry I didn't bring food," I said.

"It's fine. Can I have another?"

"Have whatever you like. Have them all." I watched him sitting cross-legged on the carpet, chomping away. "Although I'll have an orange one if one comes up."

Rob smiled and offered me the packet. "Your lucky day."

I took it. "That's a green one."

"Couldn't see in the light, sorry."

I put it in my mouth anyway. "So, none of the books on botany are the right size. Maybe any book will do, what do you think?"

"Not any book." He picked a chunk of fruit Polo out of his teeth. Those things superglued themselves to your molars. "We should make sure it's a subtle dig at this whole messed-up situation." He thought for a moment, before a grin spread across his face. "*1984* by George Orwell."

"Why?"

"Come on, Jamie. One of the major themes of that book is how the government controls access to information. They tell people what and how to think. Deviation from the accepted norm isn't allowed. *Certain ideas, or even facts, are forbidden.* Sound familiar?" He frowned. "Why are you looking at me like that?"

Two reasons, actually. The first—that was a completely stunning idea and I loved it. It was clever, it was safe (*1984* was a required text) and it made a point, albeit subtly. The second—he was being all intelligent again and, again, it was incredibly sexy. And that was why I was just staring at him because that was serious brain over-load, right there.

"I'm not some thick-as-pig-shit dropout," he said, reading my mind.

"Everyone's wrong about you," I replied, repeating what he'd written in his note to me.

Rob met my eyes and sighed.

"I'll find a copy."

As it happened, there were five on the shelves—a few different editions, and one that looked about the right size. I brought it back and compared it to the *Wildflowers* cover. "This'll do," I said.

Rob nodded and I got the craft knife, glue, ruler, and spray adhesive that I'd brought from home out of my bag to make a start. First, I needed to gently tease the fake cover off *Dance on My Grave*—tricky, because it had been glued on and made to look as realistic as possible. I slid the craft knife under one of the folded flaps—it required precision and patience—and I was finding it hard to focus. I felt bad about Rob or, more specifically, how I'd assumed things about him that just weren't true.

"I really . . . love this idea," I said, working the blade. "You're . . . good." I mean, it was a slightly pathetic effort on my part, nowhere near enough, but it was something. I glanced up and he was staring at me. "I'm sorry," I added. "I shouldn't have been surprised."

"Don't worry about it." He gave me a small smile, and I smiled back.

"So, that *Wuthering Heights* essay," I said as I continued to slowly pry up the first flap. "The one Ms. Wilkins said you copied?"

I heard him sigh again. "Everyone just wants to wrap you up in lies, don't they?" he said. "They think they know you, know who you are, know what you're capable of."

"The death theme is an unusual one to focus on though."

"Yeah? Is it? That's the thing with that book though. Everyone thinks it's about love, really over-the-top love, and it's all very dramatic, and most people—well, our class, based on what I've heard people saying—think it's pretty ridiculous, am I right?"

"Uh-huh," I said, peeling away the back flap.

"Except 'love' is just the beginning. That book is really about *loss*. And it's about the depths, the *raw depths* you can plumb when you experience the loss of someone you love *so much*, it's like your entire world, your whole foundation, just . . . implodes."

I looked back up at him again, but he was staring into the middle distance over my shoulder.

"How many people our age truly understand that?" he continued. "Some. Not many. That's why most of us think the book is melodramatic, when really it's very real. And I suppose it's why Ms. Wilkins assumed there was no way I could have come up with that idea on my own—I must have copied it from a study guide, written by someone older who'd probably experienced it, or something like it."

I frowned. "Do you mean . . . are you talking about the boy from your old school?"

"Seb?" He laughed and shook his head. "No, I'm not. God, Jamie, that wasn't anything really—that was . . . just what happens when you stick a bunch of horny fifteen-year-old boys together in a boarding school." His smile turned to sadness, and he looked down at the floor. "My mom died."

I put the craft knife down. "I'm—"

"Please don't," he interrupted. "I've had everyone say that. Everyone's sorry. Nobody can imagine what I'm going through. Last year. I should have got over it by now."

"You miss her."

His eyes met mine again, his lips parted slightly. He cleared his throat. "Let's get this done."

"OK, but—"

"Please, Jay."

"OK."

I set back to work. The second flap came away more easily, and I made fairly quick work of the rest of it. Once the fake cover was removed, I covered it with spray glue and Rob assisted as we lined it up over the actual cover of *1984*, him holding each folded flap in place as I did the next one. We were so close to each other— our fingers and hands kept brushing, our knees touching, and our heads leaning in so we could see what we were doing. Along with the cologne, he was definitely a Lynx Atlantis* wearer too—I'd have known that aquatic freshness anywhere and he'd clearly sprayed some on fairly recently. But he also smelled of fruit Polos.

We both sat back a bit and admired our work as I turned the finished book over in my hands. With the protective plastic film back on it as well, it looked pretty convincing.

---

* Whether you call it Axe or Lynx, I love the fact that for decades, teenage boys on both sides of the pond have basically smelled the same.

"Just the barcode and date stamp ticket now," I said.

"I'll let you do that—you're less clumsy than me."

"You're not clumsy," I chuckled.

"I have fat fingers."

"You've got nice fingers."

And then I shut up and pretended I hadn't just said that.

"Done," I muttered finally. "So, this goes back in Prenton's drawer, and this . . ." I picked up *Dance on My Grave*.

"You keep it," Rob said. "Memories, or whatever."

Sure. Nice to keep. The start of something? But also, massively radioactive, so I'd need to keep it hidden. I put it in my bag, along with the rest of my equipment, and we headed back to the staff area, placing the book in the drawer and closing the door shut behind us. We retraced our steps, making our way back toward the drama classroom and the fire exit. As we pushed through the set of double doors into the last hallway, Rob stopped.

I stopped too. Had he heard something? I swallowed. To be this close and then—

Rob smiled, chuckled almost.

"What?" I whispered.

He didn't say anything. He just stared straight ahead . . .

And held his hand out.

My breath caught, looking at his hand, him waiting so patiently, me . . . in some kind of turmoil, because any normal day, no way could this happen, no way could two boys hold hands in the hallway at school, except . . . no one was here, just us, but all that aside, this was fast, this was a moment, this meant something.

I took his hand.

He laced his fingers through mine.

And gently squeezed.

And my heart swelled.

How could a gesture *so small* send me sky-rocket high with more joy and ecstasy than I'd ever felt before? Was I just . . . hopelessly inexperienced? Was this doing anything for him, or was it just me who was drunk on endorphins?

He led on. We walked slowly, our clasped hands swinging slightly, me with a massive grin on my face that I couldn't get rid of. Past each classroom door, I imagined the queues of students, waiting to go inside, their eyes on us, and thought, *Wouldn't it be nice if we could do this for real?*

His hand was strong and firm, but also soft and gentle. *Warm.* Comforting. Incredibly reassuring, as if he was there for me and always would be and no harm would ever come my way because of him. And, I think, that might have been the moment where part of me fell in love with him. And there would be many more moments, and many more parts, but that was the start.

We pushed open the doors at the end in unison—a kind of celebratory flourish almost—and god, what it would be like to do that with so much confidence and pizzazz during a normal school day. We emerged into the stairwell, and he released my hand as he opened the fire exit door and we walked out into the cool night air. He trotted down the short set of steps, me following, until we stood facing each other on the path.

Silence.

Looking into each other's eyes.

Was he waiting for me to speak first?

You can feel the tension, right? This is the moment. He could kiss me. I could kiss him. Or one of us could give a long, oddly eloquent speech about our feelings, which completely ignores the fact that we're a pair of messed-up teenagers and reads more like we're in our early thirties. Sometimes you have to sacrifice authenticity for something the main readership will like, you see.*

He opened his mouth, like he was trying to speak but couldn't find the words.

Eventually: "Jay, I like you. I meant what I said in that letter I wrote, but, um . . . it's hard for me. And . . . I can't . . . anything happening just won't work." He swallowed and looked down at the ground.

And maybe that was my chance. That brief pause, where I should have stepped up and said something reassuring, just like he'd been reassuring with me so many times that day. I don't know, even an old cliché, *love will find a way*, or whatever. *We have each other, that's all we need.* But I didn't; I bottled it. I didn't know what to say, or how to help.

"See you around," Rob said quickly, turning on his heel and hurrying off up the path.

They say your life flashes before your eyes before you die. Well, everything over the last few weeks flashed before mine right then. Just the last few weeks. Maybe because that was the only time I'd been truly alive.

I had to stop him.

"Rob! Wait!" I shouted.

---

* "The teenage characters in this YA novel behave like teenagers! I, an adult, would never behave like this! One star." (Inevitable Amazon review)

He turned around and hurried back up to me. "Even if you discount the grief we'd get here—and honestly, I think I could deal with that—but even discounting that, if my dad found out, he'd stamp it all out faster than you can even imagine," he said, his voice trembling.

His eyes were wet. Glistening in the glow of the floodlights. I reached out for him, but he batted me away.

"He's an MP, Jamie. He's going for a cabinet position. He can't have a gay son. And he won't have. He's already made that perfectly clear. The electorate here would hardly approve of that, never mind the actual Conservative Party. He would ship me off somewhere very far away. Like last time. And I really would never see you again."

"But—"

"Stop it! Seriously, this won't work." He shook his head. "I . . . maybe a different time, different place, this would all have been different. But it's not. We're here and it is what it is."

"But we could keep things quiet! No one has to know!"

Rob laughed. "Because that's gone well so far, hasn't it? The close shave with Prenton wasn't enough for you? Or whoever overheard us talking in the bathroom?" He leaned in to me a bit and repeated, "It just won't work."

I tried to swallow the lump in my throat. Twenty-four hours ago, I didn't even know who he was. Now I felt like he was my everything . . . except he was only allowed to be my nothing.

"I like you," I muttered.

For a few electric moments we locked eyes.

And I honestly thought he might change his mind.

But he turned and hurried off up the path, and I watched until he disappeared into the darkness.

Chapter 23

"Oh, I know that look."

Mrs. C appeared at my side the following lunchtime as I was staring out of the library window. It was a warm afternoon again and everyone was out on the field lapping up a bit of sun and enjoying themselves. I couldn't help noticing how many couples were holding hands as they sauntered across the grass, completely unbothered by anyone. Last night I had ended up digging my notebook out from its secret hiding place under my drawers and starting a new story. The story of two boys who liked each other, and it wasn't a problem. Neither of them was consumed with guilt about liking the other, and nobody else gave them any hassle. They could hold hands in school, like everyone else. They could even kiss. They went to parties together and would share jokes, and hang out, and just *live* like everyone lived. I called them Jamie and Rob, and I hoped they existed. I read once that there's a chance that different versions of you exist in different parts of the universe—that space is so vast and infinite that, every so often, some atoms will combine in such a way that another you could be living a life very similar to yours, but any number of other variables could also change, often in good ways, and I hoped that was the case. I hoped, somewhere out there, there was a me and a Rob and things were better and easier. I hoped there was a version of this story where there's a happy ending.

Anyway, all of that only served to depress me further. Why did I have to end up as the atoms with the shitty outcomes?

"Heartbreak and angst," Mrs. C continued. "I'd know them anywhere. What happened?"

"Nothing." I shrugged.

She didn't look like she believed me. "Funny thing," she said. "I was bracing myself for the fallout from *Wildflowers*—I actually have my resignation letter typed up and in my bag—but nothing's happened." She leaned around so I couldn't avoid eye contact with her. "Hard to imagine that!"

"Hard to imagine that."

"What did you do?"

"Don't know what you mean."

"Fair enough." She smiled. "How about a cookie?"

"I'm not really hungry."

"Ohhh, this *is* bad. My office anyway. I absolutely *insist*, and as a staff member who is inexplicably still employed by the school, you really *do* have to obey me."

She smiled and sauntered away to her office. I made brief eye contact with Beth, across the library, shelving some books, then sighed and plodded after Mrs. C into the office, where she closed the door and cracked open the cookies. I plopped down on an office swivel chair opposite her.

"I'm still here, you and Rob have found each other . . . I'm clearly missing something. Why the long face?"

"I'd just hoped we . . . could be friends." I couldn't look at her. "But . . . he doesn't seem to want to be. Or thinks we can't be, or something."

Mrs. C nodded thoughtfully. "I presume you've talked a bit? What has he told you about himself?"

"His dad's the MP." I shrugged. "He's very ambitious and very anti-gay, by the sounds of it. Rob got . . . kicked out of his last school—"

"Did he say he was kicked out?"

"Well, no . . . *removed*. How do you know that?"

She smiled. "I have access to student files, Jamie. When Rob transferred here, they asked me to do a library induction with him. He was quiet and sweet and bright, and the opposite to what everyone else was saying about him. And his records from his last school told the same story—he's a straight A student. Something felt off, so I gave the librarian over there a call."

"God, you have a . . . network?"

"Of course we do! We all talk, all the time. Sharing ideas mostly, tricks to get students reading, making our libraries welcoming. But also, gossip and bitching—the most fun part. So, I learned what really went down, and that's when I recommended *Wildflowers* to him."

"Oh. I see."

"OK, so you know all that."

"And then about his mom."

Mrs. C nodded. "Very sad. And only last year."

"Must be hard."

"He's lost a lot," she said. "Uprooted from his old school, his mom. And you and him . . . it shouldn't be, but it's a risk. He stands to lose even more. You both do."

I shook my head. "It's just not fair."

"No. It's not."

Be nice, wouldn't it, if this was the moment Mrs. C dropped some nugget of wisdom that made everything click and told me what I needed to do to make things work out? What I got was:

"How about I make us some tea?"

Because when adults don't know what to do, if they're British, they make tea. One of the hardest and rudest wake-up calls you get growing up is the moment it dawns on you that there isn't always someone there with the answers. That life is fundamentally unfair, the world is full of villains and, very often, they don't get their comeuppance.*

Close-up: me, miserable as sin, moping about, but I decide to do something useful and write another letter to Speak No Monkey, begging them to play at the prom, because the only way things could get any worse was being labeled a massive bullshitter and everyone demanding refunds on their prom tickets.

Dear Speak No Monkey,

I don't know if you got my previous letter, or if my dad has really spoken to your manager, but my name is Jamie Hampton and I'm organizing the junior class prom at Market Wickby High School. I'll cut to the chase: Everyone loves your music and if you played, even

---

* What I didn't appreciate then, of course, was that Mrs. C knew damn well that one of the best solutions is giving something (or someone) time.

just one song, it would make everyone's night. Truly, it would be a memory none of us would ever forget. We don't have much money, but we cheer loudly, and the librarian here has great cookies.

If you can play, please call the school and leave a message, or write back to me.

And, if you can play, would you dedicate a song to someone for me, please?

His name is Rob West. But don't say I asked for it.

It'd really mean something if you did.

Yours faithfully,

Jamie Hampton

A bit of positive action.

It felt good.

I'd been a passive bystander all my life. A people pleaser. Never wanting to rock the boat, even if it meant losing out on things I wanted. Maybe I needed to prove myself a bit? Show a bit of fight? Because, yeah, there were things to lose . . . but maybe some of them I was *prepared* to lose.

You can probably see where this thought process is leading, but here's the key point: Very often it's not other people who solve your problems. It's you.

So, let's see how I work things out, shall we?

The moment I broke bad.*

---

* And bear in mind, this is all relative. Breaking bad for a nerdy sixteen-year-old in Lincolnshire looks very different to the hit Netflix show about a terminally ill family man in New Mexico, so relax, this story isn't about to take a dark turn, and I'm not going to set up a crystal meth lab.

Chapter 24

I received the summons to Mrs. Prenton's office during homeroom. Rob was already there when I arrived and didn't look at me when I walked in. That was probably for the best—didn't want to give the impression we were in any way a unit, I suppose.

I stood next to him, both of us facing Mrs. Prenton as she sat behind her huge wooden desk. Everything about her was just so. The coiffed hair. The two-piece suit. Blue*, of course. Maggie Thatcher would be proud. The copy of *Wildflowers* was placed in the middle of the desk. Our handiwork was pretty good, if I do say so myself.

"I must be going mad," she said.

We both stared forward.

"Or else you think I'm stupid."

I made sure to keep my face neutral. It was killing me; I craved approval, especially from anyone in authority, but I had to keep a poker face.

---

* In the UK, blue is the color of the right-wing Conservative Party and red the more liberal Labour Party—I would hate you US readers to be confused by that!

She flipped through the book. "This is a copy of *1984* by George Orwell."

"Like I said, I've never seen it before in my life," Rob replied.

She turned to me. "Jamie?"

"I didn't read it."

"Well, I know it wasn't this yesterday. So what do you think happened?"

We both shrugged in unison.

She gave an annoyed sigh. I could tell she wasn't buying this, but she was out of options. "OK, let's pretend for a moment that there were no shenanigans with this book since we last spoke. What seems odd to me, then, is that anyone would put a fake cover on this book, and that a parent would feel the need to contact the school because of the obscene content. That's quite the mystery, don't you think?"

Rob sniffed. "Is it a mystery? Isn't *1984* about totalitarianism, mass surveillance, and censorship? I feel like a lot of people would hate those themes being laid bare, especially when there are so many parallels with where our world is heading at the moment."

"I'm not following, Robert." Mrs. Prenton smiled—a dangerous sort of smile, like she was hoping he'd say too much and incriminate himself. I sort of hoped he'd shut up—we'd gotten away with it—for now. This wasn't the time to mess it up.

"I'm pretty sure there's a scene in the book where Winston has to remove references the Party doesn't approve of from a newspaper?"

"I believe there is," Mrs. Prenton said.

Rob nodded. "Right. And in the context of the whole book, that's obviously portrayed as a bad thing."

"Yes, of course," she agreed, her smile still fixed in place.

"Removing information is a *bad* thing. A thing people do to maintain power, because you can only maintain power by controlling the narrative."

I was holding my breath. Rob was like a courtroom lawyer, and I was amazed Mrs. Prenton didn't seem to see where this was heading. So, maybe Mrs. C was right—people like Prenton were so convinced they were right, they couldn't even imagine that they might be wrong.

"The book serves as a warning, certainly."

"That controlling access to information is a way of maintaining power?"

"Absolutely."

Rob nodded, satisfied. He gave it just a beat, before: "So, how is that different to what the Conservative Party did with Section 28?"

Prenton closed and opened her eyes, as if her patience was waning. "What exactly are you saying here, Robert?"

"What he's saying," I jumped in, "is that maybe the person who put the fake cover on the copy of *1984* was making a point about censorship—a kind of *protest* if you will—and maybe the parent complained because they didn't appreciate the themes of the book and felt it didn't align with their own political viewpoint. I mean, most of the people around here vote Conservative, don't they?"

"And what does voting Conservative have to do with the events of *1984*?"

"Nothing, I guess," Rob said. "One's about a totalitarian, fascist bunch of money-grabbing liars who are only out for themselves . . . and the other is a work of fiction."

Fuck's sake. Why was he determined to screw this up?

"You class your own father among all that, do you?" Prenton said, her fingers now steepled in front of her.

Rob shrugged.

"Well, you're both very pleased with yourselves, aren't you?" she said. "But don't for one minute think I'm not on to you, because I very much am. You can ramble all you want about censorship, but we don't allow books that promote homosexual lifestyles in the library for the same reason we don't allow books that promote being a Nazi—because they're damaging and dangerous. And I think you'll find, if you bother to read the newspapers, that the majority of people in this country agree." She leaned across her desk a little. "I *will* protect the students of this school from inappropriate material. And when I find out it was you who broke in here and swapped the book, you'll feel the full force of the law, because that will be classed as breaking and entering. Get to your classes."

"*You* have a death wish," I muttered to Rob as we paced down the hallway.

"You only just realized?"

I shook my head. "All that, and now you've as good as told her we did it."

"It's no fun if she doesn't know. She can't do anything about it. She has zero evidence."

I didn't understand him. On the one hand, he claimed to be scared of his dad, and desperate for no one to find out. On the other, he was happy to take a big risk. He was like someone with a peanut allergy licking the chocolate of a Marathon bar (or Snickers, as we are now supposed to call them), and getting a weird thrill out of the fact that if they licked a bit *too* much, or the wrong bit, it could literally kill them. What the hell was that about?

He stopped and groaned as we approached the door of English. "Shit, I haven't got my pen with me, I'll have to—"

"I can lend you one."

He glanced at me, seeming almost reluctant. "OK, thanks."

I tried not to smile as I reached into my backpack to fish one out. "Oh, also . . . thought you might like these." I handed him the tube of fruit Polos I'd got from the vending machine at the end of lunch. "I still feel bad for not bringing food," I explained.

He looked at the fruit Polos but didn't take them. *"Jamie—"*

"Have them."

"No."

"Why not?"

"We're not doing this. I know what you're doing, and we're not doing it."

I stared at him, then shoved the Polos into his unexpecting hands. "We're not doing anything, they're just fucking Polos, get over it."

I walked into the classroom.

Soundtrack: "It's the End of the World as We Know It (and I Feel Fine)"—because of what I'm about to do, and because, actually, I'm no longer sure how much I care.

Ms. Wilkins gives me back the essay I handed in late about themes in *Wuthering Heights*. It's an A+, even though it was late, and even though I know it's basically the same recycled garbage almost everyone else came up with. It's perfect. And just what I needed to do this.

And I tell her. I say, "I don't deserve this."

She stares at me.

And I go on: "I was thinking about Rob's angle, actually. And I think he's right. That book isn't about love. Well, maybe it is on the superficial level, but actually, yeah, it's about loss. It's about *grief.*"

"I don't disagree it's an angle, Jamie," Ms. Wilkins said. "The difference is, Rob copied his work from a study guide."

"You sure about that? And even if he did, what, mine's more original? Is it though? Is it really? Or am I just recycling the same predictable points we've been coached to make to pass the exam? Because that's what this is, isn't it? A box-ticking exercise? You can pass the exam as long as your thoughts are considered to be the right thoughts."

"You can think what you like, as long as you don't copy someone else's words."

"But that's what we're all doing! Isn't that the point? We're told what to think anyway, we're told how to answer the questions. None of us are really being original, we're just parroting what we've been told to parrot. So what does it matter?"

I might—possibly—have got away with it, had I not added "it's bullshit" under my breath by way of an ineloquent finale. That landed me in detention.*

"What the hell are you thinking?" Beth hissed as we made our way out at the end of the lesson.

---

* That's it. That's my equivalent of making crystal meth. I hope it raised your pulse as much as it did mine.

"I think I'm finally being real," I told her. "Do you hate it?"

"I'm . . . alarmed by it. Although I think I respect it."

I smiled. "Dan asked you out yet?"

"Um . . ." She blinked. I'd taken her by surprise with that question. "No. Not yet."

"Why don't you ask him?"

She stared at me.

"Take positive action." I shrugged. Then I spotted Rob hanging by the wall of the hallway, waiting for me. "I'll catch up with you later, OK?"

Beth followed my gaze to Rob, then looked back to me. "Yeah."

I waited until she'd gone, then walked up to him.

"All right, big balls, you've made your point," he said. "Whatever your point actually is."

I met his eyes but kept a poker face.

He cracked a smile, then checked the coast was clear.

"I should be able to do Monday. How's eight o'clock in the parking lot behind Shop 'n' Save?"

That felt like an eternity, but I still grinned.

"Hm. *That* put a smile on your face." He rolled his eyes and turned. "Now you'd better get yourself to detention, you bad, bad boy."

Chapter 25

It was a matter of days, but waiting for the following Monday was torture. Especially since he barely acknowledged me around school in the meantime. It got to the point where I seriously thought I'd imagined making the arrangement, but there was no opportunity to confirm it with him, and I just had to *hope*. I'd arrive and give him twenty minutes, I thought to myself. That's enough to account for any delays along the way. As it turned out, he was already waiting for me when I biked into the parking lot, leaning up with one foot against the back wall of Shop 'n' Save.

"Evening," Rob said, a small smile on his lips.

I dismounted. "Hi."

I leaned my bike next to where his was—by the loading dock. It wasn't what I would have called a romantic location, but maybe that was just me with my *expectations* again. Flattened cardboard boxes were strewn over the concrete where they'd overflowed from the big dumpster, the air slightly sour with that bin smell, and the security lights casting everything, including us, in an unflattering stark white glow. Beyond, there were no cars in the lot, and the shop was deserted since it had closed at six. There was a lonely, hopeless, bleak gloom about the place—like we were the last survivors in a nuclear war.

Why had he suggested we meet here?

Then he smiled at me, and it didn't matter anymore. He was here.

"Come on, then. I'll show you something," he said, walking over to a set of metal stairs that led up the outside of the building to the roof.

Not for the last time, I learned Rob didn't give a shit about trespassing. He had a view that it was wrong to divide up the world according to who had the money to claim it as their own, and that we all had as much right to any part of it as anyone else. I'll admit, I wasn't sure I shared his views on landownership.* I quite liked having my own space and couldn't imagine being particularly pleased to go home one day to find a couple of hippies in my bedroom "because it was theirs as much as mine," but then it turned out we didn't agree about a lot of things.†

Another surprise, dear reader? The expectation is that we'd agree, isn't it? The beauty of some common ground and shared ideals? Well, wouldn't that be boring.

After he poured scorn on my protestations about "the owner being pissed off," we ascended, up past the second floor and one fire exit, to the flat roof, where we sat down next to each other and looked out over the parking lot and the rest of Market Wickby beyond. If I had been hoping for some clichéd romantic setting (which, naturally I was), I would be disappointed (I was). There was

---

* Translation: We had a shit-ton of arguments about this.
† A few years later, he told me he hated The Corrs. Would you dare?

no sunset. No birds gently singing their nighttime songs. The sky was dark gray. There weren't even any stars visible under the low canopy of clouds.

EXT. THE FLAT ROOF. NIGHT. FANTASY SEQUENCE

Jamie and Rob lie back and gaze up at the sky. Rob traces his fingers around a constellation.

ROB: That's Orion.

[A shooting star passes by. Everything is beautiful.]

The reality:

"Granted, it's not Paris," he said.

No shit.

He pulled two cans of cider out of his backpack. "Want one?"

"Thanks."

We cracked our cans open and drank. (Me: drinking on a school night! I don't think you can fully appreciate how big this was.*)

"So . . . do you come here a lot?" I asked.

He chuckled. "Yeah, OK, I know it's shitty. That's kind of the point."

"How come?"

He shuffled over and put his arm around my shoulders, me immediately melting into his warmth and loving every second of it. "Because, Jamie, I look out there"—he swept his right hand across

---

* Sets up crystal meth lab as next logical step.

181

the horizon—"and all I can see is how crappy this town is, and it reminds me how much I want to get out."

"You come up here . . . to depress yourself?"

"No. Well, a bit, I suppose. It just feels good to stare the crap in the face and know—well, *hope*—that one day, it'll change, but in the meantime . . . it is what it is, it's my life, and I'm not going to pretend otherwise."

"That still sounds depressing to me."

"That's because you're an optimist, whereas I'm a *realist*."

I nodded. He was probably right about that.

"What about you?" he asked. "Where would you love to be if not here?"

"Oh, a city, for sure. I'm sick of the country. London looks good, but honestly, anywhere with a cinema that isn't a forty-minute drive away, and some stores that stay open after six."

"Cities are more open-minded too."

"And there's that."

"I want to travel. See the world," he said.

"But where would you want to settle eventually?"

He slightly grimaced. "See, I don't like that word. *Settle.* There's so much to see, Jay. Great big world, people, places, experiences— more than enough for one lifetime, even assuming you get your full allocation. I hate the idea of being stuck in one place, around the same people, and that's it, that's your life now."

"So, what, you'll just . . . travel about?"

"Yeah! Why not? Spend summer down in Cornwall one year, head off to the Mediterranean, spend some time in Thailand, then maybe Brazil, Mexico, travel around the US—I mean, it's endless."

"What about work?"

He shrugged. "There are people who literally travel the world following the sun, working summer seasons in bars and hotels everywhere they go."

"But don't you want a career?"

"Not especially."

"But—"

"I don't want to be a little hamster on a treadmill, Jay. What's the point?"

It was probably deeply uncool of me, but I couldn't compute any of this. I was used to being in the middle—that's where I was comfortable. And, OK, I'd recently done some things that weren't especially average: I'd read a banned book, I'd broken into school, I'd lied to Prenton, and I'd called Ms. Wilkins's approach to English "bullshit." But, fundamentally, I think I still wanted normal.

Rob took a swig of cider. "I don't want to live the life other people think I should or want me to. I'm not interested in following the crowd. I don't want to just *exist*. I want to *live*. I want to fucking *fly*."

He was like a smiling assassin. Arm across my shoulder, being all friendly, while it felt like he was basically telling me he didn't see a future with me and him. The words *being around the same people* nagged at me.

Except . . .

He was right, of course. There wasn't a future. How could there be? No one would let us. As ever, in my head, in my stupid stories, I'd imagined a world where that could be. I really had to stop blurring fantasy with reality. I had to stop being an optimist and maybe just look out there, like he did, stare the crap in the face and see it for what it was. Accept it.

So, what was this? Did he just want to be friends? Or was he just looking for some proverbial fun?

And why didn't I feel like I could be happy with either of those options?

He slid his arm away, reached into his backpack, and pulled out a Sony Discman. "Have you heard of Pulp?"

"No."

"Jarvis Cocker does the vocals. He sings like a kind of . . . dirty old man, but I love it. They just released an album, literally six weeks ago, called *His 'n' Hers*. Listen to this."

He produced two mini portable speakers, plugged them in, then fiddled around with the controls of the Discman until I heard the waves of synths, this sweeping Casio orchestra, and then this song . . . about happy endings and about . . . how they're not real, they're something you only get in films. A lump formed in my throat. Was he aware of what I'd been hoping? Was he trying to tell me this wouldn't work, but through the medium of music?

The track finished and I took a long drink.

"What did you think?" he asked.

I wiped my mouth. "It's a song about the gulf between dreams and reality."

He nodded.

"So. Yeah." My throat was so tight. I don't know why I could feel tears bubbling inside me, but I could.

Too late.

"Hey," he murmured, shifting closer again.

I wiped my eyes. "I should probably go, I—"

"Stop it." He sighed and put his arm back around my shoulders. "It *is* a song about the gulf between dreams and reality," he said. "But it's also a song about how life is an unknown, and if you don't try for a happy ending, well, you'll never know. You might get one, you might not, but . . . maybe you've just gotta try."

I sniffed and swallowed and told myself to pull it together. When I turned to him, he was staring out ahead, into the gloom. "But you don't want to try," I muttered.

He took his arm away and sat with his hands in his lap. "Do you?" He turned to look at me.

"I—" I couldn't say it. I was paralyzed with the fear of what it would mean if I did.

"You said you liked me."

"I do. I do . . . and you said you liked me. In your letter."

He nodded. "I think you're gorgeous," he said, just like that, matter-of-fact, like that was something I heard every day and it wouldn't be the most stars-in-my-eyes amazing news I'd ever received.

He chuckled. "I love how you don't quite believe that. So many guys are all ego. They honestly think they're something special. But not you. You *are*, you just don't realize it." He groaned and rubbed his face with his hands. "Aargh. Why did you have to go and get inside my head, Jay?"

"Um . . . sorry?"

"Stop apologizing." He gave me a playful push. "How about we don't overthink this? How about we just live for now? Because, at this moment, I'm sitting here with a boy I like, and I think that's enough."

"Same," I said.

We tapped our cans of cider together and drank.

"And yet, tomorrow there's school," I added.

"That's *tomorrow*, Jamie."

"So, what then? Because this is nice, but what then?" I clocked his sigh. "I'm not trying to pressure you. It's just, I don't think just one 'now' would be enough. I'm not needy, but wouldn't it be good though? A few 'nows'?"

I studied his face. *Thinking.*

"Nobody can find out," he said eventually. "I mean it. My dad is close to getting the cabinet position he's wanted for ages. Journalists are already sniffing around, just in case there's any dirt. That's what they're like. Something like . . . me could bring his whole career down. So we can't be anything at school. We can't suddenly start hanging out or people will talk. We have to ignore each other. I won't ring you, and you absolutely cannot phone me—if Dad picks up, or gets wind of it, he'll be suspicious. OK?"

I nodded. It sucked, but I could see that it was the only way. There was no version of this plan where we could be open. He couldn't be, and nor could I. And I didn't want to be, for that matter.

"We'll find places to meet up, like this, and other places too," he continued. "Could that work?"

His pleading eyes met mine. And, for a moment, I got a flash—I think—of how much he wanted this too.

"OK. Rob? Why did you decide to meet up with me after all? When you said you didn't want to? Was it what I said to Ms. Wilkins?"

"No, it wasn't!" He laughed. "Jesus, and by the way, don't go tanking your grades on my account. I guarantee you'll live to regret it." He sighed and smiled. "I couldn't stop thinking about you—"

I smiled to myself. *He did want this.*

". . . because you were doing my head in, and even though I think we're doomed, I can't stop myself."

"Doomed? Why are we doomed?"

"Oh, Jamie." He closed his eyes. "Let's be honest: We're probably gonna wreck each other, bud."

"You're such a pessimist."

"Realist."

His hand found mine and he gently squeezed it.

We locked eyes, his lips parted, his breathing . . . slightly heavier. Or maybe I was just more attuned to it.

He kissed me.

Just quickly. Just on the lips. Then pulled back, his eyes searching my face.

I smiled. I tried not to overthink it, or spoil it, by trying to remember every detail, even though I knew this was a real *moment* in my life, you know?

He kissed me again. Slower this time. Longer this time. *Different* this time.

And I . . .

Shaking.

He pulled back again, his eyes soft. "Are you cold?"

I swallowed.

"Scared?"

I barely managed to nod. Everything about this terrified me. All I could see were the headlines, flashing in my head, years and years of them. I would never admit this to him, but I was convinced if anything happened I would die of AIDS. That's what I'd been told happened to boys like me. And nobody had ever said any different.*

He moved his hand to my shoulder. "Listen, the only thing I wanted to do tonight was bring you here to tell you that maybe it's worth trying for some kind of happy ending. Except I don't like the word 'ending' because that suggests something is over, so how about . . . a happy beginning?"

I held up my can of cider and tapped his again. "To happy beginnings."

---

* This stayed with me for many, many years. I still worry today, despite new treatments meaning it's no longer something that will kill you. Hate casts a long shadow, folks.

Chapter 26

I rode my bike back through the deserted streets later that night, high on life (and also cider), buzzing, tanked up with joy, pedaling furiously, the wind in my hair, breathless and giddy with everything that was new, with feelings I'd never had and all the secrets I had to somehow keep.

And it was sweet, but it was also bitter. It felt like I'd fallen for him *so hard*, and yet I knew whatever we had couldn't possibly last. I liked the idea of a happy beginning. They're probably an easier thing. It's the endings I think are tricky.

But that night was the start. I felt it in my bones. *Alive*. And it felt good. It felt good to be on the edge for once. Where the danger lurked, where the adrenaline pumped, *where the good stuff happened*.

Electra rode up alongside me on a ridiculous Raleigh Chopper that was way too small for her. "A night to remember, kiddo!"

I laughed. Damn right. I liked it here. I liked it on the edge. I took my hands off the handlebars. "Look, Electra! No hands!"

And I rode fast, out of control, hurtling, but not scared, *free*, into the night.

Chapter 27

The handwritten sign read: "Speak No Monkey—CONFIRMED!" and had been splashed diagonally across the prom poster in the common room.

What?

The buzz was palpable, and I had to fend off about six people wanting to buy tickets so I could find out what the hell was going on, because this was the first I'd heard about it.

Debbie was pissed off when I found her in the junior class study hall. "I called your house *five* times. Your mom said you were out, so I assumed you were coming over. Where the hell were you?"

Where I was: holding hands with Rob West on the roof of Shop 'n' Save.

Where I suddenly realized I should have been: at a prom committee meeting at Debbie's.

"I'm . . . so sorry. I completely forgot," I said.

Debbie shook her head in disbelief. "OK, well. We've had some news. Speak No Monkey has agreed to play."

Time stopped. "What? Really?"

She nodded. "It's confirmed. They left a message with the receptionist yesterday."

"My letter actually worked?" A wide smile spread across my face. Oh. My. God. Oh, *thank* god. Oh wow. It had worked. I'd done it. This was going to send the prom into the stratosphere, and we'd sell every single ticket now.

But whereas I was ready to dance with Debbie and Adam around the common room, whooping and cheering, Debbie seemed to be all business this morning. "Hence the added signs to let everyone know. I've already been in touch with their manager, and Dad is sorting their rider out and all the contractual bits."

She sniffed dismissively and got back to the essay she was working on. I stood there. I'm not sure what I was waiting for, except . . . the prom was my thing. My idea. I was leading it. It was me who had written the letters to the band. I'd persuaded them. OK, I'd forgotten about *one* meeting, but did that warrant Debbie just taking it all out of my hands? I'd really wanted to make that announcement. And now she was acting like it was all her doing.

"Rather than stand there, why don't you help Adam confirm arrangements with the catering people?" she said, without looking up.

I strode away, slammed some stuff in my locker, and flopped down on a chair.

I was pissed off.

But, in my heart, I also felt like I'd let them down. I'd even written a reminder about that meeting in my Filofax.* My

---

* Leather! A present on my sixteenth from Mom and beloved by young execs in the 80s. I was never quite on trend, always a few years behind—*plus ça change!*

head was just somewhere else entirely, and, literally, it was constantly just—

Flashback: the roof. Rob holding my hand. His gentle words. The fizz when I met his eyes. His warmth. *Him.*

But, actually, maybe Rob had been right when he said I shouldn't "tank my grades" just because of him. I couldn't just throw everything away. I'd already glimpsed Rob today, acting like normal in the common room, just doing his thing, like last night had never happened and wasn't the most stars-in-his-eyes best thing ever. How could he just carry on, after *that*? Well, apparently he could. And that's what I needed to do too. That fact made even more clear to me by:

Enter Beth: on a mission, two cups of coffee in her hand (she never made me coffee—this was serious).

Location of this intervention: the junior common room, but, to be on the safe side, she suggests we sit outside, on the low wall by the humanities hall.

"What is going on with you?" she asked.

"Nothing. Why?"

"I've worked it out, Jamie."

"Huh?"

"I've seen you coming and going in the library. Your chats with Mrs. C, and then one of them with Rob West, of all people. Then you bizarrely stick up for him in English—"

"That wasn't bizarre; I genuinely feel he was wronged."

"And he's hanging back for you afterward and you chat to him then."

I shrugged. "He's an OK guy."

She rolled her eyes. "Is he? Well, it all seemed very strange to me. And, meanwhile, there's hysteria building . . ."

"Is there?"

"People keep coming into the library, asking for a copy of *Wildflowers of Great Britain*. Once would be weird enough, but ten requests in one lunchtime? *Why does everyone want to read this book?* I ask myself. So I look it up in the database. See who's taken it out to try and track it down. And I see your name and Rob's name on there."

"Oh."

She blew on her coffee and sipped it. "Are you seeing each other, then?"

I froze.

"I see," she said. "And you know who his dad is, of course?"

I looked down at the ground.

"He's met up with my dad a few times. The pair of them together would turn your stomach with their staunch defense of what they laughably call 'family values,' which is just bigotry masquerading as virtue. Jesus, Jamie. When did you start to enjoy playing with fire?"

"It just happened," I muttered. "But also, nothing much is happening. We're only talking. It's nothing. Nothing to tell. Which is why I hadn't said anything to you. Also—"

She held her hand up. "I won't say a word. Of course I won't. I'm well aware of the stakes here."

"There are no stakes if nothing's happened."

"Nothing's happened *yet*," she corrected.

I sighed.

"So, you have a secret . . . and so do I," she said. "If it would make you feel better, I'll tell you mine?"

I looked back up at her.

"I asked Dan to the prom, like you suggested," she said, a smile playing on her lips. "He said yes."

"Yeah? He did? Really?" She nodded, grinning.

God, I'm not proud to admit it, but I felt a pang of jealousy.

(Note to editor: This will be the final straw in my unlikability as a protagonist, won't it? Best to lie?)

Because, look, maybe I had Rob now. Is that what you're thinking? Except, I didn't really, did I? My jealousy wasn't that Beth had Dan, and I also wanted Dan (although Dan *was* sweet and I *did* like him, which, OK, did confuse matters), but more that the chances were, this would work out for her. And it never would for me. So she would get what she wanted, and I never could.

"He's . . . a really sweet, lovely guy," I said.

"I know." She considered me wryly. "He's got a soft spot for you too."

That made me smile.

And made me feel a bit sad, for some reason.

"*But* . . . obviously my dad can't find out. So, I suppose we're in a similar position to you and Rob—"

"I'm not sure there is a 'me and Rob'," I said quickly, panicking about how he'd made me promise no one would know.

"OK, OK, but you see what I'm saying?"

I nearly did. I nearly said "Yes." But, actually, our situations were different. She had a problem with her *dad*. One person making life difficult. Rob and I had a problem with the whole world. That she imagined we were in the same boat annoyed me a bit. It was like she didn't get it at all. But what was the point in saying anything? It was Beth. She wasn't being deliberately insensitive—she just didn't understand. I vaguely nodded, keeping it neutral, not rocking the boat (my specialty), because having a row with Beth wasn't what I needed right then.

"Me and Dan are meeting up only at his house," she continued, "and we're not going to be obvious around school; it's just easier that way, you know how gossip flies around this place. I was just thinking . . . if you and Rob ever wanted to come round—just the four of us—"

"You haven't told Dan about me and Rob?"

"No. Stop panicking. And I won't. Unless you want me to. But we're all in the same boat, Jay—"

I bit my tongue. She really had no idea.

". . . and much as I hate the analogy, isn't there honor among thieves?" She took another sip of coffee. "Think about it, that's all."

So, after my annoyance had worn off, or rather, after I'd pushed it aside, I did think about it. I didn't write it down, it felt too dangerous, but the fantasy world inside my head was rich and vibrant, down to the finest details . . .

The farm was in the middle of nowhere. There were no other buildings nearby and certainly no other people. If you wanted to hide, this place was perfect. Dan's parents were out, and were not due back until tomorrow, so we had the place entirely to ourselves. Arriving individually to avoid detection, once the four of us were inside, the curtains closed, the doors locked, we were finally safe.

Nobody could find us here.

Nobody would know.

Away from the eyes of the world, and the expectations of family and friends and enemies, we could all relax.

The wind howled outside. The rain lashed down. The storm was welcome. It not only felt like an extra layer of protection against prying visitors, but also created the circumstances for a cozy evening. Dan lit a fire, drinks came out, popcorn was made in the microwave, there were tubes of Pringles, and some frozen pizzas went in the oven. But best of all was that away from everyone else, away from parents and hatred and bankrupt ideals, we could all be ourselves. Rob and I cuddled up together just like Beth and Dan. He would casually hold my hand, like Dan did with Beth, and nobody cared. We watched The Bodyguard on VHS. As the film went on, I ended up lying against him, his arms around my waist, hands in my lap, feeling his warm breath on the back of my neck. When the famous song came on, he whispered the title track in my ear.

I will always love you.

We have many nights like that. Our own private paradise. For a few hours once a week, nobody else matters, the rest of the world doesn't exist, it's only us, and we can all be whoever we are, and nobody can stop us.

The more I thought about it, the more it was such a perfect solution. It wasn't quite the real deal, but it was something close.

I was desperate to talk to Rob.

But I knew I couldn't.

His ability to ignore me was so good, I admit I was getting worried. It wasn't that he was looking right through me or anything; it was worse, actually—he did occasionally look at me, but like I meant nothing. I wasn't expecting much, but I think I had been expecting a moment of held eye contact from time to time, perhaps a quick wink.

He was serious about no one knowing. The situation with his dad was a big deal. All the more reason for the secret get-together at Dan's house.

I found the note in my locker at the end of lunch:

Stop walking around looking so worried—I miss seeing your smile. Also, got the house to myself tonight. Fancy it? Seven-ish. Let me know that you're coming by telling Ms. Wilkins in English that your favorite book of all time is Thomas the Tank Engine.

And that's how, after a very intense and serious discussion about social class in *Wuthering Heights*, and the extent to which Heathcliff's social position is responsible for the misery and conflict so persistent in the book, I put my hand up and told Ms. Wilkins, apropos of absolutely nothing, that my favorite book was none other than *Thomas the Frigging Tank Engine*.

I felt sure she'd refer me for some sort of counseling.

That boy was making me do things.

I was under his spell.

And I bloody loved it.

Chapter 28

"Choo! Choo!"

Rob grinned at me from the doorstep as I pedaled up his gravel driveway and came to a stop outside his massive Victorian house.

"Very funny," I said, getting off my bike.

"Ms. Wilkins's face!" Rob beamed. "And then you had to justify it! *'I like trains'*!" He hooted. "I like bloody trains?! And you looked so earnest!"

"Yeah, yeah."

I left my bike propped up by an outbuilding that doubled as a garage and followed him through the front door and into a long hallway with Victorian tiles on the floor and a sweeping staircase off to the left. I caught glimpses of other rooms as we walked by—a large living room with a plush carpet, massive sofas, and big ornate lamps; a dining room with a huge mahogany table with candlesticks on it; another, smaller living room; a study; a library . . . and, I've no doubt, most of the rest of the Clue board.

"What's your dad doing?" I asked.

"He's down at the Houses of Parliament, like usual," Rob said. "It's where he is most of the week. He's currently trying to rally

opposition to a bill they're introducing to lower the gay age of consent to eighteen. It's an 'assault on family values!' don't you know?!'"
Rob shook his head. "I can't wait 'til I don't live here anymore, and I don't have to listen to his bullshit."

"And no one else is here?"

"*Relax.* I'm allowed friends around," he said. "Just as long as that's all they are, if they're boys." He winked at me, and my stomach flipped. "I must be kept on the straight and narrow; we don't want to assault family values, do we now? Speaking of which, let's have a bit of underage drinking, shall we? Want a drink? Follow me."

He led me through to the vast kitchen—fitted oak units with marble worktops, an island in the middle and a hefty-looking Aga range on one side. The far end had floor-to-ceiling windows with French doors in the middle, leading out to the lush gardens beyond, which went on for as far as the eye could see. He got out some glasses, which he filled with ice, a slug of vodka, and topped up with Coke.

"I'm only having one," he said, handing me a glass. "I've got my driving test tomorrow morning during my free period."

"Are you nervous?"

"Nah, I'm gonna pass with flying colors. I'm a great driver!" He grinned at me.

"Can't wait 'til I'm old enough to start lessons.*"

"Aw, I forget you're still sixteen, baby boy."

"Shut up." But I couldn't stop the smile that spread across my face.

---

* Took three tests, failed them all, still can't drive.

"Come on, let's sit down in the snug—let me know if you need a rattle."

"Seriously, shut up."

The snug was a little room on the left, just back up the hallway. There was a soft L-shaped sofa in it, a television, bookcases along one wall, a fireplace on the other, plus a little cart with drinks on it. On the coffee table in the middle was a wooden box filled with cigars. I'd never thought much about Rob's wealth before, but it certainly hit me then. We were from two different worlds. Did that matter? It must have done to me, as I vowed he couldn't ever see where I lived.

That was another thing about expectations, you see. Everyone always assumed, because I was a straight A student, and because I was polite and well-mannered, that I came from a wealthy family. But that wasn't true. Since Dad had left, we'd really struggled. We didn't have spending money, we didn't have fancy vacations or a big TV, just a lot of bills with scary red writing on them. I never corrected people though. It was something else that shamed me, I suppose, even though there was nothing I could do about it. And shame is what those in charge want you to feel, I realized. If you're ashamed, you're less likely to ask for help, and if you don't ask for help, then you're invisible. That's a good way of sweeping you and your issues under the carpet, pretending you don't exist, that there's no problem, and so inequality continues, the rich get richer, the status quo is maintained, and all is well. Or so they tell you.

We flopped down next to each other on the sofa. "You really got Speak No Monkey to play at the prom, then?"

I nodded. "You gonna come now?" I remembered asking them

to dedicate a song to Rob. I wondered if they would. And smiled, thinking about what that might mean to him.

"I liked that note you wrote in the book. About each having matching handkerchiefs, and being together, even though we couldn't be? That was sweet. Do you want to know something?"

"What?"

"That's when I fell in love with you a little bit." He turned to me with a massive grin on his face. "Yeah. I'll come. Everyone else is. Sounds like you actually might have put together a non-crap school event."

"I tried," I said.

"Not just a pretty face, huh?"

I met his eyes and he smiled at me. "You cannot take a compliment—you always blush. It's cute."

I looked down at my drink.

He reached over and squeezed my leg, his hand lingering for a moment, me feeling like something might happen, until a scrappy little terrier skidded in and launched itself on to the sofa, immediately wedging itself between me and Rob and settling down.

"Jamie, meet Casper." Rob's eyes widened. "Oh, are you OK with dogs?"

"Yeah, I love them."

Rob smiled. "Good, or else this probably wouldn't work out." He clocked my face. "I'm joking. Sort of. But if it was between you and the dog—"

"You'd pick the dog, I get it."

"He was my mom's, really."

"Oh . . ."

There was a moment of silence where I considered saying something like "I'm sorry" again, but I just let the moment pass.

"And now he's mine," Rob said softly.

"He's sweet. What is he?"

"Heinz 57. We're not quite sure what." He gave Casper a scratch under his ear, which he seemed to really enjoy. "Do you want to watch some TV?" He grabbed a copy of the *Radio Times** from the coffee table and flicked to today's date. "We can catch the end of *Summer Holiday* on BBC One—presented by Jill Dando— do you like her? It's *'a new series with an emphasis on what the ordinary British holidaymaker thinks. Some reports will come entirely from the public, such as tonight's report on Walt Disney World from the Wood family in Worthing.'*" He looked up. "Well, that sounds like shit. Why do I care what the Wood family think? *EastEnders* at seven thirty—*'Arthur refuses to help the aged.'* That's tantalizing!"

I laughed. "Anything on ITV?"

He scanned the page. "No, there is not. There's some sort of sci-fi film from the 60s on BBC Two." He blew out a breath. "BBC One it is, I think!"

He pressed the Power button and the TV made a high-pitched zapping noise as it came to life, the picture emerging as it warmed up. About twenty-five minutes later, I suddenly became aware that Rob West wasn't watching the TV screen, but was watching me. Our eyes locked. Then, in a moment of mutual consent, when we

---

* Despite being called the *Radio Times*, this is actually a TV guide here in the UK.

somehow both *knew* and both wanted to, we leaned toward each other and . . .

Now I would love to be able to tell you that my first what I would call *big* kiss* was by moonlight, under the stars, or a beautiful sunset. I would love to tell you that it was a perfect night, or day, that the birds were singing, there was warm evening air, or there were lapping waves, or a crackling fire.

Instead, thanks to the choices made by the TV schedulers on that fateful day, May 31, 1994, our backdrop was the soundtrack of high drama on *EastEnders* as Grant (played by Ross Kemp) punched David (Michael Ford) in the face, for the crime of dancing with Sharon (Letitia Dean) in the Queen Vic.

But still: *wow.*

It lasted all through the closing credits. And it was completely amazing.

To this day, every time I hear that theme music, or see Ross Kemp, I'm reminded of the first time I properly kissed another boy. I feel like that's the very epitome of what it means to be British, so I'm OK with that.

And we did a lot more kissing that evening.

Slow, long, breathless, frantic, tender, and, sometimes, slightly rough.

I wanted him *so badly.*

I think he wanted me too.

Don't get too excited though. I was just about to ruin it.

---

* I'm talking full-on tongues, OK? Not just lips brushing. I'm talking another boy actually clamped to my mouth for a pretty long time. Note to editor: Too much information?

Chapter 29

I felt like a new man when he showed me out of his house later that night. Well, if not new exactly, then *changed*. Is that pathetic? We'd totally kept our clothes on. Maybe the odd hand wandered a little . . . we don't need to go into it.

And, if you're a librarian, you don't need to shelve this as 16+.

Rob glanced over my shoulder, down the long drive. It curved off to the right, and we were shielded from the road by shrubs and trees, so it's not like anyone could see us, but I knew we had to be cautious anyway. "Quick action replay, then? To say good night properly."

We stood on the step, and, like before, he led the way, guiding us, setting the pace, hands all over each other, lips locked, tongues, the whole exquisite thing. Probably a minute passed, but I couldn't say for sure. His lips tenderly brushed mine, and he gently broke away. "Remember that, at school, when we can't even look at each other, remember that."

"I will."

I wanted to go in again, I wanted more, but I had to go.

"Oh, um . . . Beth had an idea. She wondered if you wanted to come round to Dan's one night. Just the four us?"

I sensed his immediate panic, the way his breath caught, and I knew I'd got it wrong.

"What?" he whimpered.

"Just, she—"

"Does she know, Jay? Did you tell her? *Dan too?*" He swallowed, his eyes wide.

"Um, no. Well, she does, but I didn't say . . . she worked it out—"

"Oh, Jesus."

"It's OK. Beth won't say anything. She heard people talking about the book, about *Wildflowers*, and looked it up and put two and two together, but—"

"And she's told Dan?"

"No. She said she wouldn't."

He ran his hands through his hair. "I want to," he said. "I . . . *really* want to. It would be amazing. But . . ." He took an unsteady breath. "I can't do this, Jay. This is exactly what I was saying. It's too risky. Too easy to slip up—"

"Yeah, but—"

"We already have slipped up—if Beth's worked it out. Who's next?" He took an unsteady breath. "How long before someone tells someone else and that someone else tells someone who knows Dad?"

"Forget I said anything."

I moved toward my bike, kicking myself for the hint of annoyance in my voice. I wasn't really angry with him. I was angry with the situation. And at myself. Because I should have realized this was a bad idea—too much, too soon. He followed me out onto the gravel drive.

"Do you understand what my dad would do if he found out? Not even found out, but just heard rumors? He'll ship me off, Jamie. He's said he would. There's some evangelical Christian school in Scotland that 'cures' boys like us, did you know that?"

I looked down. "I'm sorry," I muttered.

"I can't handle it, Jay."

"I know."

"I mean *this*. I don't think I can handle *this*."

I met his eyes, recognizing the fear in them that I was feeling.

"By 'this' do you mean—"

"It's getting late," he interrupted, breaking eye contact.

"Rob, I'm sorry, OK?"

He nodded, but he didn't look at me. "Me too," he muttered.

There was a wall between us now, and it was built from fear. Fear of the situation, of other people, and of everything that was being left unsaid. I couldn't break through it.

I took my bike and I walked it up the gravel drive, the tears springing from my eyes the moment my back was turned.

Why did other people have to make this so hard for us?

How could they think that something so beautiful was so wrong?

And had I just wrecked everything?

It was a ten-minute cycle ride home, twenty-five walking, but I started pushing my bike by foot anyway. Cycling always feels like such a joyful activity, don't you think? You never see a miserable cyclist. Or a crying one.

"This wasn't how I expected this evening to end," Electra said, appearing alongside me, also pushing her bike.

"Snap."

"I honestly thought we'd get back home, we'd put *Freedom* on your hi-fi, and we'd celebrate your first proper kiss with tongues and the liberation of it all, and, hell, get busy with the fizzy!"

"We don't have a SodaStream, Electra." I glanced at her. "What do I do now? Have I ruined everything? Just tell me. Don't sugarcoat it. Just tell me."

"You've ruined it. It's broken."

"Oh god, I've changed my mind—sugarcoat it!"

"But . . . it can be fixed."

"Can it?" I asked. "Or is that just sugarcoating?"

"For all his talk of living on the edge, of risk, he's afraid of not being in control. Of course, there are reasons for that, reasons he might share with you when he's ready, but for now, know that you stumbled into this without realizing, it isn't your fault, and what needs to happen is that he needs time. Can you do that, kiddo?"

"Give him time? Yeah."

"Without getting all depressed and writing endless love sonnets and angst-ridden diary entries, and the like? Without going on a Morrissey binge, basically?"

"I've never really liked Morrissey," I said.*

"Well, that's OK then. Now get on your bike, because it's a long walk home, cheer up and remember—you snogged another

---

* I didn't actually say this, I'm just pretending I did to account for more recent developments about Morrissey and to not be problematic. Fact is: great music. Let's leave it there.

boy tonight, Jamie. And it was amazing. And you liked it. And that, my dear, dear child, is progress."

With that, she produced a boom box*, pressed Play, put it on her shoulder, and rode off one-handed while Wham!'s "Freedom" started blaring out of the speakers. "Come on, Jamie!" she shouted.

I smiled, swung my leg over the seat, pedaled to join her, and we rode off into the night, joining George Michael on the chorus. Maybe it wasn't total freedom—but it was worth waiting for, and, I was soon to realize, it was worth *fighting* for.

Bet you're wondering how soon the shit is really gonna hit the fan, huh?

---

* Speaking of problematic, these were more often, I kid you not, known as "ghetto blasters." Casual racism, alive and well in 90s Britain!

Chapter 30

It was Mom who drew my attention to the letter. A couple of days later, we were in the living room, trays on our laps, as we were finishing a meal of Findus Crispy Pancakes (minced beef variety) with boiled potatoes and peas. Keith was away, hawking hoovers in Billericay, so no steak tonight; it was back to our normal cuisine. Weird, I realized both of us were more on edge when Keith was around—like we were putting on a show. It wasn't just the food—Mom always dressed up more and had more makeup on when Keith was home. Without him, she'd "taken her face off" the minute she came through the door that evening, and was already slumming it in her pajamas. "So, what's been going on at school, then?" Mom asked.

"Oh, the prom's going well! We've sold three-quarters of the tickets now that Speak No Monkey have confirmed." *Good old Dad*, I added in my head, because I knew Mom wouldn't like it if I spoke too kindly of him.

"Yeah, I didn't mean that."

"What do you mean?"

"There's a letter to the editor in the *Wickby Mail*—from some worried parents, about a library book?"

It might surprise you, but I'd always quite liked Findus Crispy Pancakes. OK, I was sixteen and stuck in Nowhere-ville, Lincolnshire, didn't know any better, and our European friends would doubtless be appalled, but they were very, very tasty.* Right then, however, they turned to sand in my mouth, and I couldn't swallow another morsel. "Letter?"

Mom shrugged, grabbed the *Mail* off the table, folded it over at the letters page, and handed it to me.

Dear Editor,

We write as a group of concerned parents with children of all ages attending Market Wickby High School. It has come to our attention that a deeply offensive and inappropriate book was in recent circulation in the school library. The contents of the book are rumored to portray homosexual behavior, and other immoral activities, which are not only in violation of Section 28 of the Local Government Act, but also clearly have no place in the hands of an innocent child. The Bible *makes it clear that this sort of behavior is fundamentally wrong and obscene, and as Christians it is our duty to ensure young people are raised in a wholesome environment, protected from pornographic content and lifestyle choices that are simply not permissible within the context of Christian teachings. We call upon the school to take immediate and appropriate action to resolve this alarming situation which imperils all our children.*

---

* Really though, this was probably due to the copious amounts of salt and sugar that food manufacturers were allowed to add back in the 90s. Happy days!

Yours faithfully,
A Group of Concerned Parents

My blood ran cold. I'd convinced myself that everything with the book would blow over. It was, after all, just a book. Words printed on a page. Why would anyone be worried or affronted by that? But it was clear to me: They weren't going to let it be.

But after that frozen fear . . .

Fire.

Red-hot, raging *fire.*

They could believe what they liked, but what gave them the right to push those beliefs on other people?

They were calling me immoral. They were calling me obscene.

But I was starting to understand—and really believe—that I was none of those things.

There was nothing wrong with me.

With any of us.

How dare they suggest otherwise.

I was furious. But I didn't know what to do with all the rage. I had no power in this situation. No voice.

I wanted to speak to Rob. He'd have a good take on all this, I knew it. He'd have some argument that would destroy them. But of course I hadn't pushed anything with him at school. I hoped that if he saw I was being careful, that I wasn't taking things too fast, he'd be OK with us again.

So much anger.

But no one to share it with.

Nowhere for it to go.

Beth and Dan convinced me to go over to Dan's anyway on Friday night. Dan's farm was exactly how I'd imagined it—middle of nowhere and not another soul to be seen. It was a warm evening, and we had a barbecue—just some sausages (from the family pigs, which was a bit uncomfortable, if I'm being honest), but it was nice, and seeing how Dan and Beth were acting around each other, I kept thinking how much nicer it would have been to share it with Rob. Just to have him there, joining in with the jokes and the chatter, laughing, me spilling a few more secrets about the prom (a bouncy castle—how about that?!) and everyone being excited, a couple of drinks, a bit of food . . . I don't even mean kissing or anything. Having someone around who likes you, who wants to make you laugh, knows how much you like fried onions so puts extra on your hot dog—well, I'd realized that was a wonderful thing.

After we'd eaten, we went inside. I know they didn't mean to make me feel like a third wheel, but as Beth and Dan settled down on one sofa together, cuddled up, holding hands, and I sat alone on the other, that's how I felt. I envied them.

I made my excuses as soon as it wouldn't be rude to do so, and made a hasty exit. Besides, I was pretty sure Beth and Dan wouldn't want me there *all* night. I cycled back into town but couldn't face going home to Mom and Keith, so parked up round the back of Shop 'n' Save, climbed up to the flat roof, and stared out into the darkness.

Yes, a small part of me had hoped I'd find Rob there too, also thinking, also wanting some company, but real life isn't like that; there isn't always someone else there when you really need them for dramatic purposes and to aid the narrative. There's just you, and your awful thoughts and the inescapable fact that you're just so damn lonely.

I tried to conjure the memory of him. Tried to imagine he *was* sitting beside me. Tried to remember the sound of his voice, the warmth of his breath, the Lynx Atlantis, his fingers gently stroking my cheek, his soft kisses . . .

A can of cider.

Laughter.

Lie back and look at the shitty, cloudy sky.

I missed him and I wanted him back.

And why should other people stop that?

"Quite enough angst and moping, Jamie Hampton," Electra said, climbing up the metal fire escape to join me. "What did Rob first tell you when he talked about fear and control that day?"

"Fuck the system."

"Precisely."

"How am I supposed to do that though?"

"Certainly not by languishing up here, all morose and sad. How much do you like him?"

"You know how much. A lot."

Electra nodded. "Time to put up a bit of a fight, then, isn't it?"

"I can't fight them. There are loads of them."

"Actually, there aren't. There are only a few—they just have loud voices. And then there are a lot of other people who could be persuaded—if only they heard the truth, rather than sensationalist hysteria.*"

---

* But sensationalist hysteria never goes out of style, does it?

I stared at her. *Like what, then?*

"You're a writer, Jamie," she said. "Go and bloody write!"

"Write what?"

"A letter in reply to theirs for the local paper!" She leaned toward me. "An anonymous one. Unless you fancy putting your name on it and getting your head kicked in?"

Suddenly, that burning fire in my belly had been given a rush of oxygen, hell, gasoline maybe, and the flames engulfed me. I was going to do it. I was going to fight.

At two o'clock the following morning, I made the final adjustment on the word processing file on my Amstrad PCW*, then loaded up a sheet of paper and waited for my dot matrix printer to do its thing.

Dear Editor,

I would have more respect for these "concerned parents" if they were just honest. Why don't they admit they simply hate gay people? Pretending it's about "protecting children" is nonsense. Has anyone bothered to actually ask "the children"? Do these letter writers not know that suicide rates among gay teenagers are really high, and one big reason for that is the bigotry they see everywhere and too often experience themselves? If these "parents" really cared, why don't they try to understand and help? Why don't they show some love, rather than so much hate? They claim to be Christians, after all.

---

* This "computer" had no internal hard drive, a monitor that only displayed in green, and worked off three-inch floppy disks. And I felt very futuristic using it.

And they are also wrong, whether they realize it or not. I know they're wrong because I'm a boy who happens to really like another boy. When I'm with him, everything feels brighter. He has changed me, in so many good ways. I'm happy when I'm with him. Does that upset these "parents"? That all the things they claim about us—that we're dirty, depraved, immoral—aren't true? That, actually, life is great— or at least it would be, without their hatred?

I note the "parents" refuse to put their actual names to the letter. What are they afraid of? I can tell you what I'm afraid of, why I too, am anonymous: because if anyone knew about me I would be beaten and attacked, just for living honestly, being my best self. Congratulations, "concerned parents," on making the world a worse place—because that is what your bigotry does.

Yours faithfully,

A Gay Teenage Boy at Market Wickby High School

Electra kissed her fingers like an Italian chef. I had to admit, I was pretty pleased with it.

Also, having previously scorned big gestures, here was mine. I don't know, I guess rom-coms are just in my blood. Such a hopeless, romantic optimist.

Chapter 31

But the hysteria grew. The following Monday, I'd never seen the library so busy. Kids everywhere. Rifling through the shelves, flicking through various volumes—all of them looking for *the* book. I wondered if they all wanted to find something outrageous and shocking, something smutty, or if just a couple of them secretly hoped they'd find themselves.

It was those last couple I felt for. I wished they could. Like I did.

Mrs. C was the eye of the storm—calmly shelving armfuls of abandoned books while chaos whirled all around her. "So, this is *fun!*" she said to me.

"Parents have been complaining," I whispered.

"I know," she whispered back. "And you don't need to whisper because it's common knowledge and it just sounds . . . sort of suspicious?"

I nodded. "But there's not even a book. And even if there was . . . there's barely anything in it that's wrong."

"There's *nothing* in it that's wrong, Jamie. And facts don't matter to these people. The sort of people who want to ban books are not the sort of people who are interested in truth."

I swallowed. "Is it going to be OK?"

"Yes, Jamie." She gave me a gentle smile. "It's going to be OK." Her face changed. "Oh, as long as I remember to remove that copy of *Hot Gay Sex for Teenage Boys, Illustrated Edition* from nonfiction.*" She winked at me. "Oh, bless your hopeful face. I was joking."

"My face wasn't hopeful."

"OK."

"That's just how my face is. I'm an optimist."

That optimism was tested to the max over the next couple of days. Rob wasn't in school much, but when he was, he kept his head down the whole time. He wouldn't even acknowledge me. I hated it, seeing him so scared of what the consequences might be, afraid just to look at me in case someone spotted it and somehow just *knew*.

Because that was the other thing. Rumors had now spread about there being notes toward the end of the book between two boys, and the hot topic was the identity of the "two homos." And so, like the Salem witch hunts, everyone was busy denying it was them, while gleefully suggesting it might be someone else. It felt like a clock was ticking, and eventually someone, somewhere, would hit upon the correct combination to blow the truth wide open.

On Wednesday morning, the protest started.

The group of parents were standing outside the school gates with a banner reading *"Protect Our Children!"* and an assortment of placards: *"No Homo Promo!," "Hands off Our Kids!,"* and *"Keep Gays Out of Schools!"*

---

* I was still looking for this title as late as 1998, no matter what she said. It doesn't exist, folks.

Long shot: me, Jamie Hampton, a bit of a hero, albeit an undercover one, walking past them, head not down but not exactly up either. *Do they know the enemy in their midst?*

Pan across: the protesters. Why do these people always look the same? Mean, pinched faces. An air of respectability. Middle class. A lot of women, *mostly blonde*, plus some men with awful beards.* Someone has a sign saying something vague from the Bible. Jesus is mentioned on another.

Fantasy sequence: Rob runs up to me. "Jamie! Jay! I came to say . . . screw it all!" He gestures to the protesters. "And screw them! I love you. I fucking love you! I'm so fucking gay for you!"

He shouts it mostly at the protesters, rather than me. Their chanting stops. Shock and obvious horror.

"Kiss me, big boy!" I shout back.

And, boy, does he. We are all over each other, rubbing the protesters' faces in all the gay. Tongues, everything. Before we start ripping each other's clothes off and—

Reality: I walked right by them. I didn't look. I didn't scowl. But what they couldn't know was the scene that was playing out in my head. Me and Rob. And that felt like a little bit of sweet, sweet defiance.

That's the thing, right? I didn't need a book to get "ideas" about doing stuff with other boys. I had plenty of my own. Since this whole thing had started with Rob, I'd developed a whole

---

* I promise you, look at any photo of an anti-LGBTQ or anti-abortion protest, and this is how a lot of the protesters will look.

library. A film library, mostly. In the sort of definition that wouldn't be mainstream for at least another twenty-five years.

So, that was our lovely hate montage, and now, picture that spinning newspaper that features in every film you've ever seen with some breaking news, only this is the new edition of the *Wickby Mail*, and rather than a big headline, it's the letters page, and one letter in particular.

Oh yes, it was "out there."

But while the storm raged around me (the fallout was immediate and massive—everyone was speculating about who the "Gay Teenage Boy" was; more outrage; accusations about being "anti-Christian," the lot), let us focus in on one small, very lovely, very significant moment. In any storm, it's important to find the calm. And this was it.

The location: English Lit, period 5.

The players: me—Jamie Hampton—and Rob West, the love interest. (He would kill me for calling him that; he was obviously so much more.)

Action!

Since my outburst in support of Rob's essay, Ms. Wilkins clearly thought it amusing to put us together whenever she wanted us to work in pairs. "Since your views on literature are so aligned!*" she would tell us, a sarcastic smile on her face. That day, we were

---

* Some years later I bumped into her when I was in town visiting Mom. She told me she'd put us together on purpose, because she could tell we liked each other. In all the hate, there are always people who do their bit to rebel and restore some love. I like that. And I like them.

working on the symbolism of weather in *Wuthering Heights*, and how Heathcliff is a storm, or whatever. We were getting toward the point in the semester where the actual real weather had become hotter, the seniors were all on exam leave, and nobody could really be bothered anymore. Various events loomed on the calendar: field day, the garden fete, a charity walk, *the prom*, of course, and even the lessons had taken on a more relaxed atmosphere. Hence why, despite this being an AP class, we were making big posters featuring the main cast experiencing various forms of weather—such as Heathcliff being under a thundercloud, for example. Shockingly babyish stuff, but I didn't care much, and having something that wasn't taxing to think about was a blessing.

Rob was staring down at the desk when I moved across from Beth and sat down next to him. It was undeniably awkward. But just as I was about to offer up a suggestion about starting with Cathy, he muttered, "I'm sorry."

I didn't reply. I wasn't sure I'd heard him correctly, or, if I had, that he was referring to me and him and "the situation" rather than, say . . . well, I didn't know. Or, rather, I didn't dare *hope*.

He was still staring down at the desk. "A Gay Teenage Boy?" he said. "You know how to wind up the bigots, I'll give you that."

I laughed.

And then he cracked a smile and looked at me. For a moment, he studied my face. It felt like he was seeing me for the first time, or maybe seeing someone different. I suppose I was. Inspired by him, I should add. It was funny. When this first started, I'd always seen myself as the one who was going to save *him*. This lonely boy, who I was going to help. And maybe I did, a little bit, but he also saved *me*. I sometimes wonder what the hell I would have become if I'd never met Rob West.

There was a hum of activity in the room: the general chatter of students only vaguely focusing on the work in question, mainly just gossiping. Ms. Wilkins was doing some grading at her desk. It made it easier.

"Do you hate me?" he muttered.

"Of course I don't."

"Thank you," he said. He gave me a small smile, then added, "Hey, passed my driving test, by the way."

"Aw, well done!"

"Take you for a ride sometime, then?" He winked at me.

That was it, we started to get on with the work, except for one thing: He shifted his left leg so it made contact with my right, and that's how we stayed, throughout the whole lesson, legs touching under the table, a little piece of comfort in an otherwise hostile world, and a little bit of hope that, maybe, things might be OK between us.

That evening at home, Mom, Keith, and I had just finished eating some lamb chops (yes, Keith was back), completely cremated (Mom can't stand pink meat), and, of course, totally unsatisfying—lamb chops being the frustrating intersection of too much work and not enough actual meat—when the phone rang.

"Probably for you," Keith grunted at me as he picked up a bone to gnaw on.

"864450?" I said, picking up the handset.*

---

* Yes, most people answered the phone by repeating back the number the caller had presumably called. It stopped being a thing a year or two later, and I kind of miss the formality of it.

"Hello, is that A Gay Teenage Boy?" came the reply.

I literally started choking on my own saliva.

"Who is it?" Mom mouthed at me.

I shook my head, as if to indicate it didn't matter, cleared my throat several times, and stretched the phone cord around with me into the hall, shutting the living room door between us, to afford some small level of privacy—although not much since Mom and Keith would be able to hear everything through the door anyway.

"Hello! How are you?" I said, all jolly, so no one would suspect anything. If I started whispering, or being weird, they'd know something was up, in that way moms always do.

"Ah, your mom is there, isn't she?" Rob said.

"Yep!" I said brightly. "I . . . didn't know you had my number."

"I didn't. I went through the phone book."

"You went through all the Hamptons until you found me?"

"Yeah." He didn't sound like that was a big thing.

"But there are loads of us!"

"I know. Started at the top and got lucky on number forty. Pity your mom's name isn't closer to the start of the alphabet."

I blew out a breath. That was dedication.

"It's been fine when women answered, but I've asked about ten guys if they're 'gay teenage boys' tonight, and it hasn't gone down well."

I laughed.

"Worth it for your reaction though!" he added.

"You're outrageous. And what happened to us agreeing not to phone each other?"

"Emergency. I need to see you. I want to explain. And I owe you a huge apology."

"Now?"

"Yeah. Have you had dinner?"

"Yeah."

"Main entrance of the cemetery. I'll be there in about fifteen minutes."

The phone went dead. He was always dramatic like that. Later, I learned he had a thing about goodbyes, which kind of explained it though.

I spun Mom and Keith a story about a "minor prom emergency," threw a hoodie on, and headed out.

Early June, so it was still light, and it was fairly warm. He was waiting for me just behind one of the brick pillars that flanked the entrance, grasping a bunch of flowers (for me?!), Casper at his feet, and a look on his face of relief when he saw me.

"Thanks for coming," he said. "Thank you."

"It's OK." I shrugged and eyed the flowers.

"Oh, these aren't for you." He laughed. "Do you like flowers?"

"Never been given any."

"Hm," he said.*

We walked in easy silence through the cemetery, Casper stopping to sniff periodically, and Rob pulling him on, fearful he was about to piss on someone's grave. If I'd really thought about it, the

---

* I assumed that response meant he might plan to at some point. To this day, Rob West has never given me flowers. Rob: white roses, please! Come on!

flowers were a big clue, of course, and we ended up standing in front of where his mom was buried. He removed some old stems from a pot by the headstone and put the fresh ones in, arranging them so they fell nicely. Satisfied, he stepped back, gazing softly at the grave.

"So, this is Mom," he told me. "Mom, this is Jamie."

"Hi, Rob's mom," I said quietly.

"Oh, good, I thought you might think I was weird, talking to her like that."

"Not at all. I . . . have someone I speak to as well."

He raised his eyebrows, then smiled. "Sometimes it's nice just to come down here and get it all out. I don't have anyone else I can do that with."

"Yeah, I get it."

He sat down cross-legged at the foot of the grave and patted the turf next to him, so I joined.

"I'm sorry about what happened at my place," he said, picking at some grass. "About how I reacted."

"It's OK."

"It's not OK. You were only trying to do something nice."

"It was too much. And we'd already agreed to keep everything quiet, so I don't know what I was thinking, really."

"What you were thinking, I expect, was how lovely it would be to have a little piece of *normal*. To be able to be with some friends and show them what we mean to each other. I think about that too. It's embarrassing, but I sometimes fantasize about bringing you round for supper, with my dad, and we're just open about it all, and he's OK with it, he even likes you, and we have dinner, and we laugh, and it's all just what everyone else gets to do." He turned to me. "I'm scared."

"I know, so am—"

"*Wait.* That's not it. I'm scared . . . because, I think, maybe, you've fallen for me."

I sighed.

"And I've fallen for you."

I tried not to smile at that, only because it felt like this was a *serious* moment, you know?

"By which I mean *properly* fallen for you. And that means I have to deal with the pain of, one day, losing you." He looked up and stared at his mom's headstone and sighed.

I chewed my lip, looking at him. "I'm not . . . planning on dying." I hoped that didn't sound crass.

"Neither was Mom."

"OK, but—"

"It's not even that. Mom got sick; I know that can happen to anyone. Bad luck. But, one day, you'll be taken away from me, or me from you. Because they'll never let us be together." He shook his head. "And everything that's been happening in the last couple of weeks? The *hysteria*? Over a *book*? Those parents writing to the paper and then protesting? Dad's read the letters—flat-out asked me if it was anything to do with me. Told him 'no way,' but he clearly wasn't convinced—I found the brochure for that evangelical school on the desk in my room yesterday. That's a warning, right? *A threat.* Irony is, Dad acts pure as the driven snow, but he's a hypocrite about a lot of other stuff . . ."

Rob shook his head, lost in thought, while I mused on what exactly *that* was meant to mean.

"Then some reporter from the *News of the World** turned up at my front door a couple of days ago," Rob continued. "They're desperate to get some dirt on Dad, and it's staring them right in the face; they just haven't been tipped off about it yet. It's . . . how is there a way out of this?" He looked at me again. "Realistically, I mean. None of your relentless optimism."

I nodded, glum. "On the roof, you talked about happy beginnings. So, what's this? Our unhappy ending?"

"No." He shook his head. "I don't like endings. I don't believe in them. Same with goodbyes."

"Aren't they inevitable?"

"They are *not*," he said. "When Mom was dying, I never said goodbye to her. The last thing I said was 'Have a good sleep,' even though . . . I knew. Goodbyes, endings, they suggest something is over, finished, but it never really is, is it? There is no end, because life carries on, just in different ways; someone dies, they become worm food, or they fertilize the flowers. Still life, still here, just different. Someone walks out of your life, that isn't 'the end,' that's just leaving that story for the moment and walking into another one, and maybe those stories intersect again, one day, and ultimately we're all just this bunch of captive atoms in the universe being reconfigured until . . ."

"The end?"

"Not the end!" he said. "Something will happen after the world explodes, who knows what?"

---

* A weekly tabloid newspaper in the UK that focused on gossip and sex scandals. They were always scum. The paper was closed in 2011 following an infamous phone hacking scandal.

He breathed out heavily.

"Well. I'm depressed," I said. There was a moment's silence.

"I want to be with you until the world explodes, Jamie."

I let those words sit . . .

And then I burst out laughing. "What?! I can't keep track of you."

"Seriously, I can't keep track of myself!" He sighed sadly. "I'm scared of losing you, like I lost Mom, and like I ended up losing all my friends at my last school, but then . . . if I don't do anything, then I've lost you anyway, right? *Nothing* is still *losing. Better to have loved and lost, than never to have loved at all.*"

"Shakespeare?"

"Oh, Jamie. *Tennyson.*" He glanced over his shoulder, then reached out for my hand. "I saw your letter in the paper. I read it, and I thought, when did he get so brave?"

"When I met you," I said.

"Have I finally brought the best out in someone?" He smiled, stroking my hand with his thumb.

"Hardly brave anyway," I said. "Didn't even put my name on it."

"But what you said was brave, knowing I would almost certainly read it. Admitting all that. To me. To yourself. I know that isn't easy."

"No. It's not."

"And, when I read it, I felt . . . I was beaming. So proud. Proud that you . . . were talking about me. That it was about us. And I thought, why should we have to hide? Why shouldn't we celebrate that? Who gave those people the right to decide what's right and what's wrong?"

"Right, OK, but I feel you've done a complete three-sixty here—"

"Not entirely. Everything I said is still true. The odds are stacked against us. Dad will still send me away if he knows. The press would love a juicy story. We'd both be beaten up. All that is true. Classic star-crossed lovers."

I did blush at "lovers" because we'd never gone that far.

"But I'm also sick of not living," he continued. "So, I change my vote. Let's live as close to the edge as we can. Maybe we *do* spend time with Beth and Dan, and just hope we can trust them both. We can be careful, but not to the point of not existing for each other. We speak in school. We hang out. Sit together at lunch. To everyone else, we're friends. As long as we're never caught actually . . . doing anything, what have they got on us?"

"We, *you*, especially, have to be so careful."

"I know. But what's the alternative? We don't exist just because they don't want us to exist? We can't change who we are. I don't want to change it either. I love *us*. Individually and together. I want to be with you. Whatever happens. Because having something, even for a bit, is still better than never having it. And what's the point in being alive if you can't actually live anyway? If you can't be you. If you're not allowed to love?"

I squeezed his hand.

"And, like your letter," he said, "perhaps we start to push back a bit. Because this has to change. Things have to change. Even if we do something quiet and underground—but isn't that how all revolutions started throughout history?"

"You've got something in mind, haven't you?"

He grinned and nodded. "I do have something in mind." He clocked my questioning face. "All in due course. I feel like we have some time to make up for first."

I leaned toward him.

"Not here!" he said, laughing. "Just in case. Plus, it's slightly weird in front of Mom, not that I think she'd mind. In fact, I think she'd really like you, but still . . . She's still my mom. And we're all British and massively uncomfortable with public displays of affection."

"Sorry, yeah."

He indicated the dense holly bushes at the edges of the cemetery. "But how about in there?" He smiled at me. "She won't see us, and no one else can. What do you think?"

Making out in a graveyard! That's something to tick off the bucket list, isn't it?

Did you pick up on that thing about endings, and Rob not liking them? That had a big effect on me, and I grew to hate endings too. That's why, if you read any of my books, you'll never find the words "The End" in there. Because, like Rob said, it never really is. Life goes on. Stories go on. Just in different ways. Despite that, with some of Rob's ideas, I honestly thought he absolutely wanted to bring on Armageddon, our total demise, and, yeah, The End. Get ready for it, folks . . .

Chapter 32

This is how it went down. Rob was convinced that if everyone was so up in arms about the book, then maybe they should just all *read* the damn book. It was a persuasive argument. *In principle.* If people read the book, and saw for themselves that it was nothing more than a story about two boys who kind of fall in love and explore who they are a bit, then surely everyone, or, at least, regular folk who weren't prone to pearl-clutching hysteria, would see that the complaints and the protests were unfounded and ridiculous?

I assumed what he had in mind was maybe directing people to copies in the local library or bookshop. It wasn't. He wanted to make it "easy" for people. His idea was to photocopy pages from the book and stick them up all over school.

"Let everyone read and see!"

My immediate reaction: *shit.*

My slightly more considered one: *oh wow.* What a reversal! Rob was facing his fears head-on, taking the risk, because he genuinely wanted things to start changing. It wasn't that I didn't believe what he'd said to me in the graveyard—but words can be easy, easier than actual action anyway, and I wasn't sure then just how he saw things playing out.

But he was really going for it.

I was delighted.

And I was also scared.

Monday morning. Close-up: me, Jamie Hampton, gingerly placing *Dance on My Grave* in my schoolbag, like it's radioactive waste. Sweat beads on my forehead, even though I haven't left the house yet.

Mid-shot: me, walking around school, a pulsing glow emanating from my backpack, indicating the presence of dangerous and illegal materials. More sweat. I look nauseous because I *am* nauseous.

Rewind. Replay: There's no glow from my backpack.

Everything seems normal. It's just me freaking out.

Cut to: free period. I hover outside the photocopying room. Rob arrives and nods at me. I'm doing the actual copying because I have the most experience with the machine after using it for prom committee business. It's a temperamental beast, constant paper jams, but I know how to coax the copies out of it. Rob's going to stay outside and loudly say hello to any teacher who looks like they're about to walk in so I have time to grab the book and the copies and beat a hasty retreat.

I walk into the photocopying room.

The machine was agonizingly slow. I watched the bright white light gliding back and forth under the photocopier lid, as the hot copies slid out of one end. I'd selected ten pages in total, and was making forty copies of each. Four hundred copies of the truth to put up around school.

I wished the damn thing would hurry up.

As copy number forty emerged, I flipped open the lid, flicked to the next page of the book, slammed the lid back down and hit the Start button for the next set.

"HI!"

Rob's voice! From outside.

Shit!

I scooped up the new copies, then threw the lid open, the white light blinding me as I grabbed the book and jabbed at the Stop button.

It wouldn't stop.

The machine was still whirring.

Another fresh copy emerged, which I grabbed.

"ALL RIGHT?!" (Rob, from outside.)

Another copy emerged. Why wouldn't it stop printing?

I grabbed that copy too, grasped the book and the wads of paper in one hand, and stepped out of the room.

And I make eye contact with . . .

Beth and Dan. Rob next to them, looking helpless.

Close-up: Beth: "Whatever you're doing, let us help."

The photocopier seemed to be quicker when Dan was standing next to me, with Beth and Rob standing guard outside.

"It's a good book," I told Dan.

He smiled. "I know."

It wasn't the time to interrogate him about that, but don't worry, there's an opportunity later, so be patient, and everything will become clear. It's important to leave little carrots along the way—hopefully the intrigue will keep you wanting to read on.

Back to the plan though.

We took a hundred copies each. The idea was to pin and Blu-Tack the pages up to every bulletin board and wall. No one was around because everyone else was in class, but it was still necessary to work quickly and carefully, making sure no students or teachers were in the vicinity who could possibly catch us.

We all went our separate ways.

I hurried along the English hallway. Check over my shoulder. Slam a poster on the wall. Press to adhere the Blu-Tack. Move on. No one saw. Repeat. Look left. Look right. Another poster. Heart racing. *Hot.* A door slams. Spin round. Coast clear. Slam. Press. Move. Mouth dry. *What the hell am I doing?*

Within fifteen minutes I'd plastered all the areas we agreed I would do, and I mean *plastered.* They were everywhere. Every yard along the hallway, every bulletin board, most of the doors; I even managed a few of the lower ceilings in the English hallway. I stuffed the remaining copies in my backpack and headed back to the common room, bubbling with anticipation at having distributed this oh-so-corrupt material, banned by the British government, for all to see for themselves. It felt like a massive middle finger up to Margaret Thatcher (who originally pushed Section 28) and every single homophobic bigot in power. It felt *amazing.*

. . . Until I walked through a set of double doors and saw Rob being roughly frog-marched in the direction of Prenton's office by Mr. Haskins, the PE teacher, Rob's face pale, but with an expression of grim determination as Haskins pushed him forward, keeping his arms pinned behind him.

"Leave him!" I shouted, by reflex.

Of course, that was it then. I was also bundled into Prenton's office, along with my backpack that contained the evidence of our crimes.

She read us the riot act.

She called us disgusting.

She called us sinners.

She said we were depraved.

She said we were sick.

One week's suspension.

And a letter home to our parents.

Chapter 33

My house was empty when Rob and I got there. Keith was out selling his hoovers, but now Mom had also found a sales job as a rep for
a company called SuperWare, which hawked plastic food storage
tubs and the like. I was glad for the quiet. I wasn't ready for questions, and Rob and I had a plan to sort out. I hadn't seen Beth or
Dan, so I assumed they'd got away with it, and would have the good
sense to keep quiet to save their own skins. I'd call Beth at home
later and fill her in. What else could I do? There was no way to contact her until she got home. I really wished we all had mobile
phones, like Keith had. That would have really helped.

I made Rob and me a cup of tea* and we sat in the living room.
If he was disappointed in my little house, compared to his, he didn't
show it. If anything, he looked right at home, kicking off his sneakers and sinking back into the sofa, while I fretted over the contents
of the letter Prenton had sent home with us both to pass on, along
with a promise of a phone call, meaning hiding the letter was not
going to solve anything.

---

* The best form of crisis management.

"*Promoting a book not permissible within the Christian teachings this school endeavors to uphold, and in contravention of Section 28 of the Local Government Act,*" I read out loud.

"That first bit could mean it was a book about eating shell-fish though, couldn't it? Or wearing man-made fibers. *The Sins of Polyester*. It's true—no child should be subjected."

"Rob, this isn't funny. My mom's gonna read it. She's going to ask me why I was looking at the book. What I was doing. I'm going to have to come out to her. And Keith. It's my birthday in a few days and this is how I'm starting my seventeenth year? Suspended and outed!" I sighed. "And what's your dad going to say?"

I realized then, as I watched him deflate, that all of his jokes and relaxed attitude had just been bravado. Forced cheer, or just complete denial, it didn't matter—I'd just brought him back to reality with a bang.

"He's in London for the week," he said quietly. "Prenton will call the house first, and I'm not planning on answering, so she'll leave a message on the answering machine."

"And then?"

Rob swallowed. "At some point, maybe she'll try his office, which means she'll speak to his secretary, who hates me—"

"Rob—"

He turned to me. The sadness in his face broke my heart. "We're probably safe today. But it may be tomorrow. Or the next day. So what choice do we have? Sit here and worry? We don't know how long we've got, but I do know we should live each day to the fullest. Go out with a bang. You know how prisoners

236

on death row get their special request for a final meal?"

"*That's* the analogy you're going with?!"

"Oh, come on! Worst case, we run away from home. I've been thinking about it. I'd do that before Daddy ships me off to be cured by the anti-gay evangelical cult he's lined up. Fuck it, let's party. You and me, and fuck the rest of the world."

"But, my mom—"

"Don't give your mom the letter. Leave the house like you're going to school each day, and come round to mine instead. She'll never know you're suspended."

"And when Prenton phones?"

Rob blew out a breath. "Well, you try to intercept it. But yeah, eventually the shit will hit the fan, won't it? That's life, bud. At some point, the shit hits the fan. *For all of us.* But until then, we should live. I've finally got some wheels . . ." He smiled at me. "And we have each other, and here we are, facing the end of the world, and I can't think of anyone else I'd rather do that with." He leaned in and kissed me on the lips. "Jay?"

"What?"

"When's your mom going to be back?"

"She said she'd be out all day. She's at a work training, learning how to sell egg cups and picnic ware."

Rob nodded. "I think we should go out. Have some fun. But first, I don't suppose you wanna do anything *not permissible within Christian teachings*, do you?"

That cheeky smile played on his lips, eyes ablaze with mischief and horniness.

Like I could resist those deep brown eyes anyway. Who

was I kidding, thinking I'd do anything other than follow him wherever he wanted to take me? We were going to live.

And we certainly did.

OK, we had limited resources—Rob got a generous allowance from his dad (guilt money because he was so rarely at home), but it wasn't enough to fly to New York, or go in a hot-air balloon or anything, and I had almost nothing in my bank account. But that was just fine.

"Living isn't about the big stuff," Rob told me as we sped along the country lanes in his black Fiesta with red bits. "It's what happens in between the big stuff."

"Poetic," I said, hoping he didn't notice me gripping the seat, not because I was embarrassed about not trusting him as a newly qualified driver, but because he really needed to keep his eyes on the road.

"Not me," Rob replied. "Read it somewhere. A magazine, I think." He glanced at me. "Put some music on. There are some cassettes in the glove compartment."

I leaned forward. "Um, OK . . ."

"Are you all right? You seem nervous."

"Yeah, I'm fine, it's just . . . could you slow down a bit?"

"We're nowhere near the speed limit."

"Rob, it's a safety regulation, not a challenge."

He laughed and took his foot off the accelerator. "Better?"

"Thanks. I just don't want to die."

He smiled to himself. "We're not gonna die."

We drove along in silence for a bit, and since he'd adopted a more sensible speed now, I felt able to riffle through his tape collection, and eventually put on some REM—*Automatic for the People.*

"Tell me who you talk to, then," he said.

"Huh?"

"At Mom's grave—you said there's someone you talk to."

"Ohh."

After quite a bit of silence, he chuckled and said, "Well, who is it, then?!"

"It's . . . pretty ridiculous."

"Yeah, well, we're talking about speaking to people who aren't really there, right?"

I swallowed. "Sometimes it feels like she *is* there though."

Rob nodded, taking a corner with a reassuring amount of precision. "I get that."

"It's like I can actually *see* her."

"So, what, like your grandma or something, is it?"

"It's Electra."

"I'm sorry, it's who?"

"*Electra*. From ITV's *Wave Warriors.*"

We drove in more silence for a bit, probably while he weighed up how much of a basket case I was.

"Electra specifically, or Tina Rocks, who plays Electra?"

"I'm not really sure."

"Well, is she constantly chasing you the wrong way up a waterslide, or is she offering you advice?"

"The latter?"

Rob sniffed, like all this was normal. "Sounds more like Tina Rocks—she's got a degree in psychology, I read." He nodded approvingly. "I'm not going to comment on how it all works, this talking business, but I've always thought she seems really nice, amazing hair, even when it's soaking wet, and—not that I'm an expert—*great athlete.*" He glanced at me. "You're pretty bonkers, aren't you?"

I shrugged. "Probably."

"Wouldn't want you any other way!" He smiled. "Hope she's not here now!"

I twisted round, and there she was, sitting in the back seat.

"Let him talk more about how great an athlete I am," she said.

I glared at her and she put her hands up in submission. "OK, OK. Don't want me here, huh? I know when I'm not welcome. Well, that's fine. You boys behave yourselves. And have fun."

I nodded and she vanished.

"Jay?"

"Yep, no, all good. No Electra!" I said, too loudly.

We parked on the main road in Cleethorpes*, grabbed a bag of fries each, and walked up Kings Road to Pleasure Island Theme Park.

"I'm not going on the Boomerang," I told him.

Pleasure Island had opened the year before, and while this was my first visit, I'd already heard about the rides. The Boomerang was the big roller coaster, so called because you were taken forward and back through a vertical loop and a cobra roll. *No thanks.*

---

* A seaside town in North East Lincolnshire and the nearest beach to where we lived. I'll get in trouble for saying this, but I always found it rather grim and depressing.

"Don't worry, we won't go on the Boomerang," Rob assured me.

"Promise?"

"I can't make you do anything you don't want to do, Jamie."

So that was fine. We went on a few of the more sedate family rides (the flying chairs, bumper cars, giant slide, and the furry friends tractor ride—*yes, yes, I know*), had a go on a pedal boat around the huge lake (loved that, because I imagined him reading romantic poetry to me as I let my hand drift through the water), saw the bird show and the sea lion show, and it was all great, but then I caught him looking mournfully at the Boomerang. And not for the first time either. It was like . . . he kept glancing at it when he thought I wasn't looking.

"Look," I said. "You can go on it if you like. I'm happy to stand here and watch."

"Nah," he said.

"I don't mind."

"Shame you don't like roller coasters though."

I shrugged. "I mean, I've never been on one—"

"You've never been on one?"

We locked eyes. "I don't enjoy speed. You know that from the car earlier."

"I wasn't speeding."

"No, but, I'm just saying, it makes me nervous."

"You know what they say: *Live fast!*"

"And the rest of that phrase is *die young.*"

"I prefer living fast and dying young to living slow and dying old," he said. He clocked my frown. "OK, that didn't come out quite right. I just think you can cram a lot in, do a lot of living; it's not about years, it's about what you do with them." He nodded. "I'm going to go on it, then."

"OK. I'll watch."

"Unless you want to come too?"

"I don't."

"Because this is all about stuff we haven't done before, and you haven't done this."

I looked down at the ground and scuffed my sneakers about in the dirt. "That's cool." After some silence, I glanced back up at him. He was smiling at me. "What if . . . you come with me, and because you're scared, I'll hold your hand? Would that help?"

"People might see."

"Not if we sit in the back row of the very back car."

"Even so."

He stepped toward me. "I'll look after you, Jamie. Nothing bad will happen, promise."

I took an unsteady breath. He was pushing all my buttons. I could feel myself weakening.

"I guess I just wanted us to experience it together, that's all. But if you really don't want to, then . . . we won't."

"What if it crashes?" I blurted out, unable to think with any sort of logic.

"Then we'll die. Side by side. Which is probably gonna happen in a few days anyway, so why not now?" He grinned.

"Can we stop talking about dying, please? Look, shut up, seriously, you go."

He held his hand out.

"*No,*" I said, glancing around, in case anyone saw.

He nodded. "OK, fair enough. Meet you back here, then?"

"Yeah. Good luck."

"See you then."

He ambled off toward the ride entrance.

And, of course, because being apart from him was so painful, ten seconds later I ran to catch up with him.

"OK!" I said.

He turned and smiled. "OK?!"

"No, I think this is a mistake."

"No," he replied. "I think this is love."

"Which is also a mistake."

"You don't mean that, you're an optimist."

"Well, I'm not optimistic about doing this."

He checked the coast was clear and squeezed my bottom. "You'll be fine, come on."

"Back row of the rear car?"

"If you like."

"You'll hold my hand?"

"I will."

Within minutes, we were seated in the back row of the rear car, which is when Rob turned to me and said, "When we start to go backward, expect to experience a g-force of 5.2 when we reenter the vertical loop at around forty-seven miles per hour."

I stared at him.

"And just so you know, the back row of the train, where we are now, will be the first to reenter the loop, meaning we'll enjoy one of the most forceful moments seen in steel roller-coaster design."

He nudged my leg with his.

"If you can do this, you can do anything."

And as the car started being pulled backward up the lift hill behind the station, and we were out of sight of the attendants, he grabbed my hand and squeezed.

"I love you," he whispered.

We went on the Boomerang four times. It would have been five, but Rob was starting to feel queasy. I couldn't get enough of the high. That thing blew the years of forced compliance, of expectations, of "sit still and listen" and "get good grades so you have a good future" away and made me feel alive.

Rob West.

Thank god he showed me that there can be beauty on the other side of terror.

Thank god he showed me that life could be so saturated with vibrant color it could make you breathless.

Thank god for Rob West.

Chapter 34

That evening, while Mom was distracted sorting out her SuperWare catalogs and order forms, I had a hushed conversation on the phone in the hallway with Beth. She and Dan hadn't been caught by any teachers, but even better, the stunt had everyone talking. Prenton hadn't managed to find all the copies—how could she?—and everyone was talking about the book and how "it didn't seem that bad."

"You're screwed though," Beth said.

"Thanks for reminding me."

"Why aren't you panicking?"

I chuckled, because, yeah, normally I would have been. I'd have been in a full-on meltdown. Hysterical. "I dunno, I suppose . . . Rob?"

At that point, Beth sang the chorus of that Joe Cocker and Jennifer Warnes song, "Up Where We Belong," all about how love can raise us up and take us soaring to the very heights*, and, yes, I got it, because that had literally been the case on the Boomerang,

---

* Look, just Google the song and listen to it, you know I can't quote the actual lyrics here, else I'll have to pay $$$, and I can't do that, not on these royalties.

and it was how being with Rob made me feel anyway. He insulated me against the bad stuff. It just didn't seem to matter.

The following morning, I left for "school" as usual. Mom didn't suspect a thing.

Rob answered his door wearing jeans, no socks, and a white tank top. It took me aback for a moment, because he looked . . . so damn *hot*. The tank top really showed off his arm muscles, and combined with the silver chain around his neck, it gave him a sort of bad boy vibe that I found weirdly appealing, keeping in mind that "bad boys" were not a sort I would normally be seen within a mile of . . . something else about me that might be changing, I supposed.

"Sorry, only just woke up." He tousled his bed-head hair. "Come in."

Ten minutes later, he handed me a coffee and a croissant* in his kitchen and we sat next to each other at the big wooden table. "I was thinking last night," he said, "how I basically tricked you onto that roller coaster."

"I'm glad you did."

"Hm. Not really fair though, is it? I don't want you to think you can't trust me."

"I do trust you. It's just that sometimes I need a bit of persuasion to do stuff. That's just who I am." I turned to him and smiled. "I wouldn't let just anyone persuade me."

---

* I played it down at the time, but this felt so grown-up! A croissant! Fuck me, he was cosmopolitan. I freaking loved it.

He smiled back. "OK. But today, it's your choice. Tell me something you've never done but want to and we'll do it."

"All right. OK. Really?"

"Yeah." He broke eye contact and got busy spreading some jam on his croissant. "You got something fun in mind?"

"Well, this will seem weird to you."

His head snapped up, and he leaned into me, grinning. "Ooh, I'm intrigued," he cooed into my ear. "Weird kinky, or—"

"Just weird," I giggled, spine tingling at how close he was.

"I'm all ears."

His eyes settled on my face, a little smile playing on his lips.

"I've never eaten at McDonald's."

After what might have been a shocked pause, Rob nodded and released a breath. "Right. Not where I thought this was going*, but that's OK. Wow. Never eaten at McDonald's. Really? Huh. OK, then."

Half an hour later, and Rob was still muttering in disbelief about that as we drove toward Lincoln† in his car.

"How can that be? I just don't get it. How can you have never had a Big Mac? Or a milkshake? Not even some of their fries?"

"I told you, *nothing.*"

He shook his head, keeping his eyes on the road. "I can't get my head around it."

---

* I was so naive. Obviously he was asking about something else I hadn't done but might like to. I was just so innocent I didn't realize it. It could have been a very different morning. Oh well.

† The county town of Lincolnshire, Lincoln was a half-hour drive from us. Famous for its cathedral and unlike Market Wickby, it had exciting stuff like a theater and department stores!

"Mom's always had this thing about fast food not being healthy enough, which, I mean, is ridiculous bearing in mind what we eat at home most of the time, but she won't hear it. It's why we never have orange soda."

"*What?*"

"And we're only allowed Coke on birthdays and at Christmas."

"This gets worse."

"McDonald's has always been out of the question."

"OK, fine, but you're almost seventeen. You're basically your own man. You kind of have been for a while. You could have gone yourself."

"Yeah, but I don't know how it all works."

"I'm sorry, I'm going to need to pull over if you say anything else ridiculous. *What the hell does that mean?*"

"All the menus . . . and they ask you things, right? Like what size you want. I worry I'll panic."

Rob whistled. "This'll be interesting."

"Uh-huh. I'm looking forward to it."

McDonald's was everything I had feared: bright, busy, and overstimulating.

"Decided yet?" Rob asked me as I stared at the menu while impatient customers swarmed around us.

"What's the difference between a Big Mac and a Quarter Pounder?"

"Big Mac has two beef patties, Quarter Pounder just has one."

"So a Big Mac is bigger?"

"The Quarter Pounder has more meat."

"I don't even know if I want a hamburger. What's the Filet-O-Fish like?"

"Just don't."

"OK. And the McMuffin?"

"That's the breakfast menu, Jay. It's not available after eleven."

"Huh. I see."

As I predicted, it was all too much. Eventually, on Rob's advice, I ordered a McChicken Sandwich, regular fries, a large, triple thick strawberry milkshake, and an apple pie. We found a plastic table that was free, Rob pushed the little silver foil ashtray* to the side and we both settled down with our Styrofoam boxes of food, with me copying Rob, dumping out my paper bag of fries into the lid section of the opened McChicken Sandwich, making me feel like a pro.

"Everything is so sweet," I said. Which it was—even the bun. Even the fries somehow.

"Mmm," Rob replied, sinking his teeth into his Quarter Pounder with cheese. "But do you like it?"

"Love it." Which was a bit of an exaggeration, if I was honest. It was . . . OK. The whole affair was somewhat sickly, and everything was so . . . soft. It was like food for people with no teeth. But I was at the point where anything was amazing if it involved Rob, so this was all good; it was positively *gourmet*.

That day, it felt like I had a boyfriend. An actual . . . boyfriend. After we'd eaten, we meandered around the shops. We were

---

* Wild how you could smoke in a McDonald's in the UK right up until 2007, when the smoking ban came in, isn't it?

looking at the clothes in Burton when Rob saw some vests, and said, "Something for you, Jay?"

I started blushing, remembering Jason and Scott's comments and feeling mortified that Rob might also think they looked gay. "Not really. Not anymore."

"Why not?" He frowned.

So I told him, and he hated that, and he said Scott and Jason were dicks, and I should wear what I wanted, but I told him I'd gone off vests anyway.

"Huh," Rob said. "Something else, then?"

He started looking through the racks and rails, until he found a shirt. He held it up to me and said, "This suits you. Try it on." It was red checkered flannel, not a million miles away from the one I'd admired Dan wearing, and when I emerged from the changing room, Rob told me he loved it and bought it for me.

That made me think I should buy him something too, but I didn't have much money, so I got him a copy of *A Boy's Own Story* from the bookstore, and the *thrill* I felt as we both strolled up to the Lesbian & Gay shelf in the store, and boldly browsed the available books and took a copy to the register, was only fractionally less than being on the Boomerang yesterday.

We sat on a bench by the river, and he asked me to write something in the front of it, so I put:

To Rob,
I will always love you.
    J x

He looked at it and smiled. "Are you deliberately quoting Whitney Houston?"

I realized and said, "Oh, *shit*."

And he laughed and said, "Well, I will always love you too."

We couldn't kiss, but I looked into his eyes, and I knew he meant it.

And that was it, right then, I think I died.

We were back sitting in his car.

"So did you like *The Bodyguard*?" Rob asked me.

"I just accidentally quoted it, Rob. It's not that I'm obsessed, although it's true, I do love Whitney. A lot."

He laughed. "Is there anything you're not incredibly enthusiastic about?"

"Being away from you."

He chuckled, leaned across, and kissed me on the cheek. "Likewise. I was really asking to see if you wanted to see a movie? We could drive up to the *Kinema in the Woods* since this so-called city doesn't currently have an actual cinema of its own."

The *Kinema in the Woods** was near Horncastle and was basically what it sounded like—a wooden building, built to fit a woodsy setting, that was a small cinema.

"What's on?" I asked.

Rob grabbed the copy of the *Lincolnshire Echo* he'd bought earlier and flicked to the listings. "Lucky I came prepared . . ." He ran his finger down the listings. "Ah! How about this? *In the Name*

---

* https://thekinemainthewoods.co.uk

of the Father. Came out earlier this year. Daniel Day-Lewis and Pete Postlethwaite."

"What's it about? Sounds serious."

"The Guildford Four—the IRA pub bombings they were falsely convicted of." He clocked my doubtful face. "OK, I've already seen it, but trust me, it's amazing, and I want you to see it too."

I liked that. If I did ever go to the cinema, it was only to see the latest big blockbuster release. This felt . . . like we were doing something special. Important. Something different, that regular run-of-the-mill people just wouldn't do. More than that, it was something he wanted to share with me.

"Let's do it," I said. "Back row seats?"

He chuckled and shook his head. "I had no idea how horny you actually are, *all of the time*, and also, no, Jamie, it's simply not that sort of film."

He was right.

It was not that sort of film.

I won't spoil it, but suffice to say, from about twenty seconds in, it was serious goose bumps stuff, and I was hooked.

I'd never seen a film like that before.

A film that didn't just make me jump, or cry, or laugh, but made me feel so . . . *angry.* The complete fucking *injustice* . . . the fact the police had a confession from someone else, but they buried it to save face. It was raw, brutal . . . an innocent man signing a confession that would ruin his life—because of police torture and the threats that they'd kill his father. It was a true story. How could

252

the world be like that? How was it possible? Optimistically (there I went again!), I had always started from the position that the world was a fundamentally fair place, and that the people in it were good.

But that wasn't the case.

"What's up?" Rob said as we drove back home.

"Do you think the world is a bad place?"

He smiled to himself. "I think you've just got to look for the light, Jay. Mom always used to tell me about this American guy* who used to say, if there was a tragedy, or something bad had happened, 'look for the helpers.' I think he was basically saying, in all the bad, you've still got people who care, and that should reassure you. But I actually think that's not quite good enough. You can't just *look* for the helpers. I think you've got to *be* a helper."

"Do something to make the world a better place?"

"Exactly. If everyone just stands by and waits for other people to help out, then nothing will ever change."

I nodded, thinking that one through. Mrs. C was a helper—doing her best to subvert an unjust piece of legislation. Beth and Dan were helpers—joining us for the book stunt, even though they risked being caught themselves. Electra was definitely a helper—however that was happening.

"Do you think we're helpers?" I asked him.

"If we took the next turn, and we came across an accident, I would get out and help, yeah," he said. "Would you?"

---

* His name was Fred Rogers and he hosted a children's TV show called *Mister Rogers' Neighborhood* on PBS.

"Yeah."

"Then I guess we're helpers."

"What about other stuff though? Because that's just us reacting to a bad situation. What about more proactive things. What about . . . gay rights?"

He took a deep breath. "Well, we tried that, didn't we? We did our subversive act. Look where it got us! But I think . . . we're not even eighteen yet, we're still kids, and I think there's a limit to what we can do. We're the ones who need to be helped. And I know people are trying. It's just they haven't managed it yet." He glanced at me. "You're making me sad."

"I'm making myself sad."

He hit the indicator and pulled up in a dark pull off, just a few minutes from my house. "Shall we say good night here?"

I nodded, and we unbuckled our seat belts and fell into a long, gentle kiss. He broke away first and ran his fingers down my cheek. For a moment, he looked like he was in pain.

"Fucking hell, I love you," he said.

Mom wasn't in when I got home.

But Keith was.

He was stretched out on the sofa, in his tight blue Wranglers, a pair of loafers, and an oversized, multicolored Coogi sweater that made your eyes go funny if you looked at it too long.

"Your mom's got her first SuperWare party," he told me. "She'll be raking it in soon, mark my words!"

I gave him a tight smile and made to leave for my bedroom.

"Jamie?"

254

I turned back. He was sitting upright all of a sudden.

"The school called when I was here earlier."

Our eyes met.

"Apparently . . . you've been suspended?"

I swallowed. "Yeah."

Keith nodded back. "Were you going to tell your mom?"

"I . . . I feel like she's got enough on her plate. I'm seventeen tomorrow; I think I can be responsible for my own life. And she'll worry. She'll worry, and she doesn't need to. So, no. I haven't told her."

Keith nodded again, deep in thought.

Then . . .

"Mrs. Prenton mentioned a book," he said.

I knew this was coming. It was always coming. But it still took me by surprise. Here I was, about to have everything blown apart. Everything I was, out for everyone to see, whether I wanted it, or was ready for it, to be. No choice. Boys like me didn't deserve a choice. Because we were dangerous and disgusting and we had to be stopped.

The front door would be the quickest escape route. Hopefully I could make it out before Keith could do too much damage—and hopefully he wouldn't want to punch me too much on the driveway in full view of the neighbors . . .

I looked back up at Keith and swallowed, my chest tight, breaths short. And I braced myself. For whatever was coming. Whatever words, or worse, he was going to hurl at me.

"She told me all about the book," Keith continued. "And I said to her: It's a book. Why are you so bothered?"

Uh-oh. Here it comes.

"She didn't like that. Started going on about indecency, or something." He laughed. "I told her it sounds like a good book, and I'd like to read it myself, so where could I find a copy?" My eyes widened, and he nodded. "I mean, obviously not. I hate books. I was just saying that to wind the old bitch up. She's a nasty piece of work, that Prenton. I see her and her husband down at the pub sometimes. Drinking sherry like the pricks they are. Wanna know what I think, Jamie? I think you've got the right idea. I think people should figure out their own lives and stop prying so much into other people's."

He met my eyes. "So, I told her where to shove her ignorant head. And, in case you want to know, I suggested it should be up her bigoted ass. And that's all we need to say about the matter, and your mom doesn't need to know. I won't say anything, it's all dealt with as far as I'm concerned, but, for the record, I think she'd agree with me, and the other thing is you better not do anything stupid, Jay. Like get AIDS. I don't even know how you get AIDS, but I think condoms help you *not* get it, so you just make sure . . . We don't need to talk about this, but you had better be around for years and years, and way outlive me and your mom, and that's even if . . ." He actually swallowed, overcome with emotion. "I mean, it's just a book. It doesn't mean anything."

He dropped his eyes, and carried on, "Don't you start crying . . . that's not . . . I'm not gonna hug you, that's not what men do. You just . . . fuck it, come here."

Keith gave me what must rank as the worst, most awkward hug in the history of human contact.

"You'll be around tomorrow, yeah? For your birthday? It'd mean a lot to your mom."

"Sure. Yeah."

He smelled of Brut and super-strength lager, but I didn't care. I later learned that Keith had secrets of his own—a string of failed marriages, and he was practically bankrupt, living off loans and credit cards, his vacuum cleaner business not doing anywhere near as well as he claimed. I also learned he'd had a hard life: kicked out by his abusive father at fifteen, living rough under a bridge and having to eat dog food, never finding anyone who would take a chance on him for a job because of who he was and what he looked like. Life had been a battle; he'd crawled his way to where he was now, learning that the only way was to fake it, never being able to be real. So, in a weird way, I like to think that's why he helped me. Because I was trying to be real, and even if he couldn't be, he understood someone else who was going through hell because of all the crap other people dressed you up in.*

Everyone has a history. Everyone has secrets. Everyone has problems and has faced hardships. I realized that night that judging wasn't helpful, that people weren't always who we expected them to be, and, with all that in mind, couldn't everyone just be a little kinder?

---

* Ten years later, Keith was found dead in his car, by a cliff on the coast, a Phil Collins album playing on the stereo. Turned out he had pancreatic cancer, but never told anyone, refusing treatment until he could no longer hide it and he ended it all—a faker to the end. He died with a fuck-ton of debt, but he left me and Mom a thousand pounds each in used notes, which he'd saved over the years. He was, after all, a good man.

Chapter 35

I told Rob everything when I arrived at his place the next day.

"Well, at least one of us is in the clear," he said. "Happy birthday. Was that the best present ever, then?"

It certainly wasn't a bad one, although really, it was the bare minimum anyone deserves, of course. Funny, how when you're conditioned to expect so little, you can be happy with any scrap you get thrown, rather than saying, "Hey, do you know what? I should be able to have whatever you're having!"

"Have you heard from your dad?" I asked.

Rob shook his head. "He'll probably call at some point. Prenton left a message on the answering machine yesterday, while we were out."

My eyes widened in fear for him.

"Relax, Jay. I just erased it."

I watched him pulling absentmindedly at the chain around his neck.

"She'll call again though. When your dad doesn't phone her back."

"No doubt. She'll probably call his office too—I bet she gets off thinking about how much trouble she can get me in." He sniffed. "Have to cross that bridge when it happens. No point in worrying."

"I'm worrying!"

He stopped playing with his chain. "Well, don't. It's your birthday. No worrying today. OK?"

I nodded vaguely, but I wasn't happy.

He sighed, gave me a wry smile, and shook his head. "What you need is something big to look forward to. Something fun. Take your mind off things." He met my eyes. "There's a club in Lincoln. A gay club. We could go sometime."

"They'll never let us in."

"Worth a try?"

"I dunno. What if—"

"Worst case, they'll turn us away. Best case—we have an amazing night. Think about it. Maybe in a few weeks, when all of this has blown over. Nice way to celebrate."

He gave me one of his smiles, and I already knew I'd agree to it.

"Now! What shall we do today, birthday boy?!"

Yesterday had all been about me, and OK, today was my birthday, but I wanted nothing more than to do something Rob chose. Just getting to know him, the stuff he liked, the music, the movies, anything, was a joy to me.

He took some persuasion to come round to that idea, but after a lot of sulking, and insistence, he finally acquiesced.

And that's how I found myself there.

"OK, of all the things, I did not imagine this."

"You did give me the choice," he said.

I nodded.

259

"Do you hate it?"

"I'm *intrigued*."

He smiled and held his hand out to help me over the fence. "Let's get closer, then."

We'd driven to the highest point on the Lincolnshire Wolds—a place called Stenigot, where there used to be a Royal Air Force base during the Second World War. Bordered on all sides by regular-looking fields of corn and some pastureland was a more unkempt area, covered in rubble and wild grass, protected by broken-down fencing, and even an old sign that read, *"This is a prohibited place within the meaning of the Official Secrets Act."*

"Don't worry about that," Rob said, clocking me reading it. "The site was decommissioned a few years ago."

The site in question had a huge radio transmitter at one end, and at the other, four vast radar dishes, resting on their sides, like fallen giants. And, jeez, it was creepy. While the hairs on the back of my neck were standing up, Rob seemed to be in his element as he led me over to one of the dishes.

"So, the transmitter at the far end," he said, "that was from the Second World War. It was part of what was called the Chain Home system—providing early warning of enemy aircraft. This was one of twenty sites across the east coast of Britain. There were actually four transmitters at this site originally, but only that one remains now."

"And the dishes?"

His eyes lit up. "Ah. So in 1959, everything was upgraded as part of the NATO ACE High Program. Those are tropospheric scatter dishes. They used to be upright, obviously, but, like I said, they've decommissioned it all now."

We reached one of the dishes rusting in the field. So huge. I ran my fingers over some writing on one edge: *NATO Equipment*. Rob hopped up and stood on it. "These were literally from the Cold War, when they thought Russia was going to nuke us any second."

The cold prickled through me again and I shivered.

"It's weird to think, isn't it?" he said.

I swallowed. "Why did you pick to come here?"

He jumped down from the dish. "Do you hate it?"

"No. I mean, it's . . . a bit . . ."

He nodded. "It's kind of eerie, isn't it? Knowing what these were here for. I sometimes come here, and it fascinates me . . . these dishes, just standing here, staring into the abyss, waiting . . . for oblivion." He gave me a small smile. "Happy birthday, Jamie."

"Fucking hell!" I chuckled.

"But seriously," he said, "there is a reason. You know what we were talking about yesterday? About whether the world is a bad place? Well, here's the bad, Jay. Here's war and hate and fear, right here. This is paranoia. Nuclear Armageddon. This is secrets and underground bunkers, and plans about what would happen if Russia had launched a nuke that none of us normal people even knew about. But what I think is exciting, is that in all that terror, there can still be love." He reached into his backpack and pulled out a small pocketknife, flicking one of the blades out. He smiled at me again, then cocked his head toward the radar dish, where he started scratching the knife into the rusting metal. Eventually, he took a step back and I could admire his work:

RW loves JH

"Doesn't seem like much," Rob said. "But then, maybe it is. Maybe it's a bigger statement than these Cold War dishes ever were. Or maybe it just slightly rebalances all the hate and fear. Either way, fuck hate, fuck fear, right?" He kissed me on the lips. "Happy birthday. Do you wish we'd just gone bowling?"

"No. I'm glad we did this." And I was. It felt like this meant something to him. And that meant a lot to me.

"Shall we take some photos?" Rob said.

"Yeah, OK."

Rob pulled his camera from his backpack—a nice one too, an SLR, with a lens you could twist off and replace with others—professional really, proper rich-kid gear, you know, they don't really need it, it's not a passion or anything, but they have the best stuff money can buy anyway. Still, we didn't have any photographs of us yet, and I wanted to at least chart the first day of being seventeen. Rob took one of me first, probably looking awkward and goofy, in my jeans and a gray T-shirt, standing next to the inscription on the radar dish. We swapped places so I could take one of him. I studied him through the viewfinder of the camera. He was so natural, so relaxed, and so handsome in his khaki shorts and white short-sleeved shirt that I took two. Then, for good measure, I took a close-up of the words he'd etched into the metal.*

"Let's go back to the car," he said. "This is a good time to tell you we're actually trespassing."

---

* Good thing I did. In 2020, Rob sent me a Facebook message telling me they'd taken the dishes away and sold them for scrap, and with them, our eternal love message, of course.

"Oh god!"

"I knew that would be your reaction. It's why I didn't tell you. No harm done though, huh?" He patted my bottom and strode back toward the fence, me scrambling after him, fully expecting to be shot by the Special Air Service any second.

Safely back in the car, Rob rewound the film in the camera, unclipped the back, and took it out, handing me the roll. "Can you get this developed? I can't risk Dad getting hold of them."

I nodded and pocketed the film. Meanwhile, he produced a thermos of tea, two plastic cups, and a Swiss roll, which he stuck seventeen candles into the top of—a feat of engineering that resulted in an impressive, if incredibly dangerous, amount of flames. "Blow them out, make a wish, and make it a good one," he told me.

I closed my eyes, blew, and wished, keeping my eyes squeezed shut to wish as hard as I could. When I opened them, he was smiling at me. "I wonder what you wished for?"

"I wonder."

He balanced the cake on his knee, pulled out the candles, then using another blade of his pocketknife, he cut two large chunks off, handing me a piece, along with a tissue, which was the sort of caring attention to detail I adored. He might be a bit of a live wire, but he didn't want you to have sticky fingers.

I glanced back toward the radar dishes. "Why aren't you taking history?" I asked. "You seem to know a lot about it."

"Oh," he said, munching cake, "history frustrates me."

"Yeah?"

He swallowed. "Someone, I can't remember who, it might

even have been my gran, but someone said, 'You have to know the past to understand the present.'"

"It was Carl Sagan," I said. "I use that quote a lot in history essays when they make us justify studying history."

"History must be one of the few subjects where you have to *justify* studying it."

"Probably."

"So, my issue is, we do know the past. We know it, we ignore it, and we screw the present up regardless. History frustrates me—it's all there, most of it's happened before, but we insist on repeating the same mistakes."

"Like?"

"Everyone knows they burned and banned books in Nazi Germany. No one thinks that was a good thing. Yet, here we are—basically doing it again. And when you boil it down, whether it's that, or McCarthy wanting books banned in the 1950s, or Section 28, it's the same reason: People in power are threatened by anyone who dares to think differently. I think history is interesting, it just reminds me how disappointing we are as a species." He polished off the last of his cake. "Tea, dear?"

"Thanks, dear."

Rob poured two plastic mugs of steaming tea. "It's a shame you have to be at home tonight. Are you free tomorrow though?"

"Yes. What's the plan?"

"It's a surprise, birthday boy. Come by my place. Shall I give you your present then, or do you want it now?"

"Depends what it is." I smirked at him.

"Cheeky." He kissed me on the lips. "I think tomorrow. Nice

to spread things out so the birthday fun lasts more than one day, right? Why shouldn't you have a birthday *week*?"

"I like it."

He took a sip of tea and gazed out of the window. "Oh, and . . . if you like . . . why don't you bring your toothbrush?*"

---

* Boom!

Chapter 36

I know you want to get to the "toothbrush" scene, but if *I* had to endure my birthday party at home, then so do you. You can't just see the highlights. This isn't Instagram. Besides, you know we'll have to fade to black when the really good stuff starts, don't you? And yes, I'm well aware of the irony in writing a book about Section 28 and censorship, while soft-censoring myself for the purposes of creating something that gets stocked in school libraries. Don't get me started.

Maybe, one day, there'll be a director's cut. Or a writer's cut—much better.*

Back to 1994.

It was your classic birthday party. Mom had baked and decorated a birthday cake, and there were sandwiches, scones, tea cakes, sausage rolls, and a bottle of sparkling wine, even though the drinking thing wasn't technically legal for another year—but that was Mom's way of living on the edge a bit, I think.

---

* Although it would likely be several hundred pages of unedited dirge that's deeply frustrating.

That year, Mom and Keith bought me a new hi-fi with a CD player. It was a brand called JVC, and it was compact and sleek, and loud, with decently deep speakers. Keith also presented me with my first CD—Phil Collins.

"This is what good music is, Jamie," he said. "I listen to that man, and I'm in heaven."

Yeah, OK, Keith.

Later, Beth turned up, and after a slice of cake and a cup of tea, she came up to my bedroom to help me set up the hi-fi, and to give me her present, when it became apparent there was a good reason why she'd waited and not done that downstairs in front of Mom and Keith.

"Jay?" she said, as I fiddled around plugging in the left-hand speaker. "Everyone's talking about you. And him."

"What do you mean?"

"I mean, word got round; everyone heard about the suspension, obviously, but then people put two and two together—they're saying you're the two boys sending notes in the book, you're both gay, you wrote the letter to the paper, and that's why you've been suspended—"

"Oh, Jesus."

"It's just, you need to know, when you come back next week—I think it's gonna be brutal. There was an assembly and everything—*my damn dad did a bit of it*—all about how sinful gay people are, how it won't be tolerated, and then they've literally gone through every book in the library—"

"What?!"

"Mrs. Prenton and a load of the governors—they've gone

through every book and removed anything they feel is inappropriate. Mrs. C was in tears. It's all such bullshit."

I sighed. So this was the reality. Well, I didn't want the reality. I wanted me and Rob and our adventures together. I wanted the endless days, the kisses, his gentle words, and our long discussions where I'd talk to him about the stories I'd written that I'd never shared with anyone else, where I'd read him some and he'd listen, lying back with his eyes closed "so he could picture it better," and where we'd talk endlessly about everything from god to Jarvis Cocker. This week had opened my eyes . . . and I didn't want to go back.

"Jay?"

I smiled at Beth. "Thanks for letting me know."

But Beth wasn't smiling back. "There's something else too."

I blew out a breath. "Tell me."

"You're off the prom committee. Debbie's taken over as president, with Mrs. Prenton's blessing. Debbie said you haven't been pulling your weight, and apparently there was also concern about you bringing shame to the event, and upsetting the sponsors—"

"You mean Debbie's dad?"

Beth nodded.

I sighed and shook my head. "Well, at least I got Speak No Monkey there, huh? So, if anyone remembers anything from that prom, I hope they'll remember seeing an incredible band, even if they don't remember who made it happen."

"It's appalling, Jay. The band is the reason it's totally sold out—everyone's really excited about it. But Dan and I are thinking about not going."

"Don't do that. You should go. It'll be a great night. I guess it's too late for me now though—I won't be entitled to a free committee member ticket anymore, and if it's sold out, I can't buy one either."

"Except . . . Dan and I both bought couple's tickets," Beth said. "One of which is obviously spare now."

For a second it almost seemed a perfect solution, but who was I kidding? "Not sure anyone would want me there anyway." I turned back to the stereo. "Do you want to listen to Phil Collins, then?"

"I'd rather eat my own arm," she replied. "Anyway, your mom tipped me off about your main present, so I also got you this."

She produced a wrapped CD—Deacon Blue's greatest hits, as it turned out. We lay back on the bed and I closed my eyes, listening to the first track—"Dignity"—which, to me, was all about the revenge of a life well lived, a majestic, if unspoken, "fuck you" to all the people who mocked, hated, and made life hard, because the character in the song ended up getting exactly what he wanted, and it was beautiful and perfect, even if it took many, many years to get it, and even if it was a hard, grim journey.

So. Let them. Let them do their worst.

I was not going to let them win.

Chapter 37

Everything bad melted away the moment I arrived at Rob's on Thursday evening. Yes, he'd made his house warm and inviting, with soft lighting, music, and some candles. And yes, he'd arranged a perfectly relaxed night, with Chinese takeout, two multipacks of sparkling cider, and a bunch of movies he'd rented from Blockbuster. All of that was nice. But it was *him*. I'd worried for ages about what to wear—dinner at Rob's—it felt like a big deal. I didn't want to overdo it, but I also wanted to make an effort. I opted for the red-checked flannel shirt he bought me, with chinos. He'd also gone for chinos. With a shirt and vest. Nothing needed to be said. Rob West brought the best out of me, he changed me, but he also had a way of letting me know that, fundamentally, I was OK as I was, as I'd always been, I didn't need to pretend, he liked me for me . . . and for the vests I'd stopped wearing since Jason and Scott's cruel comments.

He'd ordered way too much food: half a crispy duck with pancakes and plum sauce, sesame prawn toast, chicken dumplings, spring rolls, spare ribs in barbecue sauce, satay chicken, lemon chicken, crispy chili beef, a bucketload of rice, and several bags of shrimp chips.

"I didn't want to risk us getting hungry later," he explained. "And wait 'til you see dessert."

Dessert was a Sara Lee Black Forest gâteaux*, which had been defrosted. I was too full of everything else to eat much of it, but I managed to force some down, only for Rob to reveal he'd also bought "popcorn and other nibbles" for during the movie.

We cuddled up on the sofa in the snug, along with Casper, and Rob handed me his present—a small, wrapped box. Inside was a watch, and on the back he'd had inscribed: *To J, forever, R x*

"I hope those are happy tears," he told me.

I sniffed and wiped my eyes. "Rob, this looks expensive."

"Well, it's not about money, but I wanted to get you something special. Because you *are* special."

"Thank you. It's lovely."

"Let's put it on."

He wrapped the brown leather strap around my left wrist and secured the clasp. "There," he said. "Now I'll always be with you. *Forever.*"

I met his eyes. "I want you to be anyway, regardless of the watch."

"I know." He gave me a gentle smile and wiped a stray tear from my cheek with his thumb, and I wondered if, somehow, he knew, or had heard, about all the shit happening at school, and I wondered if he already knew our days were numbered. If the secret was out, it was only a matter of time before his dad put a stop to it all.

"Stop overthinking," he told me.

---

* This represented the pinnacle of class, and I am not being sarcastic.

271

"I'm not."

"You *are*. I can tell. Tomorrow might be anything, but tonight is tonight, and we're here, and we've still got each other, and it's good, and I love you." He kissed me.

"I love you too."

We kissed again. "Do you want to watch one of the movies?" he asked.

"No, I just want to do this."

I'm not sure how long we spent on that sofa, kissing and touching each other. It was perfect, slow, gentle, our own timeless world, and at some point, he murmured, "Shall we go upstairs?" and I said, "Yeah," and he took my hand and led me to his bedroom, more kissing, clothes off, and for two kids who really didn't know what they were doing, it felt like one hell of an epic night.

Happy birthday to me.

Chapter 38

"Exciting news," Rob said, appearing in the doorway of his bedroom the following morning, in just his boxers, carrying two steaming-hot cups of tea. "I just had a conversation on the phone with my father."

I sat up in bed, suddenly wide awake. "And?"

Rob put a cup on the bedside table next to me, then walked round to the other side of the bed, sliding under the duvet. "Is the suspense killing you?"

"Rob! Jesus, what did he say?"

"First of all, he's got what he wanted. He's in the cabinet. Education Secretary of all things. Hooray, hoorah, well done to him."

"Right."

"But that wasn't why he was calling. Prenton called his office, spoke to Margaret, his secretary, just as I thought she would. By all accounts, she was blabbering on about obscenity and vulgarity, not making a whole lot of sense, but Dad wanted to know what that was all about."

I was on edge. "Right?!"

Rob smiled. "So I told Dad I'd basically been suspended for

swearing at a teacher. Dad gave me an earful about how that's unacceptable, especially now he's Education Secretary, blah, blah . . . at which point, and I'm not necessarily proud of it, Jay, but I pulled the dead mom card. You know? How dealing with her death has left me with so much anger, it's hard for me to process it . . ."

"Really, Rob? Is that a bit—"

He shrugged. "It guilt trips him though. And I kind of feel it's OK, because Mom's not actually here to defend me, and she would want to, so this way, she sort of is? I promised, hand on heart, I'd mend my ways, control myself, be a shining beacon of virtue, or whatever, and that seemed to shut him up."

"What about Prenton calling him again though? To actually try to speak to him?"

"Yeah, I told him she'd probably try. He said he doesn't want to speak to her, because she'll just bend his ear about funding for the new performing arts hall she's after." He turned to me. "It's not a guarantee, but I think I might have got away with it."

"Fuck, yes!" I said.

We kissed on the lips, then he reached for a tea, taking a sip while keeping the playful smile on his face.

"There's more, isn't there?" I said.

"Dad's hosting a party here this weekend—it's a load of horrific political types—but he wants me there because of the whole happy families bullshit he has to portray . . ." He blew on his tea. "He said I'm allowed to bring a couple of friends. So? How about it?"

I put my tea down. "Right. So, everything about that screams bad idea to me, Rob."

"Why? It's not like I'm going to suck you off in front of the Home Secretary."

Um, OK! Noted! "I just mean, won't your dad be suspicious? If I suddenly turn up out of the blue. After everything that happened at your old school? He'll be looking out for it, won't he?"

"But what about if it's not just you? What if this is where your previous idea comes into play? What if Beth and Dan come too? Then it's just a group of friends, isn't it? The more the merrier, honestly—the rest of the company will be crusty old politicians, but the booze and food will be good."

I sipped my tea, not looking at him.

"What?" he asked.

"What's this really about?"

"Nothing!" he said, unable to stop the smile playing on his lips.

"Because it's not just about you being bored at one of your dad's parties."

He sniffed and sipped his tea.

"And it's not about looking good in front of anyone, because I'm not convinced that's really something you care about."

"Oh, you're just a little Miss Marple, aren't you?" He put his tea down. "Every single person at that party tomorrow night either voted for, or supported, Section 28. Quite a lot of them have written vile opinion pieces in the right-wing press about people like us, Jay. They're evil. They're full of hate. So, it gives me a bit of a thrill to think there could be so much love right in front of their bigoted faces, they just don't realize it."

"In all that terror, there can still be love," I mused, remembering his words up at the radar station.

"We might not be able to beat them, *yet*, but we can sure as hell keep rebelling. We can be subversive. The revolution continues. It has to."

I nodded. "OK, I just want to confirm: You're not going to pull a stunt like kissing me in front of your dad?"

"Jamie, I haven't got a death wish! I just want you there." He kissed me. "Because you make my world a better place."

I smiled and we sipped our tea for a bit.

"Jamie?"

This was another bad idea, I could sense it.

"Uh-huh?"

"How about we go into town after this, and both get an ear pierced?"

I sighed. "And you want to do that before your dad's party? Why don't we both just turn up with rainbow flags and T-shirts with 'Massive Queer' written on them?"

"I just think it would look good."

"It's really gay."

"We *are* really gay. Have you not noticed?"

"I'm not sure we want other people to notice."

"C'mon! We can tell Dad . . . that we're doing a play at school . . . about . . . pirates? And—"

"Rob. Everyone at school's talking. About us."

He went silent.

"Beth told me," I added. I glanced at him to gauge his reaction. He was staring into the middle distance. "Rob? Say something."

He sniffed and turned to me. "Let them talk."

"But—"

"Let them talk, Jay. And I'll tell you this: If we show any fear, any embarrassment, that's when they'll *know*. Until then, it's just rumor. Anyway, loads of guys get earrings, it's not a gay thing. How else do you explain the entire punk movement?"

"Isn't there a gay ear?"

"A *gay ear*?"

"As in, if the earring is in a particular ear, it's a secret sign that you're gay?*"

He shrugged. "Well, we have a fifty-fifty chance. More to the point, do you want it done?"

"Does it hurt?"

"Probably."

"And . . . you want one?"

He smiled, put his tea down again, and cuddled up to me. "It's a sort of . . . little sign, right? I would never have done this before meeting you," he said. "That's the weird thing. Never in a million years. I've always tried too hard to hide all those parts of me that people hate so much. Now . . . it's not just that I don't care. It's . . . almost as if I *want* them to see, I think. And I don't understand it, because that sounds so . . . *reckless*. Such a reckless thing to do because we know where that could lead. And still . . . for the first time, with you . . . it's . . ." He hesitated, working it out, I think. "Fuck," he said, "I think it's *pride*."

I laughed.

---

* I swear I spent as much time worrying about this in my youth as I did about quicksand and the Bermuda Triangle. Turns out none of them are really an issue. (But the gay ear thing was definitely a thing.) And it's the right ear. I think . . .

"I'm proud to be with you. Proud of . . . us. What have you done to me, Jamie Hampton?"

I laughed again. "I know what you mean. I think I feel it too. Something like I want to show you off. Be seen with you."

"And we know we can't do that—"

"So little things, like the watch, the message on the radar dish—"

"The earring?"

"It's a way of showing that. A little show of pride," I said.

He nodded. "It is." He released a breath. "I never thought . . . I would *ever* feel that." His eyes met mine. "That's you. You've done that."

"And so have you," I said. I found his hand and squeezed. "Let's get the earrings."

Chapter 39

Beth and Dan had not been hard to convince—although I think it was part unwavering loyalty, and part genuine curiosity about what Rob's house was like. We were going to be spending the evening with real movers and shakers—some of whom we would probably recognize off the news on TV, but, amusingly, that wasn't the top of our conversation topics as we walked over to Rob's on Saturday evening.

"Never thought I'd see the day when you got your ear pierced!" Beth said.

"I mean, I love it," Dan added.

"Oh, I definitely love it," Beth agreed.

Dan studied my ear. "It's . . . kinda sexy."

"Is it now?" Beth said, narrowing her eyes at him.

"Bit naughty, isn't it?" Dan said. "Suits you though." He caught my eye and smiled, and yeah, OK, my stomach did flip a little bit, but let's gloss over that.

We were all suited and booted. Me and Dan in suits (his dark gray, mine dark blue) with shirts and ties; Beth in a black dress with a shawl thing around her shoulders, carrying a small clutch. We'd got some stares as we walked down the road that evening—I guess we looked pretty dapper.

"Remember, we're all friends," I said, as we crunched up the gravel driveway,

"Which is what we are," Beth replied. "I mean, OK, we don't really know Rob, but don't you worry—I can pretend."

"I got a D in drama class," Dan added.

"Is that supposed to fill me with confidence?" I said.

We were ushered in by a hard-faced woman who turned out to be the legendary Margaret, "Sir Jeremy's secretary." She was in her fifties or sixties, gray permed hair, pleated tweed skirt and dusky-pink blouse, dripping in disapproval. She glanced us up and down with an air of disdain, told us "the alcohol is off-limits," and then took us through to the garden at the back where Rob was holding court in front of a small group of middle-aged men and women. He was in a tux with a bow tie, nicely tailored, not rented from Moss Bros like mine, and he looked stunning. His face sparkled and shone as he regaled the little crowd with some story—confident and assured, but with just the right amount of deference to his elders, he had the perfect son routine down to a T, with only that little glistening jewel in his right ear hinting at anything else.

We edged over, not wanting to interrupt, or really knowing how to, but he saw us, and smoothly brought us into the group. "These are some of my school pals," he told everyone. "Beth, Jamie, and Daniel."

My name in the middle—a deliberate attempt to hide it. I admired his cunning.

Then it was all nods and "hellos!" and excruciating small talk about what subjects we were studying, and what we planned to do in college, before Rob commented, "Oh, that's a really nice watch, Jamie!" with a look of total innocence on his face, and I saw the way the evening was going to go.

Once the adults had gone, Rob made sure our glasses of orange juice were all amply topped up with the vodka he'd hidden in the garden. It was there I met Sir Jeremy for the first time. He was an intimidating man: broad shoulders, tall, gray hair, with a face that was impossible to read.

"Dad? These are my friends," Rob said. "Dan, Beth, and this is Jamie."

Sir Jeremy cast his eyes over us, and I could see his mind working, before he settled on me as the person of most interest, his eyes drifting to my ear. "You're doing the same play Robert is?" His voice was booming and deep.

"Yeah."

"What is that again?"

"I told you, Dad," Rob chipped in. "It's a devised piece, it's really low-key, exploring elements of British society."

"So, you'll take them out, once you've performed it?"

"Yes!" Rob said, exasperated.

"Good. Because you look like hooligans." He laughed at his own joke—if that's what it was. "Nice to meet you all."

His eyes stayed on me for a fraction longer, then he sauntered off, nodding acknowledgments as he moved across the garden, before having a quiet word with Margaret.

I didn't like him.

"So, that was Dad," Rob said. "Hope you're feeling honored."

He subtly squeezed my forearm. "It's OK. If he didn't like you, you'd know about it."

I felt like I *did* know about it, but I tried to brush it off and enjoy the evening—after all, he had nothing on us. There was a string quartet; there were waitresses circulating with canapés and bottles of champagne; there were a lot of very fancy people talking very loudly and very importantly, with occasional ripples of shrill or hearty laughter; and in the midst of all this fakery (and, honestly, I don't want you to think I'd turned into Holden Caulfield at this point, but they were all absolute phonies), there we both were, the real deal, they just didn't know it, the confirmation of our love hidden on the underside of my wristwatch, and in the glances and occasional "accidental" brushes of our hands.

I had to admit, it *was* exciting. I could see why Rob wanted to do this. It was a quiet "fuck you" to the establishment, to Sir Jeremy, a way of saying, *you can make all the horrible laws you like, but you're not going to stop us.*

It was also unexpectedly sexy. Because when you're not allowed to do something, you want to do it even more, right? As the night wore on, and my drink was topped up, I started getting closer to him, touching shoulders, feeling his warmth, my stomach fizzing, chest aching for him. Standing talking to some old guy I couldn't even remember the name of, our backs against the wall, his hand drifted on to my bottom, just for a moment, sending exquisite shivers up my spine and down through my legs. This was dangerous territory . . . and I was loving every second.

Old Guy wandered off in search of a cigar. Rob surveyed the room, giving his best "wholesome boy" smile. "Do you want to go upstairs?" he quietly said, without looking at me, lips barely moving.

I kept my eyes straight ahead too. "We agreed nothing in front of your dad."

"Upstairs isn't in front of my dad. Look at them, they're all drunk. No one's gonna come up there."

I stared forward. I really wanted to.

"I don't think you have any idea how hard I am right now," he muttered. "Hi, Margaret!"

And there was Margaret, all of a sudden in front of us. She'd been keeping her beady eyes on us all night, giving the distinct impression she thought we might nick the family silver. "Hello, Robert," she said, in a tone that barely disguised her disdain for him. Margaret, it occurred to me, was someone who saw right through Rob, even if no one else did. "It's nearly eleven, so I think now would be a good time for your friends to head home and give the adults some space."

"Of course!" he chirped. God, he did the obsequious obedient son well. "I'm not sure where Beth and Dan are, so I'll go and find them and send everyone home."

Margaret nodded in approval and Rob headed out of the living room, me following.

"I think they were in the garden a bit ago," I said.

He glanced over his shoulder as we entered the deserted hallway, then grabbed me by the elbow and guided me toward the stairs.

"Where are we going?" I asked.

"We're looking for Beth and Dan. They might be up here."

Our eyes met, decision made, and we both hurtled up the

stairs, two at a time, darting around the corner at the top, down the landing, tumbling into his bedroom, where he pushed the door shut and leaned up against it, slightly breathless. We didn't need words. Within seconds we were all over each other, lips locked together as we staggered over to his bed, hands unbuttoning pants, tugging up shirts; he flopped back on the bed, me on top of him, our clothes a mess of being half on, half off, but neither of us able to fix that because we were too greedy for each other, couldn't get enough, I—

It happened in a flash.

Suddenly hands were dragging me off him.

I was thrown to the floor.

"Fuck!' Rob shouted.

"Get off him, you disgusting boy!"

Scrambling to pull my pants up, I saw . . .

Margaret.

"What the hell do you think you're doing?" she snarled.

On the bed, Rob was also scrambling to cover himself up, eyes wide and suddenly afraid.

"You filthy, disgusting perverts!" Margaret hissed. "Your father is downstairs, and you're doing *this?*"

"We weren't doing anything!" Rob pleaded.

Margaret gave a little laugh, so filled with hate and contempt it chilled me. "There are people here tonight who hold the power to make or break your father's career and everything he has ever worked for. And you . . . you *perverts* choose to come up here? And if I hadn't suspected what was going on and stopped you, would you have broken the law? The son of a cabinet minister, arrested for underage sex *with another boy?* How do you suppose that would play in the papers? With the public? *Idiot.* You should know better, at your age. You make me sick. You make everyone sick. What would your poor mother think?"

I saw how those last words wounded him. I saw how they cut him open like a knife. "Why bring her into this?" I snapped back, my voice sounding nowhere near as powerful as I wanted it to, but weak and lacking conviction.

"Shut up, get out, and never come back here," she told me.

I stared at her, shaking—rage at her unshakable righteousness or fear at the knowledge she now possessed, I wasn't sure.

She bent down toward me, her lip curling, voice mocking. "You're a silly little boy who needs to grow up and stop playing 'I'll show you mine if you show me yours' with other silly little boys. It's sickening how you're throwing away your life like this, but that's your choice. You just leave Rob out of it."

"It's not a choice," I croaked, throat thick and dry. "I didn't choose."

"Oh, you always have a choice, young man. And you chose to be weak and give in to sin. No father figure to keep you on the straight and narrow, I assume." She glanced at me like I was shit. "Now, for the final time, I want you and your diseased mind out of this house."

She spat on me. Really.

Open-mouthed, I glanced up at Rob, hoping for strength, but finding him broken, hugging his legs to his chin, staring down at his duvet. "Just go, Jamie," he muttered.

I wanted to speak, because *no*, not like this, they couldn't win, we had something beautiful and real and—

"Just go," he said again.

Chapter 40

I ran that night.

I ran from Margaret, from the hate, from the pain of seeing Rob so defeated like that, from Dan and Beth who I just couldn't face, and from myself—from the shame and the humiliation and my dirty, perverted mind.

Except . . . it wasn't my mind, was it? I didn't think that about myself, or about Rob. It was just Margaret. And the air of confidence she had because so many people agreed with her. It reignited my anger. And that's why, when Beth called on Sunday, she didn't need to talk me into it. I had fighting spirit. I was going to face whatever waited for me at school. I just hoped to hell I would be facing it with Rob, because the only thing that really scared me was what had happened to him. Had Margaret told his dad everything? Was he about to be shipped off and "cured"?

I probably shouldn't have told Beth that everything was fine. It *felt* fine, but in reality I had a target on my head, of course. Anger can give you a false sense of security.

If the symbolism of the weather in *Wuthering Heights* had taught me anything, it was that storms are bad news. The rain bucketed down on Monday, the skies dark and churning, rumbles of thunder in the distance. The bad weather meant everyone was cooped up inside all day. Students gathered in every corner of the school, the air humid, damp, stinking—BO and testosterone, a matchbox atmosphere; just one spark was all it would take. The tension was building, too much energy, nowhere for it all to go.

They found me at the start of lunch.

Like a preplanned sting operation, I realized too late that Jason was in front of me and Scott behind, and I was trapped. Panicked, I tried to swerve to avoid Jason, but he anticipated the move and barred my way.

"Not avoiding us, are you, Jamie?" he said, his smile dangerous and cold. "You've been gone so long—we've missed you."

I froze, staring at him, straight into the abyss.

Scott was behind me. His arm suddenly crooked around my neck, breathing hard. "Are you the top or the bottom, then?" he hissed. He pressed himself into me so I could feel his cock. "The bottom, I bet. 'Course you are. Oh, are you shaking? Don't worry, Jamie—I'll be so gentle."

"I like your earring," Jason said.

"Hmm, yeah, it's *nice*," Scott added.

"Makes you look more queer—is that why you got it?"

"So hot, Jamie!"

Jason reached out, fondling my earlobe, fingers dancing over the stud, while Scott held me tight, his arm still around my neck, stopping me from moving, and gripping just enough that breathing was difficult.

"Don't cry, Jamie," Jason said. "This won't hurt a bit."

I made eye contact with him—I knew what was coming—begging him not to. *"Please."*

Scott laughed. "I think he's pleading, Jase. I think he . . . wants it."

"Do you want it, Jamie?"

"Give the little queer what he fucking wants!"

"Do you want it, queer?"

"Do you, queer?"

"Queer fucking gay faggot!"

When positive and negative charges meet, you get lightning. And in a sharp flash, white-hot pain splintered through me as Jason ripped the stud out of my ear, before landing a heavy punch straight in my stomach. I doubled over, winded, choked, as blood cascaded down my neck, the guys laughing, kicking me to the floor of the hallway. I couldn't breathe, couldn't suck in any air, like my lungs just wouldn't work, and the panic of that was worse than the searing pain right then because in spite of everything I did not want to die. I wanted to live because I wanted to see Rob, and I wanted to love him. I just wanted to love him, so why did everyone have to hate that so much?

The world blurred as Scott swung his leg back and delivered a hard kick to my stomach, and I think they would have finished me off were it not for Mr. Haskins, the PE teacher, who happened to be walking by, because I heard him say, "Gentlemen! That's enough!" and voices, and talking, and I don't know what happened to Jason and Scott, but then Mr. Haskins was in front of me.

"All right," he said. "Go and see the nurse and get cleaned up."

"It was Jason and Scott," I gasped.

"Don't be a snitch, Jamie. It's pathetic."

For a moment, I forgot the pain, and the blood, because *did I hear him correctly?*

"Well, you don't help yourself, do you?" he told me.

I blinked through the tears at his cold face, also full of hate.

"Stop crying and man up," he said. "It's just a bit of blood, and if you wear women's jewelry, what do you expect?"

I stared at him. I just wanted some help.

"Are you seventeen or seven?" He shook his head and walked off.

A small crowd of students had formed around me—staring, whispering, like I was a museum curiosity. I hauled myself upright, everyone watching, and staggered down the hallway, head spinning, ears ringing, legs like jelly, guiding myself along the wall with my hands.

Minutes later, I was sitting outside the office, overhearing one of the reception staff hiss, "I'm not going anywhere near him—all that blood? What if he's got AIDS?"

I couldn't stop the tears. I was in so much pain. I just wanted someone to help me. I was shaking, scared, lonely, afraid, hurt and there was no one to turn to, not an adult, not a friend, because I was scum, I was dirty, and I deserved it. So, broken and wrecked, I got up again and used my last bit of strength to hobble to the only place left for me, the only place at school where I would ever truly be welcome.

The library.

Chapter 41

"Jamie! Oh, Jesus!"

I was a mess of tears and blood and snot and pain and hatred and hurt and self-loathing, but Mrs. C guided me into the back office and sat me down, immediately grabbing a small first-aid box from on top of the file cabinet and setting to work cleaning me up.

Beth hurried in moments later, Dan following. The word around school wasn't horror at what had happened to me—it was pleasure. I'd deserved it. It was my fault. I had it coming. Vigilante justice: delivered! Beth had already screamed at multiple people relishing the story, and had already been told she ought to stop "supporting a pedo." I'd unleashed so much hate, and they didn't just want to destroy me, they wanted to destroy anyone sticking up for me too.

"Where's Rob?" I managed to babble. "Have you seen Rob?"

Beth shook her head. "I'm not even sure he's in today."

I hoped that was true. I hoped he was safe. I wanted him here, but I'd rather he was at home, out of harm's way.

Beth held my hand while Mrs. C finished cleaning me up,

Dan with his head in his hands on the chair next to me. I understood. The situation did feel hopeless.

"It's torn, isn't it?" I said, about my ear, after she'd finished.

"Yes."

I sighed. "I liked it. Rob suggested it."

"It can be repaired. I snagged one of mine once—they were able to sort it out; it's an outpatient procedure."

"Maybe it's better out. Just makes life more difficult—lets people know, doesn't it? Brought it on myself."

"Shut up, Jamie," Beth said. "I don't mean to be rude but shut up. You have the right to wear what you like, be who you like, and love who you like. And none of those things are anyone's business but yours. And if other people don't like that, that's their problem."

"Yeah," I said. "And they'll take it out on me anyway. 'Cause they've been told they can. 'Cause they've been told I'm wrong."

Dan got up and paced over to the window, then back again. "This is so messed up.*"

Mrs. C sighed. "You're staying here until the end of school. If the other staff won't protect you, then I sure as hell will." She looked at Beth and Dan. "You can go to your classes; I'll look after him."

Mrs. C made me some tea, which I sipped as she worked out the end-of-lunch library rush, sent away assorted hangers-on and stragglers, and eventually closed the main doors and returned, making herself a cup of tea before sitting down opposite me again.

---

* I didn't realize, until years later when I bumped into him in a bar in Soho, what effect this had on Dan. Turned out he was bi and every bit as scared as me. Turned out, as well as the book itself, he'd also read the messages between me and Rob, and thought them sweet. He said they'd helped him come to terms with who he was. Funny how queer kids manage to find each other, isn't it?

She was wearing the most amazing animal-print top—zebra, possibly—and it made me smile, because it felt like a tiny ray of fabulous sunshine, on an otherwise bleak day.

"You heard about them going through the entire collection?" she said.

I nodded.

"I came this close to resigning."

"Please say you didn't. I don't think my day can get any worse."

"I didn't. But how can I do my job when I'm having to defend the books against bullies and bigots who are convinced their narrow view of the world is the only view that's right?" A devious smile played on her lips. "But we don't surrender to people like that."

She got up and pulled a stack of books out of her bag, handing them to me as I quickly put my cup down. I recognized the one on top—*A Boy's Own Story*. My eyes widened as I riffled through the others. Gay books. Lesbian books. I'd never seen so many.

"Where did you get these?!"

"My younger brother lives in London. He came down last weekend, so I asked him to bring them. There's a bookstore there called Gay's the Word—*"

I laughed. "They actually called the shop that? Don't they get bricks through the window?"

"I think, sometimes, yes," Mrs. C said. "Anyway, that's just the tip of the iceberg. I've got another stack hidden in the file cabinet. So how would you like to spend the next period taking out the

---

* And you should go and visit Jim, Uli, Erica, and the team.

title and imprint pages, and putting fake covers on them all, and we'll sneak them onto the shelves?"

I managed a small smile.

"There's the Jamie we know and love," she said.

"Won't you get in trouble?"

She shrugged. "Probably. Eventually, yes. Oh, it'll be *scandalous!* They'll want my head on a spike, but staying silent and obeying lets them win. And why should they? They're wrong. And I sure as hell don't want to live in a world where they're considered *right.*"

We spent the rest of the afternoon cutting and pasting. We removed the covers from various heterosexual romances, stories of straight people, and some Religious Education titles, and placed them on the gay books. Mrs. C said that would make them harder to find—they would literally have to read all the books to work out which ones were banned.

And it felt good. Would we get away with it? It almost didn't matter. Mrs. C had more to put out if any got discovered and removed, and she intended to carry on until the day they finally fired her. I admired her so much for that. She was prepared to put her entire livelihood on the line for something she believed in. She was brave. And she made me feel braver too.

I hung back after the last bell, hoping that Trouble would get bored and have wandered off home by the time I emerged. But, of course, Beth and Dan came back to the library for me—no way were they going to let me walk home alone. My own little army. They refused to back down, and I was grateful to them for that. Meanwhile, my heart was still full of fight, but my head was still full of worry: Where the hell was Rob?

Cut to: my question answered, as we slipped out the back exit of the humanities hall and walked along the path. We found him propped up against a wall by the temporary biology classrooms, nose bloodied, shirt torn, a swollen eye, cut lip . . . head drooped, like he was barely conscious. He managed to look up as I ran to him, and despite everything, he smiled.

"They got you too, huh?" he said.

"Fuck, let me help you."

"I'm OK."

"You're not!"

I scrambled in my bag for tissues and started cleaning him up, Beth helping me.

"I'll get help!" Dan said.

"Don't," Rob replied. "I'm fine."

He took my hand and guided it away from his face. "Don't. If they see you, it'll make it worse." He glanced at me. "Your ear?"

"They ripped it out," I said.

He closed his eyes and nodded.

"You're in pain," I said. "Where does it hurt?"

"Honestly? Everywhere. But I'll live."

"Sir!" Dan shouted across the field, seeing Mr. Haskins walking by with a bunch of soccer players, on their way to practice on the field. "Rob's hurt."

"Horseplay!" Haskins shouted back, smiling at us. "Boys will be boys. You're OK. Aren't you, Rob?"

Rob groaned, closing his eyes again.

"He's hurt, sir!" Beth added. "They did this because they think he's gay."

Haskins held his hands up. "Can't get involved with that! Not allowed to discuss being queer—it's against the law. I could lose my job." He gave her a shrug.

The soccer players were smirking, sharing digs in hushed tones, but deliberately loud enough for us to hear.

"Bunch of fucking pricks!" Beth told them.

I swear to god, Haskins turned to Scott and muttered, "Must be that time of the month!" and Scott laughed, and it was all the boys together, all the guys, all so funny, and we were just nothing to them.

Among them was Adam Henson. That stung the most. I'd always known he was one of the popular guys, but to see him part of that crowd, and not say anything? His silence spoke volumes. He looked me in the eyes . . . then he turned away. I thought he was one of the better ones. Maybe he wasn't.*

Beth froze, staring toward them as they laughed and joked and started jogging onto the field. I think, maybe, she realized what we were facing at that moment. How this hatred was so deeply ingrained, it had permeated everything, over years and years and years, and changing hearts and minds was not going to happen easily, if ever. They could get away with it. No one was going to stop them.

Well, let them hate. They could hate all they wanted. They couldn't stop me *loving*. I shuffled round and sat next to Rob on the

---

* Twenty years later, he apologized to me on Facebook Messenger. I told him it was OK. But it's not OK. I'm still a people pleaser even now, and I wish I wasn't. If you don't call it out, nothing changes. But then again, maybe he was just as scared as the rest of us, maybe he was a product of the time and the place, and maybe I should cut him some slack for that? No easy answers, no neat endings. In real life, bad people don't always get their comeuppance, and bad people are shades of gray anyway.

ground, squeezing his hand as a tear slowly rolled down his cheek. "I love you so much, Jamie," he muttered. "I only want to be with you, it's not asking much."

Tears sprang from my eyes too, and screw people seeing, I wrapped my arms around him, and that was it, the floodgates opened, and we both sobbed into each other's shoulders, until it was too painful for him, and he flinched from me, gasping and clutching his ribs.

When I looked up, Beth and Dan were crying too. They sat down opposite us, on the wet ground, the outcasts, but at least we had one another.

"So, Margaret struck a deal with me," Rob said hoarsely. "Said she wouldn't tell my dad, but I had to promise I'd cut all ties with you, never see you again, no illicit meetings, nothing at school. Said it would break his heart, as well as derail his career, and that I needed to stop being so selfish and appreciate everything he was trying to do, holding things together, since Mom died. She said . . ." He took an unsteady breath. "She said otherwise I'd be sent to that school in Scotland, and she didn't want that, and was sure I didn't, and so all I had to do was behave myself and it'd be fine."

I leaned back against the wall and tried not to start crying again.

"Don't worry, Jay. Screw that, huh?"

"You can't. You can't risk it. You can't be sent somewhere like that."

He sniffed. "I've no intention of being sent anywhere. I told you, I'd run away before that happened. And they can say what they like, they can beat me, and they can hurt me, but I am never going to stop being me and loving you and wanting to be with you, and nothing will ever stop that, so what can they do?" His voice was shaking. "What can they do, Jay? Is this all they've got? Because we're both still here! And still together."

The tears came again, rolling down my face, and streaming down his. Anger, pain, fear, injustice—all of that. And yet, buried somewhere deep, he was right, there was love, and it felt like that was somehow safe. That it was ours. And the tears were tears of love too, because I loved him so, so much.

He turned back to me. "I should get home—"

"I'll walk with you."

"You won't. They might be waiting for me just up the road. Just go home, Jay."

"*I'll* walk with you," Dan told him.

"And I'll walk with you," Beth told me. "We'll get you both home safely, and I think it might be an idea to call in sick for a few days—'til it all dies down."

"Well, fuck them. They don't get to win," Rob said. "Friday night. We said we'd go to that gay club in Lincoln—well, let's do it."

"Like this? We look like hell."

"Yes, like this."

"OK," I said, laughing despite everything. "How do we get there?"

"I'm gonna book a taxi—there and back. I'll come and pick you up around eight."

I nodded. "'Kay."

He hauled himself upright, wincing and trying to smile through the pain of his swollen eye and bloody nose. "'Til then, yeah?"

"Yeah," I said. "'Til then."

Chapter 42

Those of you familiar with story structure might be thinking that was the "All Is Lost" moment—where our hero (me, Jamie Hampton) experiences his "dark night of the soul" and everything seems hopeless, before he somehow works out what is needed to succeed, pushing us neatly into Act Three, and our finale, where our hero (me, Jamie Hampton) proves he has learned the story's theme and devises a plan, leading to the happy ending.

Well, *no*.

I'm sorry.

It gets worse. Because real life does, quite often, doesn't it? I'm convinced one reason why folks are so unhappy these days is because we've all been raised on a diet of perfect story structure in novels, TV shows, and films. Things become terrible, and then they're resolved, maybe with an unexpected twist or two in that final act, but ultimately they win through.

Reality: Things become terrible, then they become horrendous, then some other random shit you weren't expecting gets hurled at you. Life is often one bad thing after another, with no letup.

So buckle up for that.*

I spun Mom a web of lies. Yes, I'd been beaten up, I didn't know why. I knew I wouldn't be able to keep my sexuality from her forever, and nor did I want to, but I also didn't want the moment I told her to be when her son had been beaten black-and-blue. I didn't want to come out and it all be about trauma and sadness and hurt. In my head, in my beautiful fantasy world, it was a happy thing, it was positive, and it was about Rob, and love, and sharing something special, like when a boy tells his mom he'd like to bring a girl over for dinner and it's sweet, and a rite of passage, and nobody has a black eye or is crying.

Mom wasn't having it. She wanted to call the school, make complaints. That's when Keith stepped in and said he'd do it. Claimed they'd sit up and listen if a man made the call.† Said Prenton didn't intimidate him, and he'd give her a piece of his mind. That placated Mom, and Keith said he'd phone the next day. I don't think he ever did, although he told Mom he had. But there was no point anyway. Nobody at school was going to do a thing about it, and they had all the justification they needed for that.

Beth visited every day and kept me up to speed with schoolwork—and the fact that Rob was off school as well. That made me relax until I became paranoid that maybe the reason wasn't that he was staying at home and was safe, but had actually already been shipped off to the religious bigots' school in Scotland.

---

* Oh, but I do like story structure; I'd recommend *Save the Cat*, if you're interested. It may not mimic real life, but it makes for a satisfying narrative.
† The one and only time I let his misogyny go unchecked. Sorry.

I had no way of knowing, so I spent my days in my room, reading *A Boy's Own Story*, doing a bit of schoolwork, listening to music, and always, always keeping the watch on my wrist, keeping him close, *always*.

Mom was out with Keith on Friday night, so I roped Beth in, and told Mom I was going over to her house, it'd be a late night, and not to worry. I think she was pleased I was getting out of the house and having a bit of fun. My ribs were horribly bruised, and my ear still looked a bit of a mess, with some further bruising on my right cheek, but I showered, and I changed into what was now my favorite red-checked shirt, with a white T-shirt underneath, unbuttoned and untucked, with blue jeans and boots, and I felt a little more human and a tiny bit happier. I still had no idea if Rob would show up, but just after eight, a taxi honked its horn from the top of the drive, and I sprinted out and jumped in.

Fuck, it was so good to see him.

Seeing him in the back seat, black jeans, white T-shirt and black leather jacket, I almost threw myself at him and was ready to dry hump him there and then, before he must have detected my instant horniness and coughed to remind me about the taxi driver.

"All right, dude?" he said, doing an excellent impression of a straight boy.

"All right?" I mumbled back.

He had a massive black eye, and his lip still looked a bit swollen, but honestly, he somehow managed to pull the look off. "How's the eye?" I said.

He shrugged. "Sore. Nice shirt." He winked at me.

"Thanks," I said. "Girlfriend got it for me."

"You still seeing her?"

"'Til someone better comes along."

Rob laughed. "Not much choice around here, huh?"

"Not many fish in the sea!" I replied.

The taxi driver chuckled. "You boys off for a night on the town, then?"

"Something like that," Rob replied.

"Whereabouts in Lincoln shall I drop you? Are you going to Route 66?"

For a moment, I tensed. Route 66 was a straight club, and we weren't going there. But, of course, Rob had it all under control. "Can you drop us round by the train station? We're meeting some other friends there."

"No bother."

We didn't talk much on the journey—I sensed we both desperately wanted to, but we couldn't give anything away to the driver, and pretty much any real conversation would have done that. The driver had Atlantic 252 on the radio, so that was fine, and we listened to such classics as "Sowing the Seeds of Love" by Tears for Fears, while I worked myself up about being obviously underage and not getting past the bouncers of this club Rob knew about.

Cut to: Rob leading me down this grubby back alley and pointing up ahead to something that just looks like a sketchy door in a wall. "I think that's it."

"Really?" I said. It looked like the sort of place people went to get murdered.

Rob shrugged. "Let's just do a walk past."

So, we did. We did a "walk past," which revealed it wasn't just a door in a wall, but there were some windows too, albeit blacked out, and the definite thud of bass came from inside. What there wasn't, was any obvious way in—unless we were supposed to knock on the door.

However, as we walked back from the other end of the alley, the door opened, and a glamorous drag queen stepped out with a clipboard. Dressed head-to-toe in a rainbow-sequined dress, with beehive hair, massive heels, and elaborate makeup, she was entirely out of place in that grimy backstreet. She looked up, caught sight of us staring at her like the pair of wide-eyed kids we were, and rolled her eyes.

"It's eighteen and over only, chicks," she said. "No exceptions."

"We are eighteen!" Rob said, way too enthusiastically, and way too high-pitched to be convincing. He pulled out his wallet. "I have ID."

He got a card out and handed it to the drag queen, while I panicked that I didn't have such a thing, and was I expected to? Had Rob told me to get a fake ID? Had we discussed this? Or was this just one of the things I should have known?

The drag queen lazily glanced at the card, an unimpressed look on her face. "Bless your cottons, you've gone to the effort of making some forged identification—I'm honored!"

"Please," Rob said.

The drag queen studied him. "What happened to your face?"

"Got beat up," Rob said. He looked down at the ground. "You know how it is."

She turned to me. "Is he your boyfriend, dearie?"

I nodded, too terrified to speak.

"You got a name?"

"Jamie Hampton," I replied.

"And you're eighteen too, are ya?"

"Practic—"

The drag queen put her hand up to silence me. "Let's try that again. *Are you eighteen too?*"

I nodded. "Yep."

She looked me up and down. I couldn't tell what she was thinking, and half expected a quick smack around the ear, but she glanced down the narrow backstreet, then swiftly pulled us both inside, shouting, "Watch out, gentlemen, the jailbait's here!" before turning back to us and adding, "Have a good night, boys. Derek can get a bit frisky with you younger ones. Any trouble, let me know."

Inside was probably quite small, but it was dark, and there were moving disco lights, the music was pumped up, the place was hot and sticky—rammed with guys of all ages—so it actually felt *vast*. The moment we were inside, Rob took my hand, kissed me on the lips, and led me over to the bar area, where we both got vodka and Cokes in flimsy plastic cups. The night was called "Fromage," which meant the music was cheesy classics from the 70s, 80s, and from now—great to dance to, basically.

Two drinks later, we were in the thick of the hot bodies, jumping about to Yazz, Cyndi Lauper, Katrina and the Waves, Roxette, Culture Club and joining in with everyone else as we hilariously tried to sing the high note in "Take on Me."

When Wham! started singing "I'm Your Man," Rob pointed to himself on the "I," to me on the "your," and then he kissed me on "man," but before we could get too sentimental, Kim Wilde starting singing about "Kids in America," and that was such a tune, we just went with it, lost in the smoky haze that filled the air and the kaleidoscopic lights that glinted across our ecstatic faces—happy, not from alcohol, and not from drugs, but from the joy of somewhere where we finally felt free. I didn't have to look over my shoulder here. I didn't have to worry. Nobody cared that I was a boy who liked other boys, because this place was full of people who felt exactly the same. I could touch Rob and kiss Rob, and he could touch me and kiss me (and my god, we did!), and nobody even cared—they just let us be.

That place, that grim, sticky-floored, backstreet place that watered down the vodka and turned a blind eye to what was going on in the bathrooms, was a sanctuary.

I wished I'd found it a little sooner.

I had no idea what time it was. Tune after tune, hit after hit, and just when you thought you might sit one out, it was "Come on Eileen," so you had to dance to it. Every so often, they'd play one of those songs that somehow just felt like a *moment* in time, and during the whole of "Always on My Mind" by the Pet Shop Boys, Rob and I were standing in the middle of the dance floor, locked together, kissing and kissing and kissing like our lives depended on it, and when the DJ followed it up with "Together in Electric Dreams," we worked our way over to a spot by one of the walls, my back up against it, him pressing into me, mouthing along to the chorus, before kissing me again, stroking my cheek with his fingers and whispering in my ear.

I met his eyes and smiled.

And I whispered my reply.

We stumbled into the cool night air around one in the morning—dripping in sweat, our hair wet with it, ears ringing, brains buzzing. Drunk, loved-up, completely filled with joy.

Rob had arranged for the taxi to pick us up around the corner, just to be on the safe side.

I never heard the clicks of the camera.

And I never saw the photographer.

Chapter 43

Funny how you kind of know sometimes.

I'd just woken up the following Sunday morning, still on a high from Friday night, still happy because I'd seen a world where people like me could belong and not be scared, and for the first time, it felt like things might work out, that I'd get to be happy, or at least get a shot at it.

The summer sun was already streaming through my curtains, but the gentle breeze coming in through my open window was still morning-cool. For a brief, precious moment, I thought to myself, *I really am happy.*

And I believe I was.

As soon as the doorbell rang, my stomach knotted.

Sunday morning. It was unusual. Like the phone ringing after ten at night—it automatically felt like bad news.

And then hammering on the door too.

I listened as Mom opened it, heard brief voices and then thudding up the stairs, a quick knock on my door, and Beth burst in, flushed, breathless, in black leggings and a baggy black sweater that looked like she'd just thrown it on.

"You're fucked," she said, waving a tabloid newspaper at me.

She threw the paper over to me and sat on the edge of the bed. "Page five—at least it's not front page."

I flipped the pages and froze at the headline:

MP's Underage Son in Sleazy Gay Club Shame

The article, accompanied with a number of covert pictures of me and Rob emerging from the club, was an absolute barrage of bullshit, claiming Rob was not only a violent alcoholic but also was taking drugs, that the club was some kind of filthy sex den, and questioning if Sir Jeremy West MP could really be relied upon to uphold family values and "basic standards of decency" if his own son was behaving like a "delinquent degenerate" at such a young age.

I just stared at it, shocked that they would report this, shocked that it was all lies, shocked at how they were describing Rob. And then . . . the realization . . . what this meant for him. For me. Because now it was out there, in black-and-white, complete with photographic evidence, us, coming out of a gay club, the bullies were right, everyone was right, and now . . .

What now?

What was Rob going through right now?

What would his dad be doing to him?

"Jamie?" Beth said softly.

I sprang out of bed, haphazardly pulling on jeans and a T-shirt. "I have to find Rob."

Just like I had instinctively sensed trouble, I also knew where Rob would be. My heart melted when I actually saw him though, sitting in front of his mom's grave, looking completely broken. He looked so small, so vulnerable in baggy jeans and an old hoodie . . . for the first time, this boy who I'd looked to for strength, who made me braver, looked beaten and weak and . . . I . . . was . . . scared.

I walked over.

He didn't look up.

Sat down next to him.

He didn't speak.

Nor did I.

What was there to say?

We were fucked.

We both knew it.

Words would not make this better.

Eventually . . .

"Dad got briefed about the article late last night. His press officer is issuing a denial. The story will be that I wasn't aware it was a gay club, but that after Mom's death I went off the rails, and I do have a drinking problem. Dad's doing the right thing and is sending me to rehab. I think you know the place—it's up in Scotland. I'll be seeing out the semester at school, and then I won't be going back. He hopes everyone understands that all families go through difficult times, but he hopes the public can see how he's trying to do the right thing by me. As proof that I'm not gay, I'm taking a girl to the prom. There will be photos. It's the start of my rehabilitation. Her name is Katie, and she's a friend of someone Margaret knows—goes to some all-girls public school in Surrey— I've never even met her." He took an unsteady breath. "He took Casper. He's given him away. He says I'm too selfish to own a dog, and if I can't care for him properly, he'll be better off elsewhere."

His bottom lip was wobbling as he tried to hold it together. "I'm sorry, Mom," he croaked. "I'm so sorry." He still didn't look at me. "And you, Jamie, *us*, that's no more. Officially, it never was, but now . . . there's nothing I can do, I can't . . ."

"Rob—"

"I've nothing left, Jamie. I've . . ."

"Rob, no, there has to be—"

"Know what? Write your stories. Write a world where you and me can be together and everyone lets us, and it's good and happy, because that's all there is now. *Fiction*. You'll be OK, Jamie. You will. You're an amazing person; you'll do great things; the stars will always shine on you, I know it. And you'll find someone else."

I reached for his hand, but he snatched it away. "You're only making this harder. Please go." Tears were rolling down his cheeks now. "Please go, Jamie. I love you, I fucking love you, I will always fucking love you, and I need you to please go because I'm not allowed to do that, so we just need . . . to forget about each other now."

Silence.

His words . . .

Echoing around my head.

"Go," he said. "There might be other paparazzi sniffing around—it's only a matter of time before they find me. And when they do, they can't find me with you."

"Yeah," I said, getting up. "I understand."

I took a few steps away.

"I love you," I muttered. "For always."

He didn't reply.

309

I went straight up the stairs when I got home. I needed to think. Everyone else would have to wait.

I stared up at my poster of Electra.

It hadn't escaped my attention: When I was with Rob, Electra was around less. I also didn't live in my fantasy worlds so much either. Real was everything I needed.

"He saved you, Jamie, you know he did," Electra said. "And now you need to save him."

I nodded because I already knew it was true.

It was my turn now.

But how could I do that? How, when I was so powerless and alone?

Electra's eyes drifted to my schoolbag and the stack of books rammed inside that Mrs. C had given me. One caught my eye—the book on queer history. I grabbed it and started flicking through, and inside . . . a treasure trove . . . a whole history . . . the Compton's Café riots in 1966 in San Francisco; customers in drag at Berlin's Eldorado nightclub in 1929; Maureen Duffy—the first woman in public life to come out as a lesbian; Armistead Maupin; the Stonewall riots, when the Stonewall Inn, a gay bar in New York, was raided by police yet again, and this time, everyone stood up to them, with drag queens kicking police and the whole community fighting back against the brutality and injustice; The Gay Liberation Front; the first Gay Pride march in 1970; Harvey Milk; Peter Tatchell; AIDS; Section 28; and the struggles of groups all over the world, like the activists in Italy, fighting to make progress against the Roman Catholic Church. Here were stories of loss and pain and hardship and difficulty, of being hated and despised, and yet they were also all stories of strength and power and fighting spirit and, ultimately, love. It wasn't just me. There were loads of us. Thousands of us. Hundreds of thousands. Yes, I'd been looking for just one boy like me. But actually, there were people, so many people, *like us*.

The fights were different, but had so many similarities, and at their heart, one thing I knew to be true: They were all driven by people brave enough to risk it all, stand up, speak the truth, and fight for love.

And that was what I was going to need to do as well.

I had the fire, I just didn't have any weapons.

There was a gentle knock at my door, and Mom came in.

We stared at each other for a few moments. "Are you OK?" she said eventually.

I swallowed and nodded. "Have you seen—?"

"Yes, I've seen."

She hovered by the door.

"Is there anything you want to tell me?" she asked.

Nearly. There almost was. But I bottled it and shook my head.

"These came for you yesterday," she said, handing me a package. It was from BonusPrint*—it must have been the photos I had developed from the roll we took on my birthday.

(You forgot about the film Rob gave me to develop, didn't you? I slipped it in to that scene with us by the radar dishes so casually, you hopefully thought nothing of it. Well . . . surprise!)

---

* So good—you would post your film to them, and they'd send you your photos back, along with a FREE FILM so you could take more.

"Thanks."

Mom nodded, made to leave, but came back again. "Jamie? If . . . I don't know how you're going to work things out, but if . . . Rob needs somewhere to stay . . . I don't know how we'll afford another mouth to feed, but we'll do it, all right?"

I was desperately trying not to lose it, although my wet eyes must've given it away. "Thank you," I rasped.

She nodded, gave me a small smile, and turned to go again.

"Mom?"

"What?"

I opened my mouth, but—

"It's OK, Jamie," she said. "I know, and it's OK." She closed the door behind her.

I tried to steady my breathing. Then I saw Electra glancing at the package from BonusPrint. What the hell? I ripped it open and took out the envelope of photos, smiling as I shuffled through the ones of me and Rob standing by the radar dish that day.

The ones of him caught my eye, standing there, looking out, right into the abyss, as he'd described it . . . and he was smiling.

I will never forget that look. Determined. Hopeful. In the face of so much terror . . . a shrug, a *do your worst*.

I smiled too. Couldn't help it. I loved that boy so much.

Then I looked through a few more.

Different ones now, ones I didn't recognize because they must have come from the beginning of the film, sometime before I was with Rob. Family shots . . .

I stopped.

What was I actually looking at here?

I checked a few more photos.

Fuck. Really?

And I realized, Rob giving me that roll of film to develop wasn't casual and wasn't accidental. It was deliberate. He'd given us an insurance policy and the best weapon I could ever want.

Oh, Rob.

You beauty.

Fuck the system, huh?

Chapter 44

Well, here it is, folks. We've reached the finale. Well, sort of. You already know you're not getting an "end," right? Rob would hate it if I wrote one, and it's not right anyway. Don't be frustrated if you have questions—that's just real life, and real life continues, and isn't wrapped up neatly. And this has been a snapshot of real life. So, thank you for being part of it. I hope you enjoyed it[*], and, at the very least, enjoyed my thoughts on story structure. Keep your fingers crossed for the TV adaptation, huh?

OK.

So, it unfolded like this:

I called Beth and told her what I needed her to do.

And then I sat and worked out what I wanted to say and how I wanted to say it. I knew what I was going to do, I just wanted to make sure that my words were as eloquent and watertight as possible. Of course, I had no idea if Rob was going to play ball with me, but I knew I had to try.

---

[*] "I absolutely hated the way SJG constantly 'spoke' to me during this book. He's so annoying. I hated *Noah Can't Even* too, and don't get me started on Jack from *Heartbreak Boys*. One star." (Inevitable Amazon review)

Cut to: the day of the prom.

I spent the afternoon getting ready—black tuxedo, bow tie, the works. If you're going down in flames, then go down fabulous. I'd decided to take Beth up on her ticket offer and go to that prom. It was my idea. I'd arranged the whole thing. Why shouldn't I have a nice night like everyone else?

At five o'clock, Beth and Dan arrived at my front door—along with Casper. Beth was in the most beautiful ivory dress, not a huge gown, subtle, classy, her hair in ringlets; honestly, she looked stunning. Dan was stunning too, in his tux and bow tie and shiny dress shoes. Casper . . . well, just his regular fur, obviously. "Thank god you found him!" I said.

"Mrs. C found him," Dan corrected. "Her hunch paid off—there's only one animal shelter near here, the same place she got her Cavalier King Charles spaniel from, and it turns out no one wants a scrappy mongrel, so she wasn't too late. Although they still wanted thirty bucks for him." He handed me Casper's leash. "Good luck."

"Thanks. If everything goes according to plan, I'll see you both inside, OK?"

"We're happy to wait," Dan said.

I shook my head. "If I do it, I do it with him. *Together*. But thank you. It means a lot."

Dan nodded. "You look fantastic, by the way."

I smiled. "Thanks. So do both of you. Good enough to eat!"

"Please don't," Beth said.

Dan waggled his eyebrows at me and smirked.

There was one last thing I felt I should do. I went up to my room and I had every intention of taking Electra down from my wall.

315

Talking to her had helped, writing my stories had helped; gradually, I had worked out who I was, what I wanted, and what was important to me. Enough pretending. Real was what I wanted, and things were about to get very real.

But do you know what? As I raised my hand to pull off the first corner, I just couldn't go through with it. I've always been sentimental, but Electra and I had seen some stuff, we'd been through it, and she'd always been there. Electra was a strong, independent woman, and that was something I admired.

So, Electra stayed. I think that confused my mom no end, but she stayed.*

By the time I was walking down the gravel driveway at the home of Sir Jeremy West MP, I'd downed several vodka and Cokes and was feeling invincible. I stopped about five meters from the front door. Casper sat down at my feet. I didn't have to wait long. After a flicker behind some curtains in the right-hand window, Sir Jeremy himself strode out, Margaret not far behind him.

"You're trespassing!" he shouted.

"I've come to take Rob to the prom," I replied.

"How dare you. He's not interested in you. You're disgusting. Get the hell off my property."

"I've come to take Rob to the prom!"

"Are you drunk? You've got thirty seconds before the police are called."

At this point, Rob emerged. He was also in a tuxedo, also in a

---

* And I still have the poster, even now.

black bow tie, and my heart filled with joy when I saw he also had a red handkerchief tucked in his jacket pocket, just like me, just like we'd said we would. In all the hate, he'd still tried, one small piece of love, impossible to extinguish.

"Jamie?" he said, and then, "Casper?"

"Your dad dumped him at the dog shelter," I said. I met his beautiful, hopeful eyes, and I smiled.

Rob made to run forward, but his dad stopped him, before turning his attention back to me. "You're not welcome here!" He spat the words at me. "Take the dog, and yourself, and never come back. Ten seconds."

Next to emerge was some girl in a ridiculous puffy peach prom gown thing—looking every inch like a Disney princess. Presumably this was Katie, Rob's shipped-in date for the prom so everyone could see he wasn't gay. "Who are you?" she said, her voice haughty and entitled.*

"Me?" I said. "Oh, I'm Rob's boyfriend."

I didn't dare look at Rob, I just let the shocked silence hang in the air for a moment. *Enjoyable.*

"Margaret? Call the police," Sir Jeremy said.

"Ah, ah, wait!" I told her. "I think you should hear me out at least, don't you? You see, the problem is, Sir Jeremy West MP, the problem is . . . I love your son. I love him. And I know that he loves me. And when two people love each other, I think they should be together. Why can't they be together?"

He took a few steps toward me.

---

* One day, I'll write something devastating about entitled rich kids.

"He doesn't love you. You're disgusting. Leave. Now."

"I have news for you though, Sir Jeremy West MP. Tidings of great joy, no less! Your son is gay. I am gay. It's just who we are. And, know what? It isn't disgusting. It's fine. In fact, it's *great*! I've never been happier! But hey, if you still think it's wrong, or your god does, then I suggest you simply don't have gay sex. But you have no right to dictate what the rest of us do. So, here's an idea. How about you mind your own business, grow up, and get over it?*"

In the distance, I swear I heard Electra whooping and cheering.

Which was nice because no one else was.

Rob was staring at me, eyes wide—in fear?

Sir Jeremy started manhandling me, trying to frog-march me off his land.

"Get your gross hands off me!" I shouted. I twisted and shook myself free of him. Casper started barking.

Katie moved forward, seemingly gliding in her prom gown. "I'm sorry you're upset and that your crush on Rob hasn't worked out. But you really need to leave now. Because it's me who's going to the prom with him."

I shook my head. "It's just . . ."

"Go now, and there needn't be any more trouble," she said.

"It's just . . ."

"It's obvious you've been drinking and you're on some destructive streak . . ."

"It's just . . . *he gives such good blow jobs and that would be so wasted on you, Katie.*"

---

* Truth.

318

I started giggling. More shocked silence.

So I backed it up with: "Seriously, such good head.*"

I looked at Rob and shrugged. I swear, he was stifling a smile.

Sir Jeremy lurched for me again then, and despite how drunk I was, I managed to quickstep around him, and now was the time, because I'd pushed my luck, and he didn't care—it didn't matter that my argument was crass, or if it was eloquent—nothing I could have said would have made any difference. He was a homophobic bigot, and people like that will always find a reason—religion, decency, age inappropriateness, *won't someone think of the fucking children?*—to justify their hate.

So I whipped out the envelope.

The photographs scattered on the ground.

He saw.

And then he stopped.

Oh yeah, he froze deathly still then.

Covert pictures. Of Sir Jeremy West MP. Flirting, touching, and kissing . . . his secretary, Margaret. Date stamps on the photos: from when his wife was still alive but dying of cancer.

"Hypocrite," I said. "Talking about decency and family values when you're fucking your secretary while your wife is dying. But that's your type all over, isn't it? You're liars, con artists, nasty little scammers. And you call me disgusting? When all I've done is love someone who happens to be a boy, like me? When all I've done is be loyal to him, care about him, want to be with him? That's what's disgusting, is it?"

---

* Also truth.

I watched him shake as he picked the photos up.

"And by the way," I added, "I have the negatives."

He raised his head slowly and fixed me with a stare. "What do you want?"

"Oh. Just to go to the prom with my boyfriend. That's literally all. And for you not to send him away to some horrendous 'correctional facility.' You just have to let us be. That's all. We won't make your secrets public—if the people of Lincolnshire are ignorant and selfish enough to keep voting you in, that's on them. After all, we get the leaders we deserve, don't we?"

Sir Jeremy shook his head. "He won't go with you. He doesn't want to. Do you, Robert?"

I swallowed because this was the moment. The real test. I looked at Rob, I smiled, and I held my hand out.

He stared back at me.

"You said forever," I said. "You said forever, and you said to trust you. So, I'm trusting you."

He didn't move.

I took an unsteady breath, but the panic was rising. "I'm proud of you, Rob. I feel proud of you. Of everything you are. Everything we are. I love you. I want to show the world I love you. And I would like to go to the prom. So? How about it?"

Chapter 45

"Do you have any idea how sexy that was?" he told me.

Rob and I were walking along the road, toward the prom, toward . . . well, who knew? Then I smiled to myself, because there was one thing I *did* know—Speak No Monkey was going to be there, and if it was my letter that got them there, then there was a chance they would also honor my request in that letter: dedicating a song to Rob. I hoped they would. And I hoped he would love it. I hoped it would make up for just a little bit of all the horrible stuff.*

"At what point did you decide you'd come?" I asked.

A smile played on his lips. "I wanted to the moment you showed up."

"Yeah?"

"But I only knew I *could* when you produced the photos."

"So, about them?" I said.

He took a deep breath. "I've had them for ages on that roll of

---

* Folks, they didn't just dedicate a song to him, they only went and played an early version of "Next Door's Dog" a full ten months before it was released to the general public on their iconic *Songs from the Sofa* album, and dedicated that to him! It became our song.

film. I knew they could bring him down, but it couldn't be me. Despite everything you think, you're stronger than I am. At least, when it comes to my dad you are. Plus, he can't control you like he can me. You're a loose cannon. And he can't mess with you." He stopped. "But this isn't about the photos. You really were something just then."

"Well, you're really something too. That's why I wanted to fight for you."

He quickly kissed me, and we carried on walking. I could already hear the low thud of bass in the distance.

"Regardless of Dad, they'll still drag us through hell, you know," he said.

"I know."

"But you still—"

"If I'm going to be dragged to hell, I want to be dragged there with you. But, you know? It won't always be like this . . ."

He smiled, but shook his head, like he didn't believe me.

"No, no, it won't!" I insisted. "In twenty-eight, twenty-nine, thirty years' time, imagine how much better it'll be. So many people are fighting and campaigning—I read about it—things will be different by then. Gay people will be free to be themselves. Books won't be banned. Nobody's gonna be talking about 'indoctrination' because people will accept that some people are different from them, and it's not about choice, it's just about who you are. I think people will learn from history.*"

"You're saying, when we're in our forties, in 2024, or whatever, we won't be repeating the same tired arguments, dressed up slightly

---

* Ignorance is bliss, folks!

differently, but rooted in bigotry just the same as they always were?"

"Uh-huh!"

He shook his head. "I love you, but you're bonkers. People never learn from history. *Never.* I told you."

"I bet you!"

"OK," he said. "I'll bet you. If what you say turns out to be true, then we're fine, we're all happy, and that's enough of a prize for me. But if you're not . . . if it's history repeating . . ." He thought for a moment. "Then you promise me you'll write our story, put it out there, warts and all, and maybe someone will read it, and maybe someone will stop and think and see that we're just human and we have feelings. And maybe, if people can simply open their hearts, maybe one day they'll learn."

I shook his hand. "You have a deal.*"

We'd arrived at the entrance to school. I don't think either of us was expecting a warm reception—in fact, personally, I was expecting to be kicked out. But it had to be done. We had to try. Because every revolution starts with small moments of dissent. Small acts of rebellion.

"Forever and always, Jamie."

"Forever and always, Rob."

He took my hand.

We stared, apprehensive, but determined, right into the abyss.

Smiling.

And we walked.

Onward.

---

* And here it is, Rob. With love, with admiration, and with thanks. Forever and always, Jamie x

ONLINE RESOURCES

https://www.cdc.gov/lgbthealth/youth-resources.htm

https://libguides.usc.edu/lgbtq/links

https://thesafezoneproject.com/resources/

https://www.glsen.org

https://www.asexuality.org

https://lgbtqreads.com

https://www.thetrevorproject.org/resources/

https://www.glaad.org

ACKNOWLEDGMENTS

I'm incredibly grateful to the US team at Scholastic for bringing this very personal story of mine across the pond. My heartfelt thanks to Andrea Pinkney, David Levithan, and Jennifer Thompson—I love working with you all. Thank you also to the design team, Elizabeth Parisi and Maithili Joshi; Janell Harris in Production; copy editor Marcia Santore; and proofreaders Cailin Evans, Shannon Sturk, and Priscilla Eakeley. Special thanks again to Jacob Demlow for all his feedback on this American edition—and hey, whether you call it "Lynx" or "Axe" it's still unmistakably pungent!

Thank you to all the team at Scholastic UK: Linas Alsenas, Sarah Dutton, Sarah Baldwin, Harriet Dunlea, Hannah Griffiths, Ellen Thomson, Catherine Bell, Antonia Pelari, my agent Joanna Moult at Skylark Literary, as well as Sarah Counsell, Beau, Dolly, Betty, and all my family, friends, and fellow authors—especially The Gay YA Club!

Thanks to Aislinn O'Loughlin for coming up with "Speak No Monkey" after my call for help on Twitter (so much easier to outsource writing a book!) and to Afrori Books for the album name *Songs from the Sofa* and Ritch Ames for the song title "Next Door's Dog." Let's form a band—yay!

I'd like to thank everyone who campaigned against Section 28 back in the day—people and organizations like Stonewall, OutRage!, *The Pink Paper*, *Gay Times*, the Lesbian Avengers, Peter Tatchell, Sir Ian McKellen, Michael Cashman, Simon

Callow, Helen Mirren, and so many more. And to those who supported Section 28—including every single MP who voted for it, the Salvation Army, the Christian Institute, the Muslim Council of Great Britain, the Pentecostal British Union, groups within the Catholic Church and the Church of England, as well as Baroness Young, Brian Souter, and newspapers like the *Daily Mail, The Sun,* the *Daily Record,* and *The Daily Telegraph*—shame on all of you.

A special thank-you to Corinne Forde, Alison Tarrant, and all the school librarians, teachers, individuals, and organizations who supported me during 2022, which turned out to be an "interesting" year.

To all the brilliant booksellers and bookshops out there—thank you for continuing to champion LGBTQIA+ books and authors.

This book is dedicated to librarian, and all-round wonderful person, Alice Leggatt. Turns out Rob was right—people don't learn from history, and librarians, teachers, and educators across the world are still facing unprecedented challenges about LGBTQIA+ books in school libraries. The arguments and the rhetoric surrounding these challenges are straight out of the late 80s when people campaigned for Section 28, and when you strip it all away, it still boils down to the same old ignorance, the same old lies, and the same old bigotry.

So, I'd also like to thank all of you who are fighting for the simple right of being able to read whatever book you'd like to read, and for making sure that all young people have the chance to see themselves, and their lives, reflected in a book, and that those young people also get the opportunity to read and learn about people who are completely different from them too.

Section 28 destroyed lives. Its legacy lives on today. I never want another generation to be harmed through ignorance and fear. I'm so proud of us all, standing together, determined to make the world a happier, better, more understanding place. We'll never let hate win.

Simon

ABOUT THE AUTHOR

Simon James Green is an award-winning author of books for children and young adults. He has been shortlisted for the YA Book Prize, the Diverse Book Awards, the Lollies, has won the Bristol Teen Book Award, and been three-times nominated for the Carnegie medal. He has written seven young adult novels, including *Noah Can't Even, Alex in Wonderland, Heartbreak Boys* (an Indie Next List pick), *You're the One That I Want, Gay Club!* (which received starred reviews from *Kirkus* and *Booklist*), and *Boy Like Me*. His first middle-grade novel, *Life of Riley: Beginner's Luck*, was shortlisted for the Blue Peter Book Award and won the Fantastic Book Awards 2022. *Sleepover Takeover* won the InspiRead Book Award 2023 and featured in the Great Book's Guide from BookTrust. *Finn Jones Was Here* was selected as Book of the Month by the Booksellers Association. Simon has also written two picture books, illustrated by Garry Parsons: *Llama Glamarama and Fabulous Frankie*. He lives in London.

For more information on Simon visit: www.simonjamesgreen.com

ALL OF US, TOGETHER, ALWAYS

In this achingly honest dialogue, Simon James Green and David Levithan share insights, reflections, and hope for a new future as books with LGBTQIA+ themes continue to come under attack. At the same time, the stories and experiences of gay youth shine a positive light for young readers. David is the *New York Times* bestselling and award-winning author of *Boy Meets Boy*, *Two Boys Kissing*, and numerous acclaimed books that feature LGBTQIA+ characters.

David Levithan: I'm going to start at the sadly obvious place to start: As we're sitting down to talk, a number of states in the US have passed laws that look and act like Section 28 (a legislative designation for a series of laws across Britain that prohibited the "promotion of homosexuality" by local authorities). It's no surprise that history repeats—but a lot of us have been surprised to see it repeat so soon. What has it been like to see your "historical fiction" take on such present-day relevance?

Simon James Green: It's completely horrifying, but it's also what inspired me on to write the book. *Boy Like Me* was written during the summer of 2022. I'd wanted to write a novel about what it was like growing up as a gay kid in the 90s for a while, but I wasn't sure if teenagers today would really connect with it. And then the book bans started happening. And Florida's "Don't Say Gay" law. The hateful rhetoric I'd heard in the 90s was making a comeback, both in the UK and the US, and I realized those teenagers *would* connect with it, because it was happening right now, in their schools, to them and their friends. I wanted to equip those teenagers with some context, and a bit of a road map about how you deal with it, because we've been here before, and history can show us how to work through it.

DL: I think what's interesting to me, as a fellow teen-of-the-90s, is while the book banners' rhetoric has remained largely the same, the teens they are using it against have changed. When we were teens, the banners were trying to keep us in the closet. But now, they've largely lost that battle, and they are trying to push us back in the closet . . . which (I hope) is a much harder thing to do. And certainly there are so many LGBTQIA+ teens who are standing up for themselves and their literature. When you were writing this book, were you often struck by how different the story would be if it were set now?

SJG: One hundred percent. Back in the 90s, I felt hugely isolated. There was no sense that anyone else might be gay; you were completely alone with your feelings. Now, even if you're physically isolated, maybe somewhere quite rural, there are so many communities online. It's much easier to find your people, but also to unite and fight. We're now in a position where a generation of LGBTQIA+ young people have had access to the books they need, they've seen positive representation in TV and films, they've been taught about LGBTQIA+ history and lives in schools, and, increasingly, many have been able to be more visible. And non-LGBTQIA+ young people have also experienced that. So, there's been a huge shift, and you're right, there's no getting all that fabulousness back in the closet now. But I still think there's a lot of fear that queer young people today can experience. And a lot of prejudice and hate. So, there's a lot of nuance here. I think Jamie would still feel a lot of the same things if the book were set today, but I suspect the way he goes about dealing with them, the exact nature of the shame and fear he feels, and how he ultimately fights back would all be different.

DL: One of the themes of the novel is the power that books contain—not in and of themselves, but because of the remarkable reaction that can take place when a reader finds the kind of story that unlocks parts of their lives they didn't fully know they'd had locked up. Are there any books that you feel helped you unlock your own identity?

SJG: As a teenager in the UK during Section 28, access to LGBTQIA+ books was difficult because there was nothing in the school library. I'd managed to read a couple of books featuring gay teenagers, but they were adult novels, often quite literary, and they weren't about the here and now. But in the mid-90s, a play came along called *Beautiful Thing* by Jonathan Harvey. It was made into a film, which I saw, and I then bought the script. Finally! A story about two sixteen-year-old boys falling in love, set on a council estate in London in the 90s! That play changed everything. It made me realize that's what I wanted too, and it made me want to write those sorts of stories.

DL: This answer makes me so happy—I literally have the CD cover from the *Beautiful Thing* soundtrack up on my wall in front of me as I type this. I keep it within view as I'm writing because it was such a revelation to me, and is the DNA of so much of what I write.

It's something I think about all the time—how we didn't really have queer YA love stories when we were growing up, so had to basically figure it out on our own, or try to translate straight YA love stories (hello, John Hughes) into our own queer versions. Which is no longer the case, in a world with our novels and *Heartstopper* and countless other depictions of queer love. The love story within *Boy Like Me* is so tender—and so predicated on secrecy. Considering that this interview will be in the back of the book, so we don't have to worry about spoilers, can you talk a little about your choice to play it out the way you did?

SJG: Readers will know from the note at the front that some of this book is based on real-life events, so some of the way it plays out is literally just . . . how it really played out. I was very keen we should see a fairly long period of simply not knowing who the other boy was. My overriding memory of that era was that sense of mystery—the not knowing who might or might not be gay, and the resignation that you probably were never going to find out. When we find out it's Rob, we have two characters who are chalk and cheese—they couldn't be more different, and Jamie himself feels they're unsuited. This was another thing I really felt in the 90s—there was this sense that if you wanted some kind of connection with someone, a kiss, a cuddle, maybe a bit more (winky face!), then there wasn't much choice. In the unlikely event someone else at school had come to terms with who they were, and was prepared to do something about it, they would probably be the only other one. I wanted to show how Jamie and Rob would never ordinarily be a thing, but circumstances make them into one, and they then discover they do have things in common, and they slowly start to mean something to each other. But it's tentative. And it's very slow. And it had to be instilled with fear and doubt because the consequences of anyone finding out were so high, and the level of ignorance about how you did anything, and what was safe, was huge. I remember feeling a sense of being doomed—that nothing could possibly last because it wouldn't be allowed to, the hate was too much, and ultimately, the fear and pressure to conform would get to us both and put an end to everything. I peppered in some of that sense of dread throughout. That's really what the Cold War nuclear bomb dishes the boys visit are about—this sense that you're just "waiting for oblivion," as Rob puts it.

DL: One of the things I've always felt was particularly insidious about Section 28 was that it was passed at the height of the AIDS crisis—information about our lives was withheld from students at exactly the time that information was particularly lifesaving. In the novel, AIDS seems to hover as a threat, and also as a source of misunderstanding about gay people. I was wondering if you could talk a little for current readers about how HIV/AIDS shaped Jamie's generation of gay men in the UK.

SJG: Do you remember the fear when COVID first appeared? Here was a virus, and nobody knew too much about it, but it was killing people, and there was no real cure or treatment, and it was terrifying. Now, by the mid-90s we did know more, and we knew how HIV and AIDS could be spread, but while we were edging toward treatments, this was still something that would ultimately kill you if you caught it. The newspapers were full of stories of gay men dying—and they would report on that in the most hateful of ways, calling it a "gay virus plague" and suggesting we only had ourselves to blame. Meanwhile, the few gay heroes we had—like Freddie Mercury, the lead singer of Queen—were dying from AIDS-related illnesses. I'll never forget the shock of Freddie dying, his gaunt and emaciated face all over the tabloids. And if you put all that in the context of Section 28, of no one at school being able to talk about any of this, of no information, support, or reassurance, nothing to keep you safe, you can hopefully understand just how frightening it was for a lot of us. It felt like being gay was a death sentence, and if it could happen to Freddie, a global superstar, then it could happen to any of us. That made many of us scared to be gay. It made some of us pretend we weren't. And, like Jamie says in the book, that fear doesn't leave you sometimes, and it can still impact you even now, when AIDS absolutely is treatable and when it's no longer an illness that will kill you. The men who died were mostly older than me, and I never had to go through the trauma of seeing close friends lose their lives to that horrible disease. But we shouldn't ever forget what some people in the community have been through, the fights they've had, and what they have lost.

DL: In your acknowledgments, you thank a number of organizations and people who fought against Section 28. One of the things I love about queer protest of this era was that they could be very creative. Do you have any protests in particular that are favorites?

SJG: Oh, yes! When Section 28 was being debated in Parliament, a group of heroic lesbians abseiled into the chamber from the public gallery, using only a washing line, to protest. Then, on the night before it became law, and frustrated by a lack of publicity, another group of lesbians invaded the studio where the BBC News was being broadcast, calling out: "Stop Section 28!" They continued the broadcast, while one of the newsreaders sat on one of the lesbians. You can see it all on YouTube. Absolutely brilliant.

DL: You mention the "interesting year" of 2022, when you came face-to-face with a censorship challenge. Could you talk a little about that, and the effect it had on you as a writer?

SJG: I was banned from a Catholic school in South London where I'd been booked to do an author visit. Various reasons were given along the way, from my books not being acceptable within the teachings of the Catholic Church, to accusations of obscenity, pornography, and eventually being offensive to their religion. The story became national news and I was featured in the press and on TV, after which came the death threats. What really upset me though was knowing the effect it would have on some of the students at that school. Regardless of your religion, you can't help being LGBTQIA+—it's not something you have any control over, and my heart broke for those kids who would be seeing and hearing all this hate, and what message it sent to them. That really galvanized me. It made me more determined to get LGBTQIA+ stories out there and to fight against bigotry and book censorship. They want us to hide ourselves away, be silent and pretend we don't exist. No way! Pushing back and being louder and prouder than ever is the only answer. I'm not interested in the pathetic excuses people use to justify their hate. LGBTQIA+ people are a fact. We exist. We're not going anywhere. Understanding ourselves and other people is a good thing. It makes the world an easier, and happier, place to live. Grow up and get over it.

DL: I love that the book is dedicated to a librarian—that seems very fitting! Are there any particular moments you can share where a librarian made a difference to you, as a young reader and/or as an (ahem) older writer?

SJG: The librarian in the dedication is the one from the Catholic school who stood alongside me and stuck up for me, eventually resigning and moving to a new school. We're now really good friends. But my love of librarians comes from all the school visits I've been on over the last six years since my debut was published, and seeing all the good work they do. These brilliant people make all sorts of kids feel welcome in their libraries, making them a safe space, a space of discovery, a space for finding yourself and finding others . . . it's a beautiful thing, and they're the folk who make it possible.

DL: Amen to that! Now, an extremely hard and deeply personal question for the end—if you asked this of me, it might take me years to find an answer. But I shall ask you anyway. If you're given a whole library to choose from . . . what book would you leave a secret message inside, and what would that message be?

SJG: Right now, it would be *1984* by George Orwell. And I would write: *Read this and see how people hell-bent on retaining power behave. Understand how they try to control the narrative through the media people can have access to. Understand how, like con artists, they distract you. Realize how all that is designed to benefit them, whatever excuses they might use. It's not about protecting anyone or anything but their power, their money, their privilege, and their control. Don't fall for it. Don't let it divide us. We fight back. All of us, together, always.*

I feel
like this
too.
Anyone
else?